To Steve
All you
ever wanted to
know about
cricket ---

David Brophy

BODYLINE
THE NOVEL

Paul Wheeler

faber and faber
LONDON · BOSTON

First published in 1983
by Faber and Faber Limited
3 Queen Square, London WC1N 3AU
First published in this edition in 1984
Filmset by Goodfellow & Egan Ltd Cambridge
Printed in Great Britain by
Richard Clay plc
Bungay, Suffolk

The excerpt from Neville Cardus, Cardus on Cricket,
is reprinted by kind permission of the Literary Executor of
Neville Cardus and Souvenir Press.

British Library Cataloguing in Publication Data

Wheeler, Paul
Bodyline
I. Title
823'.914[F]   PR6073.H/

ISBN 0-571-13383-5

Oh, for the old days, the good days, the days of our strength!

RUDYARD KIPLING

The author would like to express his gratitude for the assistance he received from the participants in the 1932/3 teams, whose recollections were the starting point for this fictional account of the events that year.

Chapter One

Play was suspended briefly at 3.30 on the second day and both teams were presented to King George in front of the pavilion. They put on blazers and stood in two lines facing each other while the old man, stooping now and showing his age, shuffled past, shaking each by the hand. He seemed to be in a hurry; a fleeting smile, a muttered welcome and on to the next player, accompanied first by Woodfull, the Australian captain, then, along the other line, by the towering figure of Percy Chapman. The royal briskness might have been interpreted as boredom; as if the men were minor civil servants at a Buckingham Palace garden party. However, everyone present, including the large crowd who stood silently watching the presentation, knew of the King's passion for the game. One of the few monarchs to love cricket, he regarded it as much a part of the Empire as *Pax Britannica*. The haste he encouraged was prompted by a desire to return to his seat and let them get on with it.

As Chapman escorted him to the clutch of waiting equerries, the King murmured: "Are we in trouble, Mr Chapman?"

The scoreboard showed England had made 425 in the first innings and so far Australia had replied with 150 without loss.

"I'll be happy to get Bradman out cheaply, sir," Chapman replied.

The old King stopped and glanced back at the Australian line. His rheumy eyes rested a second on the short, grinning young man at one end. When they swung back to Chapman, the England captain detected a gleam of irritation. What had he said? For a moment he felt himself whisked back to a headmaster's study, a frightened boy about to be scolded for insolence—

"Bugger Bradman," His Majesty grunted, and beneath the clipped grey beard his lips parted ever so slightly.

Chapman relaxed: "I'll do my best, sir," he said and giving a short bow, returned to his team.

The crowd settled back into their seats and waited for the umpires to reappear. A euphoria bathed the ground as warm and comforting as the blazing sun that had shone uninterruptedly since dawn. Now, as the shadows of the western stands began to move slowly across the outfield, a faint wind brought the afternoon to perfection. Give an Englishman a hot summer's day tempered by a mild breeze; give him a Test series with the old enemy, a respectable score to defend, and a glimpse of royalty. Give him all this and nothing short of an earthquake could jolt him from a mood of peace and complacency. Even if Australia were starting well and had not lost a wicket. All they were doing was adding to the pleasure; they were making a game of it. No one wanted to watch a walkover. The Aussies were fighting back and all credit to them. After all, they were one Test down, beaten at Trent Bridge, and had lost the last two series in '26 and '28. The press had written them off as a side with one or two players of promise but with no coherence as a team. Well, on this grand day, at Lord's, the Mecca of the cricketing world, they were putting on a decent show. As the umpires walked to the middle and the King watched from high in that glorious pavilion, as the breeze dried the perspiration on the forehead and the clock showed at least another two hours' play, few people present were thinking of the Depression and the dole queues. The nation was well poised and having itself a bit of a fling.

Shortly after play resumed, Jack "Farmer" White, recalled to the England side to replace an out-of-form Larwood, had Ponsford caught at slip. 162 for 1.

"A handshake from old King George and look what happens!" someone yelled and everyone laughed. Ponsford acknowledged the applause with a modest wave of the bat and clattered up the steps of the pavilion. A quiet descended. The next man in was the reason why a great number of the crowd had come, and their anticipation hung in the air like a heavy mist. They were theatregoers waiting for the entrance of the star—

Up in the journalists' box, Neville Cardus heard the initial burst of clapping and, craning his neck, watched Bradman emerge from the pavilion to begin a long, measured walk to the centre. He doodled on his notepad, turning over in his mind what he had previously written about the 22-year-old from New South Wales. He had watched him make 236 in almost as many minutes during the tourists' first game at Worcester. While the other Australian batsmen looked stiff and out of touch, the "Boy Wonder", as some newspapers dubbed him, had thrashed Fred Root who, four years earlier, had ignominiously skittled out the visitors. This time he could only manage 2 for 112. Then, in the very next game at Leicester, he had seen Bradman knock up an unbeaten 185, followed by 252 against Surrey and 131 in the First Test. "Boy Wonder" gave way to a new nickname: the "Run Machine".

Cardus had no trouble accepting that the man had an all-round ability with the bat unequalled in the thirty years he had been observing cricket. A magnificent defence, a mighty pull, the hookshot, the cut, the glance—the straight drive. He also possessed that touch of unconventionality which marks the great from the merely good: Percy Fender had cast doubts on Bradman's use of a cross-bat to deal with deliveries short of a length on the offside. Cardus had seen the finest batsmen since the turn of the century, and all of them displayed some eccentricity, a quirk which added to the excitement of their performance. Bradman was no exception.

Added to all this was the footwork. His feet moved so quickly, bringing him down the pitch after the bowler's moment of no return when the ball has left the hand, to send it skimming through the covers before the fielders could move. Sometimes he leaped into an extraordinary position, yards outside the off-stump, to pull the ball across the wickets towards an unmanned part of the legside. He seemed to know where the ball would land before it was bowled.

Cavalier batsmen have always been present in cricket. They are the men who empty the bars, whom young boys imitate, who capture the imagination of the sports writers. They are the life blood of a game that can suffer from over-caution. But, like cavaliers in other spheres, they often burn themselves out prematurely. Taking risks is good for the spectators, but selectors are unimpressed. Cardus had seen many bright young hopes suddenly disappear. A run of bad form, an injury and they are no longer on the Possibles list. Soon they are just another statistic in *Wisden*.

While Bradman ambled to the wicket in his characteristic manner, allowing his eyes to grow accustomed to the light, Cardus was troubled by a niggling doubt. Where would Bradman be in five years? Glancing at his notepad, he discovered he had doodled a series of question marks down one side.

Standing at extra cover, Chapman waited patiently as the new batsman ran through a series of gestures that was becoming his hallmark. After the leisurely stroll to the crease—some ascribed his dawdling not to the need to get used to the light, but to the fact that everyone who came from Bradman's part of Australia moved slowly when a heavy task lay ahead—he took guard, pulled the peak of his cap, flexed each hand inside its protective glove, looked around at the fielders, shrugged his shoulders to loosen the muscles, patted the top of his pads and finally settled into position, the bottom of the bat placed oddly *between* his feet. During this performance, a broad grin never left his face. Bradman possessed yet one more uncommon trait: he always looked as if he were enjoying himself.

Jack White flipped the ball from hand to hand while he waited, and even when the umpire half-turned to indicate play, remained at his mark for a few seconds to underline his lack of concern that the maestro had arrived and was now ready. Two years previously, White had exploded the myth that slow left-arm bowlers were of little use on Australian wickets and returned as England's most successful wicket taker. Now almost 40, he was in his prime, a serene and cheerful man with the rosy cheeks of a Somerset yeoman farmer. Choosing his moment, he advanced to the wicket and swung his arm over in the casual manner for which he was famous.

The ball was well pitched-up and Bradman met it two yards down the wicket. The crack scattered the pigeons at the Nursery end in all directions, and before any of the England fielders could even sight the direction of the stroke, the ball tripped over the boundary rope at long-off and bounced into the crowd.

When the teams went in for tea forty-five minutes later, Bradman had reached his 50 without giving the remotest chance. With his unusual grip, the top hand further round the handle of the bat than usual, it was almost impossible for him to hit the ball in the air unless he meant to. At the same time, he whacked it so hard that the fielders were unable to cut it off unless it came directly at them. From the very beginning, anything short was pulled to the leg boundary. It was as if he were setting the record straight for future years. Before his innings at Surrey, the home captain, Percy Fender, had queried his ability in print. Bradman's answer had been to score 252, reducing the Surrey attack to a shambles. Returning to the pavilion he had thrown down his gloves with a grin and remarked, "I wonder what Fender will have to say in the morning paper *this* time."

What the crowds at Lord's witnessed on that late June day was the arrogance of genius. After tea, Bradman advanced to a chanceless century and by 6.30 he had made 155. Not once did the ball go where it was not intended; each stroke forced it down on to the ground where it remained, speeding across the turf as if held down by a magnet. When Chapman moved his men round, it travelled to where they had been standing. The field fanned outwards until there were only the wicket-keeper and slips on the square. Chauvinism was forgotten in the stands as the exhibition continued unabated. Who cared that at the end of the day Australia were only 21 runs behind? Here was a spectacle that those present would talk about for years. Not since Gilbert Jessop's century in 1902 could anyone recall anything like it.

Cardus certainly couldn't. After the field emptied at the close of play he remained seated for a long time, the buzz of excitement from his normally phlegmatic colleagues in the press box a distant blur to his ears. Finally he picked up his pen, turned his notepad over and wrote slowly in firm capitals: "THIS BRADMAN IS A GREAT PLAYER FIT TO BE MENTIONED WITH THE BEST OF THEM."

When play resumed the following Monday, Bradman took his

score to 254 before being dismissed by a miraculous catch at extra cover from Chapman. But by then the damage was complete and Australia went on to win the match by seven wickets.

The defeat plunged the country into a state of furious self-criticism. To his surprise and despair, Chapman found himself pilloried in the newspapers, moving overnight from the swashbuckling hero who could do no wrong, to the lacklustre skipper unable to resist the onslaught of a mere boy. Why had he behaved like a punch-drunk boxer as soon as Bradman began to open up? English cricket had been successful in the past by using intricate fielding techniques: leg-traps, inner and outer rings, cunningly deployed silly mid-ons and mid-offs, aggressiveness, close-in catchers—the principles of chess, forcing the opponent on to the back foot, cramping his style, beguiling him out. Yet what did Chapman do? Sent everyone to the boundary! It was humiliating, a deplorable exhibition of weakness—from a team that had whipped the Australians for six years!

The Third Test took place at Headingley. Away from the effete south, the spirit of Yorkshire would lend the kind of support to the England side they didn't get at Lord's. None of this "well played, Bradman" lark. Down south cricket was a game. Up here, it was a religion, and you didn't hear too many Methodists say "well played, Catholics". Harold Larwood, unarguably the fastest and most accurate bowler in the world, good old "Loll" from the Nottinghamshire pits, was back in the side. So was Dick Tyldesley from Lancashire, a right-arm slow bowler who would, the northern crowd agreed, do what Farmer White and his Somerset cutters had so miserably failed to pull off in London—have Bradman back where he belonged, on the dressing-room balcony.

Australia won the toss and batted. At lunch Bradman reached his century. By tea he was 220 and at the close of play had scored 309 out of a total of 458. Having made a hundred in each of the three playing sessions, he equalled Trumper and Macartney's innings in the morning, and had beaten R.E. Foster's Test record of 287 by six o'clock.

Cardus and his colleagues searched the Thesaurus for new words to describe what they witnessed, but in the end could only come up

14

with variations of "remorseless". The Boy Wonder simply went on and on; there seemed no reason at all why he should ever get out. Nobody came near to containing him. At one stage Geary and Tyldesley bowled with a man on the boundary behind them as well as a long-on and long-off, such was the severity of Bradman's driving. Neither bowler had ever been treated like this before, and when Larwood returned with the third new ball his field was equally unprecedented, containing only one slip and a gully, with an extra cover and extra, deeper square leg. But, as at Lord's, none of the fielders ever seemed to be in the right place and time after time Bradman drilled the ball clear of their outstretched hands. At one point, a perspiring Tyldesley finished up sprawling among the front row of spectators, having failed once again to catch up with a boundary.

"Never tha' mind, Dick, lad," called someone. "If tha'ad had a handicap, tha'd a beat t'ball."

Only once, when Kippax was out, did the young Australian show any sign of weariness. He lay down motionless on the grass until McCabe arrived, but soon was up again continuing as he had all day, driving, hooking, cutting. The next morning he took his score to 334 before he was caught behind off Tate. The match ended in a draw due to rain but remains a landmark in the history of cricket, a monument to a man eager to prove he was no flash in the pan.

Neville Cardus at any rate was no longer in any doubt:

It isn't true [he wrote] that Bradman has inaugurated a new era in batsmanship; he is substantially orthodox in technique. Nearly all his strokes at Leeds would be usable as illustrations to Fry's thoroughly scientific and pragmatic book on batsmanship. But Bradman shows us excellencies which in the past we have had to seek in different batsmen; nobody else has achieved Bradman's synthesis. It is, of course, a synthesis which owes much to the fact that Bradman stays at the wicket longer than most of the brilliant stroke-players of old ever dreamed of staying. Perhaps he is marked off from the great-ness of his predecessors not so much by technique as by temperament. . . . The really astonishing thing about Bradman is that a boy should play as he does—with the sophistication of an old hand and brain. Who has ever heard before of a young man, gifted with quick feet and eyes, with mercurial spirits and all the rapid and powerful strokes of cricket—who has ever heard of a young man so gifted and yet one who never indulged in an extravagant hit high into the air? . . . . If Bradman develops his skill still further—and at his age he ought to have whole worlds to conquer yet— he will in the end find himself considered not so much a master batsman as a phenomenon of cricket.

The selectors dropped Larwood for the Fourth Test at Old Trafford where rain caused another draw, but reinstated him for the final game at the Oval when they transferred the captaincy from Chapman to Wyatt. None of these panic-ridden measures made any difference at all. Bradman scored another double century and except for a period when a damp surface made the ball rise from Larwood, nothing halted the Australians, who gained a huge victory by an innings and 39 runs and the return of the Ashes.

A season that had started on the crest of a wave for England ended in bitter recriminations and the effective end of more than one Test career, including that of poor Chapman. As in politics, defeat in Test cricket results in the tumbling of heads and the digging of graves. In the August of that long summer of 1930, the post-mortems were more severe than ever before. England had lost the Ashes many times in the past, but never so unexpectedly. What had happened? A proven side faced a demoralized eleven containing a number of inexperienced boys, and was annihilated! Where had things gone wrong? Why had Chapman gone off the rails? Why had morale crumbled in the England dressing-room to the extent that rumours had circulated of arguments and even fist fights?

The public at large compensated for the loss of national prestige by showering Bradman with attention. Wherever he went everyone wanted to shake his hand, to win his autograph. A quiet, reclusive figure off the field, he appealed to the English respect for

16

modesty. In return he showed himself to be deeply impressed by England and its traditions. He read avidly, absorbed her history and customs, assimilating facts and figures about London while the remainder of the Australian side went off on holiday or visited relatives. He became that rarest of heroes: the kind who can humiliate the English and yet remain in their good books. As a rule, they do not warm to show-offs. Unquestionably Napoleon and the Kaiser would have been better regarded had they not constantly tried to demonstrate how clever they were. Bradman was different. With his diffident attitude towards adulation, with his quiet smile and self-effacing manner—why, he was an honorary Englishman.

Watching the crowds gather round the Oval pavilion to hear the customary speeches, sat a tall, well-dressed man. His back erect against the seat, he projected a military bearing as he leaned his weight very lightly on a walking cane set vertically between his knees. Under the hat the first signs of grey flecked his sideboards, but there was no doubt in the mind of anyone who might have noticed him that he possessed the body of a fine athlete.

Sitting there, still as a rock, he displayed none of the good-naturedness of those around him who were laughing, making deprecatory jokes about England's performance, shrugging and in general congratulating Australia on a job well done. His hands tightened on the knob of his cane as the players lined up for the press photographers. He should leave now, before the final speeches, the grovelling and the cant that goes with the acknowledgement of defeat. But something prevented him. Perhaps he needed to see it through to the bitter end, taste the salt tears of humiliation if he were, one day, to seek and exact his revenge.

And so he remained, while Woodfull declared how happy he and his side were to regain the Ashes and how he had enjoyed the hard-fought but always sportsmanlike encounters; how the spirit of this grand game had been maintained throughout and how he looked forward to 1932 when next they would meet their England opponents in Australia. The man looked on as Wyatt echoed the same sentiments but hoped next time it would be England's turn to triumph. He caught sight of Pelham Warner standing to one side—Warner, the grand old man of cricket, the apostle of the faith that preached fair play and good sportsmanship. Behind him stood Percy Chapman, whose international career was wrecked because he had pursued these very ideals. And lost. Good old Percy, good old Plum. The world was one huge cricket match where differences were settled by a handshake; where nobody questioned the rules or argued with the umpire; where honour was more important than victory; where to be gracious in defeat was a sign of good character; where to covet winning was the mark of a boor.

A burst of applause signalled the end of the formalities, and the crowds slowly dispersed while the Australian side waved and grinned for the photographers. The man stood up quickly and edged past the other members towards the aisle. He had seen enough, heard enough. The elderly spectators scarcely glanced up as he went by, too busy exchanging pleasantries about how there was no other game in the world which typified so clearly the Christian virtues. He reached the steps and for a second looked back, registering their contented faces, the complacency and cheerful resignation in their voices. The pit of his stomach was in turmoil and he wanted to take his cane and bring the end down hard onto their heads. But he himself was English, one of their stock, he was guilty by association. If one was ashamed of one's country, one left it. Or sought to bring about a change. There was no other alternative.

He caught an old fellow, an acquaintance, eyeing him curiously as he stood biting back the tears, so he walked briskly up the steps to an exit. There he turned once more, glancing at the members' enclosure.

"This must change," he thought. "This will change. Your days are numbered, old men of goodwill. The sun is setting on your world. And I will dance on its grave."

Chapter Two

Kirkby-in-Ashfield is a town 10 miles from Nottingham on the borders of Derbyshire. A settlement had been there since the days of the Danelaw but it was not until the nineteenth century and the volcanic eruption of the industrial revolution that the place grew large enough to be noticed. "Kairkby", as it is pronounced in the broad accent of this part of Nottingham, the dialect of the men and women of D.H. Lawrence's novels, became synonymous with coal. Soon after rich seams of anthracite were discovered, the village changed out of all recognition; a scattering of thatched and slate cottages disappeared under the foundations of the tight lines of back-to-back housing for the hundreds of men and their families who came to hack and pick their way deep into the earth. Cobblestones strengthened the roads. The undulating green hills were obscured by slag heaps and the sky turned grey from dust.

In this respect Kirkby was no different from any other coal-rich town. A price is always paid for prosperity and few of its people minded. There was little to recommend the life of a farm labourer tied hand and foot to the land. What if the arrival of coal brought new kinds of illness?: pneumoconiosis, failing vision from years spent in underground darkness—were these any worse than rickets and starvation? The mines guaranteed employment, and regular money cushioned the blows of a hard life. Kirkby grew fast. A brick industry flourished, providing more jobs, further incentives to move there. By the 1930s there were more than 17,000 souls living in its crowded, bustling streets and the town enjoyed a reputation of solid working-class respectability in Nottingham circles. Even among those who followed the centuries-old lace-making trade, whose elaborate middle-class ways and over-furnished parlours around the Ropewalk and the Castle gave rise to derision in the public bars of the Flying Horse and Old Salutation taverns. Both sides of the industrial coin shared the Midlands admiration for hard and honest toil, and the difference between ending the day covered in soot or with fingertips lacerated by needles was not made a serious issue.

However, by 1932 Kirkby had been no more successful than any other industrial town in avoiding the consequences of the great economic collapse. The work force at each pit was reduced by over half in two years and no miner knew from one week to another whether it was his turn next. The pin-neat streets grew untidy with increasing numbers of men standing at corners, leaning on the railings of the recreational park, aching for the day to pass; at night the unemployed were less conspicuous, but in the broad light of the afternoon everybody could see who wasn't bringing home the groceries. Surprisingly, there was little resentment between those who were out of a job and those who for some lucky reason still clocked on. The new shift clattered towards the pit while those on the dole catcalled and waved.

"Hey up, mister, carry yer snap tin, then?" "Left yer missus on her own have yer, Sid?" "All right for some, intit—"

The fortunate ones grinned and muttered silent prayers that they wouldn't be on the wrong side of the fence soon. And when the morning shift disappeared and the roads grew quiet again, the men outside the gates fell to talking of what they could do to spend the long hours ahead.

During the summer, the smarter ones took themselves out of local public view and went into the city to watch the cricket at Trent Bridge. The game had regained its popularity in the county in 1929 when Arthur Carr led Notts to the championship for the first time in twenty-two years. In addition Kirkby's greatest celebrity, Harold Larwood, was back at the top of the national bowling averages.

This particular Saturday afternoon the vast reaches of Trent Bridge were more populated than usual. It was one of the last games of the season and the day was clear and fine. Surrey had won the toss and elected to bat. The Trent Bridge wicket was docile at this time of year and many batsmen looked forward to playing there and adding a few more points to their averages.

The championship race was over and Notts had recently been knocked out of the running by Yorkshire. Surrey had enjoyed a reasonable season, but this game was not going to affect the placing of either team. However, the men from Kirkby trooped into the city to get lost in the crowds and cheer on their old mucker, Loll.

They were glad to find the home side in the field and wondered what Surrey would do with Larwood and Bill Voce. It was widely assumed that both the Notts fast bowlers would go to Australia that winter; Larwood was a certainty, of course, but there was heavy betting on Voce who, at 23, had proved himself in the current home championship averages, in the West Indies three years ago and in South Africa the following winter, ending each tour as the chief wicket-taker. Five years younger than his friend and partner, "Tangy" Voce had started his career as a slow left-arm spinner but Carr had prevailed upon him to use his height and strength to more effect and turned the lad into an intimidating over-the-wicket quick bowler.

And today, with the likelihood that there was at least one Test selector in the crowds, Voce was keen to earn his passage down under.

Surrey batted slowly but without loss until lunch. After the break, Carr used his spinners for a few overs before tossing the ball to Larwood.

"Seen the patch on the leg stump?" he muttered.

"Aye."

"Ten bob if you can hit it five times out of six," Carr said, moving back to mid-off.

I don't need a bribe, Larwood thought, as he went back seventeen paces to his mark, but ten bob always comes in handy. T'skipper were often doing suchlike. A quid here, a couple of bob there if he can knock someone's cap off or gerrim caught in t'slips. Sort of unofficial bonus money.

The batsman facing was Douglas Jardine, recently appointed captain of Surrey, taking over from Percy Fender. Jardine had topped the national averages in 1927 and 1928 and had been vice-captain on the last England tour to Australia. But as an amateur, his appearances were spasmodic and Larwood had not bowled at him for almost a year. He was particularly good on the leg, moving the ball towards square or fine with a contemptuous flick which perfectly fitted his cold, precise manner.

Hit the legside patch but keep the ball away from Jardine's favourite shot—hardly a piece of cake, Larwood pondered as he waited for the batsman to receive him. Well, it's ten bob against six fours—

Coming in with his "carpet slipper" run, Larwood raced to the bowling crease, leaped high into the air and stabbed his left leg stiffly into the ground. The action caused a catapult effect on the ball which left his hand at 95 miles an hour. It sped down the wicket and hit the worn patch Carr had pointed out, kicked up high, missed Jardine's left elbow by a fraction, and slammed into the gloves of the wicket-keeper as he leaped full stretch above his head. The delivery had taken a half-second and drew a shout of approval and surprise from the crowd. Until that moment, none of the bowling had come up higher than the waist, presenting no problem to the batsmen. Now, Larwood let go a "special" which had Jardine staring hard at the spot on the track in front of his legs and caused Carr to grin and hold up one finger to his fast bowler.

The next ball found the spot again and this time rose into the batsman's body as he went on to the back foot to fend the delivery away. The third flew past his chest, and the fourth over his head as he ducked low. The fifth hit him in the side with a loud thud.

Jardine felt the ball crash into his ribs and an excruciating pain flash across his chest. While Larwood looked on from the bowling end, he forced himself to straighten. More than anything he wanted to rub his side, to bend over and try to relieve the agony. He wanted to close his eyes tight shut and grind his teeth, perform all the natural, if pointless, functions of someone in pain. But that would have pleased Larwood and he was damned if he'd do that. Or Carr. The bastard had put the fellow up to it, of course.

"Do you wish to go off, Mr Jardine?" asked the umpire.

"No, thank you."

"Very well."

The last ball of the over dropped precisely on the patch and Jardine played it hastily down the legside.

"Ten bob, I owe you, Harold," said Carr as they crossed, and the stocky fast bowler grinned.

"I got six out of six, skipper," he replied. "Ten bob was for only five."

"Then I'll throw in a pint as well," Carr said. Passing Jardine he smiled.

"All right, Douglas?" Jardine prodded the wicket with the end of the bat and nodded.

"Yes, thank you."

Jardine's partner lasted three balls from Larwood's next over before deflecting a rising delivery to leg slip. Two balls later the new batsman took a wild swing and heard his middle stump torn from the ground and go cart-wheeling past the wicket-keeper.

Fender, watching from the dressing-room balcony, said, "If someone doesn't do something, that little sod will run through us like a dose of salts."

"Oh, Douglas is doing his Horatio-on-the-bridge act, don't worry, Percy."

But Fender was unconsoled. In this mood, with the pitch helping him, Larwood was the most frightening prospect in the game. Often in the past his speed had been neutralized by an easy wicket. Two years ago Bradman had slaughtered him at Leeds. Quickness in itself was only of limited value. But Larwood possessed an accuracy unheard of in someone of his pace. He could hit a sixpence over and over again. On a damp pitch he could even make his own mark on the pitch by a relentless pounding in an area less than 3 inches wide.

When the outgoing players relayed the bad news about the worn patch, Fender's concern grew, and the rest of the side left him alone to lean forward on his chair and stare at the batsmen, as if willing them to stay in.

By tea, Surrey were 140 for 6, Larwood having removed five of their batsmen for 33 before resting. Voce took 1 for 40. Jardine came in with 53 not out and walked stiffly up the steps towards the dressing-rooms.

Fender greeted him with a broad grin: "By God, Douglas, that took sheer guts."

"Would someone close the door, please?" Jardine said.

His voice was clipped and sounded as if he were holding in his breath. One of the men pushed the door to with his foot. Immediately Jardine fell heavily on to a bench and closed his eyes. Fender bent forward to catch him before he slid to the ground.

"Douglas, what's the matter—?"

Someone pointed to a red mark on the left side of his woollen sweater. Fender raised it and gasped when he saw a blood-stain on the shirt about 2 inches across. With careful fingers, they helped to ease the shirt out of the waistband and roll it up. A large purple bruise, long and curving under the ribs, surrounded a cut about an inch long. Rivulets of blood had coagulated down Jardine's side.

"Why the devil didn't you come off, you bloody fool?" Fender murmured, peeling the shirt gently over his head. Jardine opened his eyes and gave the tightest of smiles.

"What—give in to that little bastard?" he whispered. "Never."

"Well, there is no chance of going on after tea," said Fender. He turned his head and called: "Someone, get a car, ring the nearest hospital—"

Jardine stood up and detached himself from the helping hands. "Percy," he said quietly, but with the cold tone they were used to hearing when he was annoyed, "the only place I'm going after tea is back out there. Or this club can find another captain."

At the end of the day, Surrey were all out for 243, Jardine making 85 before being caught in the slips off Voce. The Notts openers played out time and were 15 at the close. Alf Jackson, a friend of Larwood from his pit days, took three of the others round to wait outside the professionals' dressing-room.

"Fancy a jar, Loll?" he grinned as Larwood and Voce appeared lugging their cricket bags.

"Heyup, Alf, what you doing here? An' Jim, an'all—"

"Reckoned as how we'd watch someone else work for a change," Alf grinned.

They crossed over to the Trent Bridge Inn. Jardine and Carr

were standing in the lounge nursing whiskies. Larwood caught the Surrey captain's notice as they passed the open door to go into the public bar.

"Well bowled, Larwood," Jardine called, giving no clue to the pain he felt under the bandages.

"Thanks, Mr Jardine," Larwood answered. "Well batted."

He moved to the front and bought a round of Shipstone's Ales and they went over to a corner table.

"Ode Sardine can hardly stand up," Voce muttered, grinning.

"Why?" Jim asked. "What you mean?"

"Loll gorrim smack in t'ribs," Voce said. "Daft bugger carried on like nowt were wrong. Couldn't hardly hode his bloody bat."

"Din't look like it," Alf remarked. "If he got 85 hardly able to hold his bat, what would he have done if he'd been fit?"

Voce shrugged. He wasn't one for giving credit to his opponents. He had never seen the point. Especially amateurs. They played the game when they felt like it, displacing pros who needed the money, kept to themselves in their separate changing rooms and talked to you like you were muck on their boots. Well, most of 'em did, any road. Arthur Carr, though, were different. He may have been to a posh school, but he played t'bloody game like it mattered. Wonder what he and Jardine were jawing about next door? Mebbe Arthur's putting in a good word for him to go to Australia. Odds were Jardine'll get job of captain, or so everyone said. Mebbe he should go and have a listen round t'door—

"Whose shout is it?" someone said, and he came out of his thoughts to find them all looking at him, wiping their mouths.

"Wait on," he replied, "I ain't finished."

"Then sup up." Alf grinned. "Never known anyone hode a pint longer 'n you, Tangy, when it's your turn."

"Can't stay," Larwood said as the new ales arrived. "Lois'll have summat to say if I'm late."

"Tode yer wives'll gerrin t'way of drinking," Voce laughed as he sat down. "But you wouldn't listen—"

Alf and Larwood took the tram to the Mansfield Road station and found a Kirkby bus just pulling out. Alf ran into the middle of the street forcing the driver to stop with a squeal of brakes. He put his head out of the window and started to swear, then saw Larwood.

"Oh, it's you, Harold," the driver yelled. "How'd yer gerron today?"

The next morning he and Lois took June, their 4-year-old daughter, along to feed the chickens at the poultry farm they had recently acquired. Lois had something on her mind and talked little, occasionally saying something to June, telling her not to spill the chicken feed, or to mind the road, or to be careful of falling over.

"What the matter, duck?" Larwood said eventually, knowing she was ill at ease. Lois didn't answer, but drew her coat a bit tighter round her.

He knew what the matter was, but there was nothing he could say that he hadn't said before.

"Alf said he'll give you a hand wi' the chickens while I'm gone," he said.

"We can't afford to pay anyone," Lois answered.

They reached the farm and she unhooked the gate. The chickens raised a howl of chatter.

"He don't want money," Larwood argued. "He said he'll do it just for the eggs."

But Lois shook her head.

"I'll manage," she replied, filling June's little seaside bucket with feed and letting her run on ahead, flinging handfuls through the cages at the squawking birds.

They wandered silently down the rows, watching the fowls squabble among themselves and throw themselves at the wire as they passed. Lois finally said:

"I hate it when you have to go away, Harold."

"I know," he replied uneasily. "How d'you think *I* feel?"

"It's different for you," she said. "You have distractions. Different countries, and your friends an'all round you all the time. Me, I'm stuck here, nowt else to do but look after June, who's getting old enough to look after herself now, she don't need me every minute of the day, not like when she were a baby. And these daft chickens. It's different for you."

26

He felt anger in her voice and stayed silent. Then she softened, and took his hand:

"Don't mind me, love," she said, "I'm a selfish bitch. Always want to have my cake and eat it."

"Nowt wrong wi' that," Larwood grinned. "If you can manage it."

"It's just—I mean, *six months* away!" she cried, squeezing his hand fiercely as the thought took hold of her. "I can't stand it when you go away three days for a game. But half a year on t'other side of t'world—what if owt happened to you? Or to me or to June—you'd be so far away—"

"Nowt'll happen to any of us," he replied, putting an arm round her shoulders, pulling her to him. "We're lucky, us Larwoods. Always was, always will be. You'll see."

June was tossing grain into the far run and shrieking with laughter as the chickens fought over it.

"Not so much now, our June!" Lois called. "You still have a lot to do yet, all up t'other side!"

Larwood stared at the colliery wheel off to the left, still and silent for the only day of the week. Next to it, a monument to the hard graft of the Midlands, stood an enormous slag heap. He wondered what the countryside had been like before coal.

"Alf's no nearer gerring back down to t'face," he said, conscious that his wife was watching him. "Could be he'll never get back, way things are going."

"Things'll change," she replied, but not with much passion. "They've just got to, han't they? I mean, there's been lay-offs before, and men went back to work. Can't go on like this for ever, now can it. Stands to reason—"

Her voice trailed away. As far as anyone else could see, things *could* go on like they were for ever. Thank heaven they weren't with the rest of them. She had no idea how she would face life on the dole. Apart from with anger and resentment. If anyone told her she'd have to go careful on what she spent feeding her family, on clothing June—she would start throwing things, she was sure of it. Not that *that* would do much good.

No, they were lucky, like he said. The Lucky Larwoods. . . .

"It were cricket gorrus out of t'pit," Harold was saying. "It were cricket gorrus the chicken farm, gorrus a bit of security, Lois. The game's been good to us."

"I know," she answered. "Don't think I'm not grateful to it, 'cos I am. But I still hate having you go off like this. I'm never going to like a game that makes you a stranger to your own daughter."

They turned at the end and began slowly to walk up the other side, Lois occasionally filling June's bucket.

"You've done your stint of tours," Lois went on. "Why can't you tell them you want to miss this one? They know how much time you've put in wi' cricket."

Larwood laughed and gave her shoulders another hug.

"Oh aye," he scoffed. "I can just imagine what they'd say to that, all right!"

"Well, there'd be nowt wrong in just *asking*, would there?"

"Be like saying to t'gaffer in t'pit—'D'yer hear, Jack, I'll not be in next week, feel like a bit of a lie-in.' Talk sense, Lois."

"I *am* talking sense!" she exclaimed. "There's plenty of others could take your place."

"I'll be too ode and put out to pasture soon enough, me duck," he said. "Let's not rush it."

Some of the lads were in the Newcastle Arms as they passed on the way home. Lois felt guilty about having gone on about the Australian tour, and said why didn't he stop off for a quick one.

"But mind, dinner's on t'table in half an hour."

The public bar was packed with miners. Spruce and neat, their shirts fastened to the neck and crinkly with starch, they stood in tight groups playing spoof, or sat at the scrubbed bare tables, heads down over dominoes, or threw darts. Everyone drank from straight-up pint glasses. Tucked away round the corner stood a Ladies' Snug, where half a dozen women of uncertain ages sat with their handbags held firmly on their laps and a stout or a port and lemon on the table.

The mood was boisterous; the one day off the men enjoyed and the one hour in the day when they could say to hell with their problems, we'll have a jar or two. Every so often a roar of laughter erupted from a crowd in the corner and when it subsided someone continued talking in a low, conspiratorial voice. There then followed another burst of glee. The jokes were being passed round. There was a commercial traveller with them who had just come back from London with a new batch and each one was a winner. When the men laughed, half the women in the Snug would peer round disapprovingly, knowing exactly what was causing the mirth and trying mutely to put an end to it. But by now the mild and bitter had oiled the funnybone and the men were immune to their frowns and pinched expressions.

Alf Jackson, part of the noisy group, saw one of them glare across and gave her a jaunty wink.

"Heyup, Missus, come over here and I'll give you summat to laugh about!"

The woman pulled in her head like a startled tortoise and muttered to her companion, who tutted and said something about "that Alf Jackson, cheeky monkey, he'll come a cropper one of these days—"

When Larwood threaded his way to the bar, Alf saw him and squeezed among the drinkers.

"My shout today, Loll," he called.

"Nay, Alf, it's all right, whorra you drinking—"

Alf fiddled for some coppers and banged them down in front of the landlord.

"Pint o' Shippos, Arthur," he said firmly, turning to Larwood with a grin.

"I've still gorrenough to pay my whack at t'bloody counter," he said. "You bought 'em in town yesterday, you and Tangy. A fool and his money are soon parted, me ode Granddad used to say—"

They took their drinks back to the joke session but as soon as Larwood arrived, they began talking about the Surrey game, then about the tour.

"Who'd yer reckon'll skipper, Loll?"

"I dunno. S'hard to say—"

"Reckon Chapman's had it, then—"

"Aye. Pity, though. Grand bloke, Percy. Everyone liked him, even down under. Papers an'all. Never got slagged by the crowd."

"What's Aussie pubs like, Loll?"

"Not like here."

"What's Aussie ale like?"

"Not like here."

"What's Aussie women like, Harold?"

"Not like here—"

"How'd you know then, you dirty ode devil? Tried 'em, have yer—"

Another gale of laughter brought the heads round from the Snug again before Alf stuck his hand on his hip and wiggled his body at them, whereupon they retired once more to mutter about that awful Alf Jackson and how one of these days—

Larwood settled happily into the corner with his pint and listened to the fast, cheery backchat. When they asked about cricket, he would answer briefly, not wanting to dominate the conversation but also not wanting to show off the fact that he was in work whereas most of them weren't. Not only that, but he was paid to play a game, a far cry from hacking chips of coal in the blackness a hundred yards below ground.

The men continued to tell stories, breaking off frequently to make sure Larwood, who could never remember jokes, was not being ignored. He kept assuring them he was having a grand time and that he was sorry he didn't have any tales of his own. He was never happier than in the midst of his friends, some of whom he had known in Nuncargate when they ran in ragged short trousers over the fields, fishing for newts in Jeffreys' pond or scrumping Ma Derby's apples. Conversely, the men of Kirkby all liked Loll because he might be a national figure but he never put on any side. He was just the same as always, paying his way in the pub—sometimes a bit more—never talking about himself except when he was asked. Some blokes had their names mentioned once in the local rag and started acting like the Prince of bloody Wales.

Two strangers came in. One of them recognized Larwood and whispered to his mate who looked over and said loudly, "'Im? Larwood? Can't be. Don't look more'n knee-high to a bloody grasshopper."

Alf heard the remark and turned round to be met by two sullen faces.

"Do owt for yer, John?" the same man asked. Alf guessed they were drunk already and turned away. The man gave a short laugh of triumph and when they bought their drinks, he and his friend sat down at a table.

"Take no heed of them," Alf told Larwood, who also had heard the comment about his height. "One smell of t'barmaid's apron wi' some blokes."

An uneasy ceasefire passed for a few moments.

"I dunno," one of the newcomers bellowed for the whole bar to hear, "All right for some, intit? You get some nancy boys paid to gallivant all over t'bloody world hitting a daft ball wi' a piece o' wood. While others stand on t'dole queue wi'out enough to feed theirselves."

A couple of men made a move, but Larwood pulled on their sleeves and shook his head. When the man at the table looked at him to pinpoint his accusation, he gave an easy grin.

"It's not all beer and skittles, my friend," he said. "I don't see my wife and kiddy for days on end, sometimes months when we travel abroad."

"Oh, poor ode devil!" the seated man wailed, wiping his eye with his hand. "Shurrup, you're mekking me cry!"

"Sound like you can't wait to get back down t'pit," the man said.

"No, not me," Larwood answered.

"Why, pit too good for t'likes o'you, now your pictures in all t'papers?"

Alf began to pass across a new round from the counters. When he came to Larwood he passed the glass over the head of the man who had been doing the talking and tilted it slightly. The fellow rose with a roar of anger as the ale ran down his ear.

"Here, what's your bloody game, then?" he shouted.

"Sorry," Alf said, looking at Larwood, not the complainant. "Waste of good ale. Here, have some of mine—"

He tipped a few drops of his own into Larwood's glass, again over the man who had sat down wiping his neck. Some more went over him and he stood up again quickly, ready to take on the whole room.

"You done that on purpose!" he snarled and reached out to grab

31

Alf's lapel. Alf knocked his hand carelessly away and turned his body.

"Think I'd waste my drink on you—you must be daft as you look," he said dismissively.

For a second the man deliberated whether it was worth continuing. There were at least four of them willing to have a go, and this was a strange town to him. He was passing through, looking for work. Lack of success kept his temper high, and a fight would ease his frustration. Even if it ended with him being beaten black and blue. But he thought again and resumed his seat, muttering.

When Larwood finished his second pint he put it on the window sill. "I've gorra go," he said. "Lois'll have t'dinner on t'table."

Alf swallowed his drink and said he had to go as well, and the two of them left the pub and walked slowly up the cobblestone hill to their houses.

They passed a knot of children playing cricket, the wickets chalked on a wall. When the boy bowling saw Larwood he went back ten more paces and came in hurling the tennis ball so fast it hit the wall half-way up and rebounded into an alley opposite. The other lads raised a howl of protest and said he had to give away four wides as a penalty. The row was still going on by the time the two men had reached the end of the street and turned the corner.

"Wonder if any of them will end up bein' paid to gallivant all over t'world," Alf remarked.

"Hope so," Larwood replied with a chuckle.

Alf gave his friend a sideways glance:

"Here, Loll, don't mind that silly bugger in t'pub—"

"I didn't."

"He were only ninepence in t'bloody shilling—but there *was* summat in what he said."

"What's that?"

Alf stopped by some allotments and looked over the array of garden sheds and serried rows of cabbages, their leaves eaten by insects into delicate lace patterns.

"Well there's no denying about t'dole queues," he murmured.

"I'm not denying it," Larwood answered; he was going to say something more when Alf held up his hand.

"Don't lose yer rag, me ode," he said. "All I'm trying to say is nobody minds you blokes going off round the world playing cricket. Everyone'd give owt to changes places wi'yer."

"Well, then?"

Alf chose his words carefully. He knew his friend well. Off the cricket field, there was no one more agreeable and accommodating. He had never heard him utter a malicious word about anybody. That was why he was so popular. Talking cricket was another matter, though. You had to be careful. Loll wasn't just a keen sportsman; the game was his life's blood. It was as important to him as anything, except his family.

"If you beat t'Aussies," Alf went on, "the world'll say, 'Good lads, you earned your snap, three cheers for the lot o'yer and have the next pint on me.' But you lose like you did last time, and folks are gonta start wondering why the bloody 'ell they *should* fork out to send you swanning round the place playing games. That's all I'm trying to say. Don't take it the wrong way. Two years ago you got hammered. Nobody could understand why. We all thought you'ad it in yer pockets. Then Bradman murdered you. Could be, some folks thought, could be you've all got a bit soft going first class on t'boats and trains and staying at fancy hotels. They'll not be looking to be clobbered again, Loll. This time you've just *got* to win."

Larwood tapped the railings with his fist and knew every word Alf was saying had been said before. Not so directly, but bits here and there. Two years ago, nobody would have tried to rile him like the man in the pub. But since then, there had been a couple more years of depression, lay-offs in the mines and the factories. The mood was now more sour, less optimistic. People looked round for a whipping boy. Cricketers led the life of Old Reilly. Well, as long as they kept winning then they deserved it. But when they started losing—how many times after the 1930 series had he heard men say: "Blimey, *I* could a'done better'n that lot—" And they believed it. Bitterness led to envy and envy led to hostility. "It's not how good you play, it's how well you're in with the nobs—"

"Aye," he said as they resumed walking. "I know."

Chapter Three

Pelham Warner instructed the reception clerk at his club to bring Mr Jardine through to the garden where he would be waiting. He had every reason to be pleased and showed it as he flicked through *The Times*, enjoying the warmth of an Indian summer.

Things had gone well at the Selection Committee meeting. There had been reservations about his enthusiasm to appoint Jardine captain of the tour, but nothing he had not been able to handle. Perrin had been concerned that the man had had little Test captaincy experience—three matches against New Zealand in '31 and the single Test against India that summer—but was unwilling to support any of the other possible candidates. Chapman was finished after the Australian débâcle in 1930; Wyatt was captain of Warwickshire but had lost the '30 Oval game when England relinquished the Ashes. Fender and J.C. White were now in their forties, and it was felt that public reaction would be hostile to the appointment of men almost twice the age of some of the Australian team.

However, Jardine presented other problems to the Selection Committee besides his limited international experience. True, he had recently taken over at Surrey and there was no question that he had a shrewd tactical brain. But the trouble was, as Higson, the third selector, pointed out, the man was too bloody clever by half. Warner had countered that that was precisely what they required in an England skipper but knew what Higson meant. There were very few players in the game who actually admitted to *liking* him. Hitherto, England captains had controlled their side by a sympathetic presence. Cricket traditionally was a game played among friends, and the skipper of a side was chosen for his social as well as tactical qualities. The boyish, genial figure of Percy Chapman personified the popular hero, the amateur cavalier conjuring up images of schoolboy idols immortalized by the comics of the period.

Douglas Jardine didn't even *look* genial. Tall and slim, he held himself erect, and his aquiline features with the close-set eyes over the thin prominent nose made him look permanently contemptuous. Born in India of Scottish parents, he had attended Winchester and later Oxford, where his cricket had been consistent but undistinguished. His austerity came from within himself—his father M.R. Jardine had been a popular captain of Oxford in the 1890s—and seemed to manifest itself in an unwillingness to be impressed or overawed. Some put this down as a typical Wykehamist trait; certainly on intellectual matters it was apparent among many former pupils of the school. But Jardine carried it into all aspects of his life. He made no concession to popular sentiment. Indeed he often sought to provoke it. He rarely, for example, wore the M.C.C. cap during a Test match. Instead he preferred the Harlequin colours of his university days, a conscious badge of his intellectual superiority. Some said that in the company of his own kind he could relax and even become responsive and witty, but this was invariably reported at second hand.

That morning Jardine's personality had been discussed at length by the three selectors. Six months was a long time for men of all stripes to be thrown together. How, for instance, would Jardine cope with men like Tommy Mitchell, Voce, Larwood and Bowes?—all fine upstanding sportmen but as different from the Surrey captain as chalk from cheese. "Gentlemen," Warner started, "I would venture to suggest that what we are looking for is someone who will lead from the front. We need a skipper out on the field, not in the pavilion."

He was referring to the uneasy rumours of the Oval Test in 1930 when, after having removed Chapman, the selectors had sent out messages to the stand-in captain Bob Wyatt about how he should conduct the side. Like most rumours, this was only partly true, but even the suggestion had cast a derisory shadow over the M.C.C.

The arguments moved back and forth for an hour, but there was little passion in them; Perrin and Higson knew what Warner was driving at, and with Jardine's immaculate record in the four Tests he had so far led, they realized there was no serious alternative.

And so it was with a feeling of justification and inner pleasure that Warner sent a note to Jardine and asked him to lunch in order to relay their decision. His open and hospitable view of mankind meant that he took pleasure in announcing good news. For most of his life, and he was now almost sixty, "Plum" Warner had personified the very best privileged upbringing. Tolerant to a fault, unwilling to say a malicious word about anyone, his had been an extraordinarily untarnished life. Born in Trinidad of a father who was an Attorney-General, captain of cricket at Rugby, an Oxford blue, he had first toured in 1896 with Lord Hawke's side in the West Indies. Since then the game had been his entire world. He had captained Middlesex until 1920 and had been elected at the age of 31 to the committee of M.C.C. He had come to conduct his life according to the conventions of his beloved game. Neither required many written rules. Indeed, they both suffered if they were too highly regulated. It was enough in life to observe the traditions of fair play as it was on the field. There were things one simply did not do; everyone knew what they were, or if they didn't, they would find out after a few innings. Disputes took place in an atmosphere of quiet civility, and a handshake was all that opponents required to resolve differences.

The reception clerk appeared, followed by Jardine, still walking a little stiffly after the recent game against Notts. Warner laid his paper aside and stood up.

"Morning, Douglas."

Jardine nodded briskly.

"Good morning."

"Simpson, don't go away," Warner held out a hand to the steward. "Would you organize a couple of scotch and sodas? Out here, please."

"Certainly, sir."

Warner waved a hand at a chair and Jardine sat, grimacing a fraction as his side gave a twinge of protest.

"How're the ribs?" Warner asked.

"Fine. Just bloody sore, that's all."

He peered round in the bright sunshine, gazing at the other tables set out on the small lawn. He recognized someone from Oxford days and in the corner a friend of his father waved.

"You ought to become a member here, Douglas," Warner said. "You always seem to know more people than I do. I could put you up, you know. There wouldn't be any trouble."

"Thank you," Jardine answered with the merest of smiles. "But I don't think so."

"Why on earth not?" Warner felt a moment of displeasure. The man sounded as if he didn't like the place, whereas he hardly ever came except occasionally when he was invited for lunch.

"Don't be upset," Jardine added, his smile broadening a little. "I like it here. I like the people, the food and the furniture. If I joined anything, it would be a place where I could enjoy the company of men like you, Plum. But the truth of the matter is, I'm not very clubbable."

"Oh, what rot!" Warner scoffed. "Really, Douglas, there are times when I believe you are engaged in a lifelong prank against your fellow beings! Not clubbable indeed! It is an odd sort of chap who doesn't relish the company of his peers. And where better to do so in surroundings like this? Think about it, Douglas. I would personally regard it as a very great pleasure if you would let me put you up."

"I got your note," Jardine said, making it plain the matter of club membership was boring him. "Written on M.C.C. paper, I noticed."

"I've been at Lord's all morning," Warner explained, and a thrill of expectancy danced through his stomach. "Talking about the Aussie tour."

"You mean you've been talking about Bradman."

"Bradman and others, yes."

"Plum," murmured Jardine, placing an elbow on the table to ease his injured side, "there *are* no others. Whatever side you pick will be required to play Bradman plus ten extras."

"Oh, come now, that is hardly the case," Warner protested,

then realized he was being distracted from his principal reason for asking Jardine to come and see him. "However, that's neither here nor there. We discussed the team, naturally, but so far we've not really come to any definite conclusions. As a matter of fact at the end of the two hours, we only arrived at one clear decision."

A waiter was advancing towards them with a silver tray bearing two whiskies and a soda syphon.

"And what was that?" asked Jardine, sounding as if he were only mildly interested in an answer.

The waiter slid the tray on to the table and placed a whisky in front of each of the two men.

"That you should lead the side," Warner announced. He waited for a response. "The decision was unanimous, of course," he added.

Jardine shook his head briefly at the waiter who was offering the soda syphon.

"I'm sorry, Plum," he said briskly. "But I must refuse."

Warner sat perfectly still for a moment, looking as if he hadn't heard. His expression turned blank.

"I beg your pardon?"

The waiter was now looking at him, a hand on the lever of the syphon.

"Sir?"

Warner came out of his trance and looked at the man and then the syphon.

"What—oh, ah—just a splash—Douglas, what did you just say?"

The waiter fizzed some water into Warner's drink and stood back, holding the tray.

"Will there be anything else, sir?" he asked. Again Warner took a moment to refocus his attention.

"Sorry—? Oh, no, no, thank you, that will be all."

"Thank you, sir."

The waiter moved away inside.

"Douglas, for God's sake, what do you mean you *refuse*?" he cried, bringing a head or two round from the neighbouring tables.

Jardine sipped his drink as if they were talking about how splendid the hollyhocks were.

38

"You must find someone else," he replied quietly. "I'm naturally flattered by the offer and I thank you and the selectors most sincerely. But I have to say no."

"You don't have to say anything of the kind! No one has ever *turned down* the M.C.C. captaincy, ever!"

"I'm sure that isn't entirely true," Jardine replied mildly.

"I mean turn it down as you have done!" Warner almost shouted. "Without any kind of explanation. Any *reason*! What's the matter? Business? You've never let business interfere with cricket before. Is there any *personal* reason why you can't go—? Douglas, wipe that absurdly silly smile off your face and be good enough to tell me what you mean. I wouldn't put it past you to be pulling my leg. If you are, stop it. I have as good a sense of humour as the next man, but there are matters one simply does not joke about."

Jardine let him go on for a while, teasing him by his silence. Finally, when Warner dried up, he placed his drink down and leaned an elbow on the table. This was the only position that lessened the burning ache in his side.

"You'll recall that I toured Australia four years ago," Jardine began.

"And did very well on their hard wickets," Warner responded.

"Whether I did well or not is beside the point," Jardine continued, and the teasing quality in his voice had gone now. "The point is that during that tour, I arrived at one unalterable and undeniable conclusion. I came round to the view that your average Australian male is an ill-mannered, foul-mouthed, detestable lout. I endured insults and personal vindictiveness from those apes they dare to call cricket enthusiasts to a degree that no human being should be exposed—"

"Oh, you mean the barracking," Warner intervened. "Good Lord, Douglas, is *that* all? Look here, I first toured down there in 1903 and they were just the same then. It's nothing to get worked up about, for heaven's sake. We all go through the mill with the drunken larrikins on the Hill. No one minds."

"Wrong," Jardine said tersely. "*I* mind. I mind being called filthy names for no apparent reason except that I don't pretend to enjoy the experience. You will say, of course, that if I were to turn round and give them back the same kind of thing, they will love me for it—"

"So they will," Warner protested. "Why, Maurice Tate, Leyland—they told them where to get off in no uncertain terms and they're positively worshipped—"

"Worship from imbeciles is something I don't seek," Jardine answered. "Besides, it's not only barrackers and their foul language. I dislike *everything* about Australians. I detest their false bonhomie and hearty handshakes, their excruciating slaps on the back. I hate their raucousness, the way they conduct their lives at the top of their voices—"

"Douglas—"

"No, Plum, you're wasting your breath. I play cricket because it gives me pleasure. If it does *not* give me pleasure, *ergo* I don't play. The last tour of Australia gave me no pleasure at all and I have no reason to believe that the forthcoming trip will be any different. So I thank you and the selectors for your very great compliment, but I must regretfully refuse—"

"But can I not just say—"

"And there," said Jardine, finishing his whisky and placing the glass down with a significant firmness, "we might let the matter rest."

Warner gave up. Perhaps the others had been right. God knows what morale would have been like in the dressing-rooms with this fellow in charge! And yet, and yet. . . .

As they wandered into the dining-room, Warner regarded the rigid back of his guest. He was the only person in the country to lead a team that would have any chance of winning. Of that he was certain. Percy Chapman had tried to do it on charm and failed. What was it Teddy Roosevelt had once said? Speak softly and carry a big stick. Warner had no trouble imagining Douglas Jardine charging full tilt up the hill at San Juan. The fellow simply had to be persuaded to change his mind. However, as he well knew, that was no task for ordinary mortals.

Chapter Four

"Order, order, order, ORDER!"

The Speaker of the House of Commons was having trouble. For a start, no one was listening to him, although that in itself was not unusual. When members grasped the bit between their teeth during debates his presence was little more than ceremonial. If order *was* restored it would be because *they* wished it so, not through any deference to his authority. Not that he wasn't enjoying himself. That little sod Thomas was getting everything he deserved—

"Order, ladies and gentlemen, please—order!"

Gradually the braying subsided, and he was able to announce one of the many members who were frantically waving order forms in his direction. The man stood for some moments until the others regained their seats and quietened down. "Mr Speaker, is not my Right Honourable Friend in the same position as the doting father who gives his growing children the key to the door, only to find himself one night locked out of the house?"

A gale of laughter, hooting and cheers filled the hall, and once more the Speaker vainly tried to make his voice heard above the din. Democracy produced the effects of a barnyard at times, he had always thought. A little more discipline would give him fewer headaches.

He glanced down at the object of the derision. J.H. Thomas, Secretary for the Dominions, sat with his hands thrust deep into his pockets, glaring at his tormentors over the round wire glasses he habitually wore half-way down his nose.

Serve him right, the Speaker said to himself. Give a man enough rope—

"May the house be graced with an answer from my Right Honourable Friend?" the M.P. who had just spoken added, yelling above the noise. "May we hear if he now regrets having given our colonies such wide-ranging freedom in the conduct of their affairs in the light of their recent unreasonable behaviour at the Imperial Conference?"

Thomas waited until the catcalls subsided, then rose very slowly to his feet, keeping his hands deep in his trouser pockets. Ramsay MacDonald, two places along the front bench, gave him a worried glance. Say something good, Jimmy, he pleaded silently. Don't leave me naked.

Thomas looked round him for a full twenty seconds until the last insult died. Then he said simply, "No," and sat down again.

The baiting roared back into top gear and little else of significance was added to the debate before the Speaker directed the House on to other matters. Thomas pulled his papers together. Those nearest him could tell he was seething with anger, because he was chewing the end of his walrus moustache. There were few men present eager to cross swords with this odd-looking, rotund man in the funny glasses when he did this. A hard apprenticeship served in the National Union of Railwaymen before his negotiating abilities brought him a seat in Parliament had left him with a biting wit and a quickness to retaliate that usually left opponents staring vacantly, or eyeing the door.

Jimmy Thomas was one of those rare creatures in government— an authentic "character". Born illegitimate in a Welsh slum, he had started work at 9 years old, eventually moving to the railways first as a driver then as a trade union organizer. Twenty years later he entered the House of Commons and began an inexorable rise to the top, arriving in the Labour Cabinet of 1924 as Colonial Secretary. Throughout his career, Thomas had never tried to conceal his origins. His accent was more Cockney than Welsh and included a flaw that he was never able, or never willing, to correct: at times, he could not always put his aitches in the right place. Jokes abounded about this. It was said that once he sat down heavily in the House and confided to his neighbour, "Blimey, I've got an 'orrible 'eadache," and received the answer, "Never mind, Jimmy, just take a couple of aspirates."

When he entered Parliament in 1910, a story goes that he met

Lord Birkenhead, then F.E. Smith, in the corridor and said: "'Ere, cock, where're the lavs?"

"Go down this corridor," Smith instructed, "and you will come to a door marked 'Gentlemen'. But don't let that put you off."

Neither doors marked 'Gentlemen' or anything else put the ambitious 35-year-old off, and soon F.E. Smith came to admire the thrusting and often ruthless nature of the newcomer both in debate and in committee.

When Ramsay MacDonald formed the National Government in 1931, Thomas went with him, continuing his role as Secretary of State for what was now called Dominion Affairs. He was a popular, no-nonsense figure with whom the public could identify, an uncommon trait in politicians of the day, but of late the increasing aggressiveness he had experienced from some of the emerging Dominions, in particular Canada, South Africa and Australia, was sapping his efforts to remain so. The move to a National Government was widely regarded as a sell-out by sections of the Labour Party and his loyalty to the Prime Minister lost him considerable respect at large, especially abroad. On the other side of the world, the Colonies watched with anxiety the throes of a political system that had once effortlessly controlled an immense empire. Confidence in Parliament weakened as parties disintegrated in the face of economic depression and mass unemployment, and coalitions desperately struggled to keep a semblance of order.

The world depression had affected all the Colonies, but it was to London that they looked for a remedy. When it was not forthcoming, a feeling grew that the home country was no longer the wise arbiter of their problems. In themselves, many of these far-flung possessions were neither bankrupt nor starving. Resources were plentiful under the soil, and farms teemed with livestock. What the Colonies required were markets and the wherewithal to exploit their potential wealth, and when they didn't receive them, they began to make trouble. Trouble which ended on Thomas's desk.

He had tried to meet them half-way and in the process allowed a greater autonomy in the handling of their economic affairs. A series of Imperial Conferences had witnessed the larger Dominions

43

gradually consolidating these concessions and inevitably using their newly acquired strength to demand more. The world was in a terrible state and the only viable national policy was one that recognized the need to get in first. It was dog-eat-dog these days, with no excuse to be found for the sensitivities of an Imperial institution that had outlived its effectiveness.

Needless to say, there was a lack of support for this view in the Commons. Thomas himself certainly never subscribed to it, he simply tried to do an impossible job. Consequently, as he left the Chamber after an hour of the most severe mauling he could remember, his sympathies did not lie with any of the countries over which he wielded a diminishing control

His private secretary, Edward Marsh, heard him stump down the corridor and enter his office. Marsh knew at once the afternoon had gone badly by the sibilant muttering he could hear through the plaster walls and stood ready for the shout he knew was already rising in his master's gorge: "Heddie! Get the 'ell in 'ere!"

A crash signalled a waste-bucket had been kicked flying as the Secretary of State marched to his overflowing desk. Marsh took a deep breath and went through the interconnecting door.

"Do I take it the House was unimpressed by the antics of our far-flung Empire?" he said.

"I know where I'd like to fling it," Thomas snarled. With a sweeping movement he dashed a column of folders Marsh had placed on his desk to the carpet and turned to glare at a long wall-map showing the Colonies and Dominions marked in red. Bringing back an arm, he thumped Australia with such force that the blinds on the windows rattled.

"The bleedin' nerve of those ex-convicts!" he thundered, a gob of spittle sticking to the map above Pitcairn Island. "They blame *hus* for their hunemployment, *hus* for the Depression, *hus* for not buying their bloody sheep, when the price they're asking is daylight bloody robbery! I tell you, Heddie, we should never have taken off their leg irons. I mean that."

You don't, Marsh thought, but you're putting on a good enough performance. The two men were completely different in temperament; Thomas the self-made man with the baggy suit and

44

cheap spectacles, Marsh the urbane sophisticate with immaculate diction. But Marsh relished the aura of raw power that surrounded the Minister. Even when besieged on all sides, he displayed a fierceness that some victims had underestimated to their cost. He could never imagine Thomas throwing in the towel. When he came to die he would doubtless first arrange his interview with the Almighty on his own terms. He admired the fact that his boss never seemed to lose control of any situation; he might rage and kick things, but these actions were all part of a charade. Old Jimmy was a street fighter who had never lost the ability to hit below the belt when all else failed: the very stuff of political success. He would not want to work for anyone else, that was certain.

He knelt and retrieved the folders from the carpet and replaced them on the Minister's desk while the older man continued to glare at the wall map, as if willing the red parts to disappear.

"Back on the railways," he muttered, more to himself than his assistant, "if you gave a bloke a rise, he was more likely to do what you expected of him. Go up to management and doff your 'at and show you wanted to talk about shorter hours in a reasonable hand civilized manner, more likely than not they'd give you 'alf an ear. They'd listen, they would. They'd listen and meet you 'alf-way. But with this bleedin' lot—"

He waved a hand vaguely at the wall: "—'old out your 'and in friendship and they'll chop it off."

Marsh knew the storm would blow away as long as nothing was said to prolong it; and so he remained silent, flicking through the top file on the desk. Finally, Thomas sighed and turned round.

"What's all this bumf, then?" he grunted. Paper work bored him and it took every ounce of Marsh's diplomatic skills even to get a few signatures.

"Nothing that won't wait, sir," he said casually. "You have an hour tomorrow morning before your meetings start. Perhaps we could go through them then—"

Thomas reached out and took the folder from the younger man's grasp. If there was one foolproof way to gain Jimmy's interest, Marsh knew, it was to pretend the issue at hand wasn't important. He watched his boss open the folder and adjust his glasses.

"What the 'ell is this?" he muttered, sitting down.

Marsh pretended he could not recall and leaned over to check.

"That—oh, just an *aide-memoire* from the Governor of South Australia."

Thomas peered through his spectacles, bringing the paper closer to his face. Marsh recognized the gesture; whenever Thomas wanted to show contempt for something he was reading, he would pretend his sight was so poor that nothing short of pressing his nose to the paper would enable him to see the words.

"What in God's name is Hore-Whoosit rabbiting on about?"

"The Governor is making one or two oblique references to the forthcoming cricket tour, sir," Marsh explained.

"Oblique is the word for it," Thomas replied. "I can't make head or tail of this. Translate it for me, Heddie."

Marsh took the folder and glanced at the report. Sir Alexander Hore-Ruthven was an effective, if long-winded representative, but had gone down quite well in South Australia since his appointment. However, his writing tended to suffer from prolixity, and Marsh was usually called upon by his master to paraphrase his letters.

"The Governor is musing on the possibility that we might be beaten heavily again as we were in 1930, sir," he said.

"Very interesting," Thomas sniffed. "I'm sure we are all better men knowing his views on cricket."

Turning the pages, Marsh continued, "Well, sir, he does have a point which might bear considering."

"What's that?"

"He points out the obsession that most Australians have about sport, Minister."

"Ho?"

"Yes, sir. Actually I see what Sir Alexander is driving at. The Americans are the same."

"Nothing else to think about," Thomas grunted. Apart from horse-racing, sport was of little interest to the Welshman. As for cricket, he had never been able to interpret the printed scores. 180 for 3 declared, so-and-so 50 not out, rain stopped play in the second innings—it was all gobbledegook to him.

Marsh persisted.

"They really are quite single-minded when it comes to competitive games, sir. As this report explains, the Australian cobber-in-the-street, as it were, doesn't read a newspaper for its editorials or the business or the arts news. He reads it for one thing only—sport. If he wants to hear about wars he turns to the sports columns—chaps are much the same here, but less so, if you see what I mean. If England loses at cricket or rugger, or ping-pong, nobody really minds, not for long anyway. In Australia or America losing is a reason to hang the flags at half-mast and for the entire nation to go into a prolonged state of mourning. It's all here in Ruthven's report."

"But why is he banging on about this?" Thomas persisted. "It may be all most enlightening about the Horstralian mentality, but frankly I don't give a toss *what* they feel about games or the playing thereof."

"Sir Alexander makes the thought-provoking point", Marsh carried on, regardless of the looks he was getting over the wire rims, "that had Australia not beaten us so comprehensively in 1930, they would not have behaved quite so arrogantly at the Imperial Conferences."

"Poppycock—"

"He may be overstating the case," Marsh said, "but there is a grain of truth in what he says."

"They win a game of cricket, so the price of their bleedin' sheep goes hup? Heddie, you need a rest."

Marsh smiled.

"It's all a question of morale, Minister," he went on. "The Australians destroyed our supremacy in the cricket world when we were least expecting to be defeated. At a stroke, we are relegated from the pinnacle of success to just another mediocre team. They have Bradman, not yet 25 years old, generally regarded as invincible and likely to remain so for the next fifteen years. *That* is what your average Aussie is reading in his sports papers. And *that* is the reason, this report suggests, why they are being so bloody-minded."

Thomas said nothing for a time, alternating between looking at the papers in Marsh's hand and the wall map.

"And you reckon we're going to get clobbered again, this cricket lot we're sending?" he asked finally. His secretary nodded.

"It's on the cards."

"Why? Can't we find *any* good players *anywhere*?"

"Not good enough. Oh, we have some quick bowlers and even now Hobbs has retired, Herbert Sutcliffe and Wally Hammond are there to stiffen the batting, but seeing what Bradman did the last time—the other thing, of course, is Jardine has refused to go as captain."

"Refused?" Thomas raised his eyebrows. "Why?"

"He doesn't like Australians very much, apparently," Marsh replied.

The Minister gave a snort. "I know how he feels."

"I've been told he cracks the whip a bit, old Jardine, which is just what some of our chaps need," Marsh reflected. "It's all very well having some decent players, but cricket's an odd game. A side can easily get demoralized if there isn't a strong hand in control. The psychological aspects of cricket are really quite remarkable—"

"Wait a second, hold on," Thomas breathed. "Let's not get carried away. As far as I can see, cricket is a bunch of blokes decked out in white trousers chucking a ball at three sticks, and another bloke with things strapped all over him flinging a bat round his head trying to stop them. All right, so I'm just another of them ignorant buggers who never went to the proper schools, and maybe all this psychological argy-bargy is lost on my simple brain, but as far as I'm concerned, the only hinteresting part of your explanation of that there letter is the bit about the Aussies thinking they're the dog's bloody dinner just because they won. And that if this Jardine fella was in charge, we'd stand a better chance of beating the sods. You did say that, didn't you?"

"Not quite in those words, sir, but, well, yes—"

"Then the way ahead is simple and obvious," Thomas said, entwining his fingers over his chest and tapping his forefingers together. "Get Jardine to change his mind."

"Easier said than done, sir."

"Why? Stubborn, is he?"

"In comparison, I'm told, the Rock of Gibraltar is a gadfly."

Thomas leaned forward and his eyes glinted. "Tell 'im I'd like a word."

"I ought to warn you, sir," Marsh said, "Jardine is a law unto himself. He isn't going to be impressed by a tour of Parliament and lunch on the terrace."

Thomas untangled his fingers and gripped the edge of his desk, beaming up at his assistant.

"Heddie, it has been my experience that when you want somebody to do you a favour which they are not, at first, willing to perform, all you 'ave to do is mention the Honours list."

Marsh met the open grin with a slow smile. He laid the folder on the desk on top of the others and went out to make the necessary arrangements.

The meeting was shorter than Thomas anticipated. Eddie Marsh telephoned Jardine directly; the two men, having met in the past, were sufficiently intimate to nod to each other in the street.

"What on earth does the Secretary of State want to see me about?" Jardine asked.

"I've no idea, Douglas. He rarely acquaints me with his inner thoughts."

"I don't suppose this has anything to do with the tour?"

"Couldn't say."

"Tell him I'm not going and then let me know if he still wants to meet."

"I think he knows you aren't, Douglas. Look, you would be doing me a favour if you came. If you don't, he'll accuse me of not pulling my weight and I rather like it here. I should hate to be transferred."

Thomas was waiting for him on the first bench inside St James's Park from the entrance at the Foreign Office end. Marsh made the introductions then mumbled an excuse and walked back up the Clive Steps. Thomas took Jardine's arm but let go when he felt the man instinctively stiffen at the contact. He walked slowly, toying with his cane, keeping a pendulum movement going between his thumb and forefingers.

"I'm not a regular cricket watcher, Mr Jardine," he explained as they walked along the side of the lake. Some workmen were using a long hose to clean out the jetsam watched by a gaggle of geese from the bank. "I have to tell you that at the start."

"A great many people aren't," Jardine replied blandly.

"But I've got a great respect for it," Thomas continued. "My private secretary Marsh is dead keen. You know 'im, I gather."

"We have met."

"Oh, he's a real enthusiast. Keeps me up to date with everything."

"That must be very helpful."

The older man gave his companion a sideways look, catching the condescension, the twinge of sarcasm. But he let it go for the moment.

"Oh yes, oh yes, Heddie is a treasure. I don't know where I'd be without 'im. Knows about all sorts of things. All sorts."

They walked on a way in silence.

"He tells me you aren't going to Australia," he said casually.

"That's correct."

"Might I ask why, Mr Jardine?"

Jardine told him.

"My word, you don't beat about the bush, do you?" Thomas exclaimed, when Jardine finished an undemonstrative account of his feelings towards Australia and her people.

"No, Minister. I've never learned the lexicon of the politician."

Thomas beamed. "I admire your frankness."

"There isn't much to admire," Jardine replied. "I am merely stating a point of view."

"And one I'm sometimes inclined to share," Thomas chuckled.

"Really."

"Yes, really. Running the Colonies, the Dominions, whatever you want to call them, is a thankless task, Mr Jardine."

"I'm sure it is, but from what I have seen, you do it very well."

"Thank you, I do my best. We can but do our best."

Another twenty yards went by in more silence.

"Is your reason for not going", the Secretary of State went on, "anything to do with the general view that we are going to have the pants licked off us once again by these buggers?"

"No, that isn't so," Jardine answered, with some restraint.

50

Thomas detected a frosty tone and smiled:

"Oh, don't get the needle, my boy, don't fly off the handle," he urged, putting up a hand soothingly. "I'm not suggesting you were *afraid* to go—"

"I've just explained why I refused."

"So you did."

"As it happens I think we have a decent chance of winning back the Ashes," Jardine added, but not with much conviction. He was concerned to think that his decision was being interpreted as cowardice.

"But what with these Bradmans and, whatsisname—Kippax and—and—" Hell, what *were* the names Marsh had mentioned? "—and so on, we're not what you might call favourites, are we?"

"Perhaps not."

Thomas nodded and gripped his cane more firmly, running the tip along the top of the railings that border the grassy banks of the lake.

"I'll be candid with you, Douglas—do you mind if I call you Douglas?"

"No."

"My job brings me into touch with a great number of Horstralians, New Zealanders, 'Ottentots and what have you," he confided, "and they've all got one thing in common—give 'em an inch and they'll take a mile. Now I'm not complaining, it's 'uman nature after all to grab what you can, but I've got to find a way to stop 'em. Otherwise we living here in old England aren't going to have two ha'pennies to rub together. We'll be so busy giving millions away, we'll not have anything to spend on ourselves. And I don't need to remind you of the present state of our economy, now do I? Unemployment two and an 'alf million—we simply can't keep sendin' money half-way across the world to satisfy a few loudmouths who think they have a divine right to it. D'you get my drift, Mr Jardine?"

"I get roughly about half, Minister," Jardine answered. "What I don't get is why you think I can help you."

Thomas stopped walking and gripped Jardine's elbow fiercely.

"You can help me, sir, by one very simple favour."

51

"Which is?"

"Change your mind," he whispered, breathing a kind of urgent evangelism into the discussion which might have seemed ridiculous in a less accomplished actor. "Go and beat these hoity toity buggers. Oh, I know they gave you a bad time, called you names and all that. But don't you want to get revenge? Don't you want to get your own back? Eh? Go down there and show 'em who's boss."

"Minister," Jardine interrupted the flow of zeal. "What you say is all very well, but *how* do we beat them? The side we have is just not good enough. Privately yes, I *do* believe we shall lose. But I believe we would lose even if I were a member of the team. So, if the prospects are not good, and if my presence would not make any difference to the outcome, then why spend your valuable time trying to persuade me to change my mind?"

Thomas retained his hold of Jardine's elbow. Before he replied he looked about the park as if afraid they might be overheard.

"Jardine—Douglas, listen to me. I don't know anything about cricket, but I do know something about *winnin'*. Now and again, you have to, well, bend the rules. Do you know what I mean? I mean to get your own way, to come out on top, you have to find a way of doin' things that other people haven't thought of. I'm sure that applies to cricket as it does to anything else. Isn't that so?"

Jardine delicately disengaged his arm and they carried on walking along the meandering path.

"Actually, no," he said quietly. "It doesn't apply to cricket. There are certain rules and there are a number of conventions which the players observe. If they break the rules, or don't observe the conventions, then they stand out like a sore thumb. You cannot disguise foul play in cricket, Minister. Remember the phrase: 'It's not cricket.' We all use it when we disapprove of some poor behaviour or other. Rugby, soccer, tennis—nothing else has such an aura of sanctity about it. Don't tell me we can win if we bend the rules. There are precious few to bend, and anyway there are umpires to ensure it doesn't happen."

Thomas recalled Marsh's view about this man's rigidity and started to think he had vastly understated it.

"I could be very grateful if you did change your mind, Douglas," he said quietly.

"I'm sure you could be, Minister."

"What I mean to say is, well, you don't see many sportsmen in the Honours list, now do you?"

He raised an eyebrow and looked at Jardine who nodded.

"And quite right too. Sport is played for amusement. Not for medals."

Back at his desk Thomas turned his fountain pen over and over in his hands remembering the conversation. Eventually he wrote on a memorandum pad: "Write to Hore-Ruthven. Tell him we shall lose again."

* * *

The man waited until his secretary came in to say good night and add the usual, "Will that be all for today, sir?"

"Thank you, Miss Stevenson, that will be all. I'll lock up."

"Goodnight then, sir."

"Goodnight. Oh, Miss Stevenson—"

"Yes sir?"

"I have a short letter to write—"

She turned to retrieve her dictation pad from her office, but he put up a hand.

"It's—ah—it's a personal note, please don't worry—"

"Oh, very good, sir."

"Except I would rather like to type it, if I may."

"Of course, sir."

"My handwriting is perfectly awful and it is rather important for the letter to be legible."

The secretary smiled and went back to her desk, uncovered her typewriter and laid out some paper.

"Do you know how to use one of these things, sir?" she called.

"Oh, I'll get the hang of it," he replied. "It's only a short letter anyway."

"I've left some paper here for you."

"Thank you, Miss Stevenson."

"Good night, sir."

He waited until she closed the outer doors before bringing out from a drawer a large, leather-bound book of press cuttings and opening it across the desk. They were all cricket reports with photographs of various players. There was Larwood. And Voce. And Foster, Gregory, MacDonald. There was Arthur Carr standing with the Nottinghamshire side that won in the 1929 championship. Turning the heavy, stiff pages, he came to an account of the 1930 Oval Test with a headline: "AUSTRALIA REGAIN ASHES". For a long time the man studied the cuttings, sometimes crowding a page, with the longer columns gummed at the top and folded over loosely, falling down like a Jacob's ladder. The reports gave him no pleasure, but as he continued: "JARDINE APPOINTED CAPTAIN AGAINST NEW ZEALAND" and "HOBBS SUBJECTED TO FAST LEG THEORY" and "PELHAM WARNER CONDEMNS SHORT FAST BOWLING"—a look of serious determination took shape. When he came to the final page, he closed the book and heaved it to one side. Quickly, he ran through the points in his head to make sure he was word perfect.

Then he cranked a sheet of foolscap into the typewriter carriage and with careful probing forefingers, started to compose the letter.

* * *

Warner had just arrived at Lord's for another Selection Committee meeting when a steward told him he was wanted on the telephone.

"Who is it?" he asked.

"Mr Jardine, sir."

He hurried into the office and picked up the receiver.

"Hello, Douglas?"

"Plum," the abrasive voice sounded a little hesitant over the line: "Is that offer you mentioned the other day still open?"

For a moment Warner couldn't understand what he was talking about.

"Offer?"

"The tour, the winter tour," Jardine replied.

Warner felt a ripple of excitement.

"Why—ah—yes, as a matter of fact, we haven't—ah—

discussed anybody else yet. In fact, I was just about to meet Perrin and Higson this morning—why, Douglas, what is it?"

The reply took a few seconds.

"If it's all the same to you," Jardine announced, "I'd rather like to change my mind."

"You—you mean you accept the captaincy?"

"Yes."

Chapter Five

Dear Jardine [the letter started],
You must excuse the quality of this typing, indeed, I hope you will excuse the bad form in sending a personal letter in typescript at all, but I would prefer for the time being to remain anonymous, a state that would soon be ruined were you able to recognize my handwriting.

I am addressing you on a matter of some importance. I would say it's a matter of "vital" importance, but I do not wish to sound more melodramatic than is necessary, especially at the outset when you may reasonably decide that you are looking at the ramblings of a lunatic and deposit this letter into your dustbin.

The subject of concern I wish to discuss is the state of cricket. More specifically, the present state of English cricket. Even more specifically, the state of English cricket *vis-à-vis* Australia, since there can be no doubt that it is between these two countries that the finest moments of the game are encountered. In 1930 England were reduced to a shambles by a side which came over here with precisely one single advantage. This was the inclusion of a phenomenally good young player named Bradman. Remove him and Australia is left with a fair-to-middling eleven which would, I submit, provide only ordinary problems to a side selected from the fruitful crop of current English players.

After the débâcle two years ago, it became widely assumed that Bradman was omnipotent. Miles of newspaper columns described his invincibility, his contemptuous treatment of our bowlers, and waxed eloquent about the likelihood of a further ten or fifteen years in which England would be confronted with this superhuman figure.

I watched many of his innings in that year. I admit the man is a superb player, the best in recent times. However, I watched his final innings at the Oval and despite the huge score that he made, I became aware that Bradman has a weakness. Furthermore, it is a weakness which can be exploited. I will go as far as to say it is a weakness which, if exploited properly, could haul him down from Olympian heights and dump him back into the ranks of the average Test players who come and go, whose light shines momentarily and then sputters out. England possesses bowlers in their prime who can attack Bradman's fault and effect this result. She also has a captain capable of directing the attack and pursuing it to a conclusion.

For an hour during the last Test in 1930, Bradman faced Larwood on a damp wicket. The state of the pitch made the ball fly. Several rose awkwardly on his legside and he could do little more than push them away in a hurried and ungainly stroke. There is a cinematic newsreel account of this in the archives which I recommend you see. Both Bradman and Jackson were greatly discomforted during this spell and their scoring rate considerably reduced. However, since by then the game was already a lost cause, few of the spectators took much notice and merely waited for the inevitable defeat with cheerful stoicism which made me ashamed to be an Englishman.

Bradman, therefore, is suspect when receiving a fast rising ball on the legside delivered by a man as quick as Larwood. In this respect he is no different from any of us. No one likes to be hurt and as you have discovered in the past, Larwood's pace can inflict painful damage should the batsman fail to get out of the way quickly enough.

Let us discuss Larwood for a moment. He is not only the fastest bowler in the world, he is also incredibly accurate. Told to hit a patch on the wicket time after time, he will do so. Put Voce at the other end, follow them by two other pacemen who can also make the ball fly, and you have an answer to our "run machine". Bradman cannot score off a short ball rising into his body. If the ball is pitched short enough, it will fly high over his head—he is only 5 feet 7 inches tall—and thus stay out of his reach. We have all witnessed his footwork, but a step has not been invented which will allow him to climb 3 feet into the air. Secondly, if the ball does not rise quite that high, it is likely that the sheer speed of a man like Larwood will intimidate the "boy wonder" into either moving out of the way, or fending off the ball to a waiting fielder. Thirdly, and here we move into an area where my anonymity becomes understandable, if the ball does not go above Bradman, if he does not move out of the way or succeed in using his bat to defend himself, it is likely that he will sustain an injury which would put him effectively out of the game. Given all these eventualities, it is clear that what I am suggesting cannot fail to contain a man whose Test average against us last time was 139.

It is in your power, Jardine, to do it.

I am offering a solution which offends every convention of the game. Were I to stand in the Long Room at Lord's and give voice to it, I would be horsewhipped.

But I feel I am likely to receive a longer hearing from you, Jardine. Read the following statements and put a cross against those with which you profoundly disagree:

I always play to win.
I will do everything in my power to avenge the humiliation of my country.
I do not care about public opinion nor court popularity.
Sport is merely war continued by other means.
Sport means more to Australians than anything else.
I dislike Australians.
I will do anything within the rules to beat them at cricket.

Perhaps I am wrong, Jardine, but I do not think you have marked a solitary cross. I refer you to the last statement. When I said earlier that my ideas would offend the *conventions* of cricket, I did not mention breaking the *rules* of the game. For, as we are aware, there is no rule to prevent a player bowling in an intimidating manner. The fact that it is just not done is neither here nor there. It is only not done by men who do not care about the result of the game, just so long as they enjoy a jolly contest and shake hands with their opponents at the end.

That does not apply to you, Jardine. I believe you are the only person in the game today determined enough to beat Australia at any cost. Think about your decision not to lead the tour this winter. There is still time to change your mind.

Chapter Six

It was going to be a busy week and one in which he expected more than a little opposition. The prospect didn't daunt him since he had always, ever since Winchester, relished arguments. When his personality started to emerge from the chrysalis of childhood, he was surprised to discover how much he enjoyed imposing his views on others, and how relatively simple it was to do. The secret, he learned, was to avoid locking horns with one's opponents; simply stand back and *tell* them. There were several fellows more articulate than he; several more with better memories for facts and figures. But there was none with the physical presence that, by the age of 17, he was able to display to great effect. Tall, angular, with a nose that was made to project an intimidating glare, he found he could quell opposition at a glance.

Such qualities often produce an autocrat; a severe headmaster or a demonic politician who governs with the arrogance of the patrician. But side by side with the austere streak in his nature ran something else which he recognized as both a matter of concern and of pleasure. Towards his senior years at school, Jardine came to acknowledge in his character an inclination to rebel against the established authority. Somewhere at the back of his mind a small but firm voice whispered radical thoughts which he was unable to resist. Why should a tradition be venerated merely because it had been so for generations? Surely everyone must be judged on his merits, not on his position in society. Had not his father always maintained that the first test of a person's worth was to see if he looked you directly in the eye? If he did not, never mind if he was a senior judge, Prime Minister or archbishop—treat him with caution.

There had been one incident at Winchester which demonstrated this almost subversive need to show his objective view of life. In his last year, he had established himself as one of the finest young batsmen in the school. His reputation within his House secure, he was asked to follow a hallowed tradition of posting up a Roll of the current House cricket XI in order of merit, using full initials. As it happened, the side had played badly the week before, except for himself and one other. When the notice went up on the board, a moment of considerable excitement and expectation, it read:

C House Turner Cup 1920
D. R. Jardine
W. M. Leggatt
The following might have been included had they not been unable not merely to bat and bowl, but even to field:

There then followed nine names listed without any initials.

Nothing remotely like it had ever been done before, and he had been subjected to a barrage of abuse from boys and masters alike. The experience might have blighted the rest of his life; a youthful prank which misfired to cloud a promising career. But Jardine remembered it warmly, and the memory never failed to provoke a quiet smile of satisfaction.

His manner was no good in debating societies which he avoided, but worked miracles with those who shied away from personal confrontation. It worked in a country like England where, on the whole, people would sooner die than make a fuss in public, would rather steal away and spend a sleepless night brooding over a slight than face their foe and trade punch for punch.

By the time he was 32, he had honed his technique into such a keen-edged weapon that he could say with justification that he knew of no one, except his father, who could withstand his arguments or convince him he was mistaken. Once he made up his mind, all that remained was to persuade everyone else involved to agree. And as he entered Lord's on Monday morning for his eleven o'clock meeting with the Selection Committee, the issue was the names of the bowlers to go to Australia.

"May I say," Perrin remarked as they sat down, "that we are delighted you have agreed to lead the side, Douglas?"

Jardine nodded impatiently and drew out a folded piece of paper.

"Thank you," he said, opening out the sheet. "I have here a list of bowlers we will need if we are to do anything about Bradman. They are Larwood, Voce, Bowes and Allen. With Hammond's medium pace, I think we can all agree this is the best attack we have to offer."

Warner blinked. Higson glanced at Perrin and coughed.

"Bowes?" he queried. "And I take it you mean G. O. Allen of Middlesex."

"Of course."

"Larwood and Voce, certainly," Warner intervened. "But, well, Bowes is a bit of a surprise, Douglas, I must say—"

"Three days ago he took 7 for 65 against the Rest of England. Yorkshire won the championship to a great extent by his bowling."

"Yes, yes, I know, but good God, Douglas," Warner went on, alarmed, "*Another* Yorkshireman? Sutcliffe, Verity, Leyland—and now Bowes?"

"Verity? Why?"

The astonishment of the other three members became clearly audible.

"*Why?*"

Jardine shrugged.

"Yes, all right, Verity," he conceded, in a way that suggested that the inclusion of the finest slow bowler in the country was of no interest to him. "But I want Bowes."

Warner groaned.

"Four Yorkshiremen, two Notts, Duckworth and Paynter from Lancashire—I hate to think of the stick I'm likely to get at the club."

"Plum, whether we have northerners or southerners shouldn't be of the slightest concern," Jardine snapped.

"No, of course not, but—well, dammit Douglas, why Bowes?"

"Because he's 6 feet 5 inches tall, that's why," Jardine replied. "And on those rock-hard wickets, he'll be devastating."

Warner sniffed.

"Never thought a fellow's height would determine whether he was picked for England," he said mildly.

Instead of replying, Jardine turned to Perrin.

"You raised an eyebrow over Gubby Allen," he said, the Bowes issue settled as far as he was concerned.

"Well, it *is* rather sudden, don't you think?" Perrin answered, failing to keep his eyes directly levelled at Jardine's imperious stare. "Besides, the man was born in Australia. He even has an uncle who played for them."

"I was born in India," Jardine reminded him. "Does that make me a bloody wog?"

"No, of course not—"

"Douglas, Gubby is a fine bowler when he's on form, but the fact is", Warner added, but started to quaver when he now received the full tilt of Jardine's nose, "his appearances are often few and far between. As an amateur he has other commitments and, well, his record is hardly consistent."

"I played almost no cricket in 1930," Jardine reminded them, "but you picked me to lead against New Zealand."

The logic silenced them.

"Four fast bowlers," Higson remarked looking at the names he had written down. "Five if you include Hammond. No side has taken four quickies before."

"No side has had to face a man like Bradman on Australian wickets before," Jardine replied coldly. The discussion was already boring him. He knew they would agree sooner or later and regarded the rest of the meeting as wasted time.

"You think fast bowling is the answer then, Douglas?" said Warner, twisting his pencil round nervously.

"I have no answers," he snapped. "But I have suggestions. However, if you can convince me that back-of-the-hand tweakers will tie up Bradman, McCabe, Kippax and Richardson on wickets the texture of reinforced concrete, then I'll scrub my list and take whomever you say."

An hour later the team was complete: Jardine (Captain), Wyatt (Vice-Captain), G. O. Allen, the Nawab of Pataudi and the young Surrey star Freddy Brown made up the amateur contingent.

The pros were Sutcliffe, Hammond, Leyland and Paynter, batsmen; Duckworth and Ames, wicket-keepers; Voce, Larwood, Bowes, Verity, Maurice Tate and the diminutive Tommy Mitchell from Derbyshire completed the bowling attack. Pelham Warner would return to Australia for the first time in twenty years as co-manager of the tour with R.C.N. Palairet, and the scoring and baggage-handling was to be in the hands of Bill Ferguson. As they rose, Higson tried to lighten the mood.

"Happy now, with your bowlers, Douglas?"

Jardine clipped his fountain pen away in an inside pocket and picked up his papers.

"Frankly," he said as they made for the door, "I doubt if Verity or Tate will get a game. If I had my way, we'd take two more pacemen."

Warner shot a glance at Jardine and wondered why he had accepted the job of tour manager. If the bloody fellow was already behaving like some Mongolian warlord, God knows what he would be like by Christmas! "If I had my way" indeed! What had the last hour and a half been except a ruthless demonstration of him getting his own way?

The newspapers picked up the speed content of the selected players but drew nothing from Jardine other than general observations about the pace of the Australian wickets and the need to push the ball through more quickly than at home. When one reporter reminded him that Bradman scored most of his runs off fast bowling, he replied that Australia had no one to match the quality of men like Larwood, Voce and Bowes. However, as always with this fascinating game, he added, we must wait and see. It is a rash fellow who tries to forecast the result of a Test series, there were many slips between cup and lip—

His next call was a small flat near Chancery Lane. A board beside the main entrance read: Foster—3B and he found the door on the first floor at the top of the stairs.

Frank Foster opened the door almost immediately and welcomed Jardine with a brisk handshake.

"Come in, come in," he said, almost pulling him through before slamming the door. "Before anybody sees you."

Noticing Jardine's bemused look, he grinned quickly. "Sports reporters get everywhere these days," he announced. "God knows what they would make of you coming to see me."

"I should think they would get it right first time," Jardine said as he was shown into a neat, comfortably appointed sitting-room. "After all, they've seen the team."

"Four quickies and a medium pacer, with Tate able to fling the odd one down," Foster mused, heading for a drinks cabinet. "And D. R. Jardine was seen entering the premises of one F. R. Foster known back in the Punic Wars as a practitioner of fast leg theory. Reads well, that. Scotch?"

Jardine studied the man as he mixed the drinks. He was 43 or so now but his body was still well proportioned; he had the stance of an athlete and only a few wisps of grey in his tidy hair betrayed the passing of the years. Yet his career had ended when Jardine was only a boy, cut short by a motorcycle crash early in the war, and all that was left of his fabulous years, when he and Sydney Barnes won the Ashes for England in 1911/12, were the accounts in *Wisden* and the memoirs of contemporaries.

They had met occasionally in the past and Jardine had detected a trace of bitterness in the ex-Warwickshire captain. Beneath an outwardly companionable manner lay a melancholy which appealed to the younger man, who understood why a brilliant sportsman should resent a world which cut off his life's passion at the age of 25.

He took the generous whisky and raised it a few inches.

"Nice to see you again, Frank."

"Here's to you, Douglas."

They drank for some minutes and exchanged pleasantries until Foster eased himself down into a chair with a grimace. "Bloody autumn—always gets the joints creaking," and then stuck out his chin, looking across at Jardine, and said "So what are you going to do with all these speed merchants? Knock Bradman's bloody head off?"

Jardine started, reacted a second, and put down his glass as Foster gave a short, loud guffaw.

"Oh, come on, Douglas," he exclaimed. "Don't treat me like an imbecile. It's probably the only way you'll get rid of the little bastard. Fast leg theory, correct?"

Jardine recovered and nodded, as if reluctantly yielding a secret.

"You pioneered fast leg theory, Frank," he said. "I want to know what you need to make it work."

"Only one thing is absolutely essential." Foster replied, picking up his glass and allowing a dramatic pause while he sipped the whisky: "And that's a skin as thick as a rhinoceros. How does yours measure up?"

"It's thick enough."

"There are other requirements which come in handy," Foster went on, grinning cheerfully. "Like pig-headedness, determination and, seeing how you intend to use leg theory in Australia, a working knowledge of all-in wrestling won't come amiss."

"Don't worry about me," said Jardine. "What do I need on the field?"

Foster stood and opened a writing desk, returned with a pad of paper and a pencil. He pulled his chair forwards and sat down again, using the coffee table to write on.

"Bowler, batsman—" he murmured, drawing two sets of stumps, then placing crosses for the men mentioned: "three forward short legs, three behind, a square and a deep square."

"That leaves one man on the offside," Jardine muttered in surprise.

"If your bowlers do their stuff, even he is one too many," Foster replied. He threw down the pencil and leaned back.

Jardine looked up, puzzled.

"Is that all?" he asked.

"What else do you need?" said Foster, shrugging. "Fast leg theory means precisely what it says. The theory is, if you bowl fast on the legside sooner or later the batsman will hole out to one of the fielders. What more do you want—a whole lot of psychological claptrap?"

"No," Jardine answered slowly. He gazed a long time at the paper and the arc of crosses.

"It will work if you can keep them coming down on the spot," said Foster. "If you can't, you might as well award the other side 300 runs before you start." He leaned over the table and picked up the pencil. "Anything loose, a bit too short, a little too wide—even an ordinary batsman will pull it clean out of the ground. The question you have to ask yourself when you set this kind of field, is 'How many runs can I afford to give away?' If the answer is not many, forget about the whole thing."

"But it worked for you."

Foster smiled and Jardine once again detected a trace of melancholy in the look.

"I was nowhere as quick as Larwood or Voce, or Bill Bowes," he said. "I never *frightened* the batsman. It worked sometimes, it didn't work others. For me, it was a device designed to push the man into a hurried stroke and let him put up dolly catches to the close-in fielders."

"Precisely," Jardine nodded, pointing to the crosses on the paper representing the short legs. "Isn't that the basis of the theory?"

Foster finished his whisky and nursed the glass in his hands.

"It was the basis of *my* theory," he said quietly, "because a catch was all I could hope for as a medium pacer. But you, Douglas, you have Harold Larwood in your armoury. You have Voce, left-arm over the wicket, hurling the ball in towards the batsman at a speed I couldn't have reached if I'd thrown it. You have Bowes, the tallest chap I've ever seen on a field banging them down from the clouds—oh, by all means put your fielders round about. But with men as fast as that, don't be too surprised if there aren't more who leave retired hurt than caught at forward short leg."

He studied Jardine as he spoke and detected no sign of surprise, or disapproval, or even disagreement. He sat, his fists under his chin gazing at Foster's diagram for a long time. The air grew chilly in the room as the sun disappeared behind the buildings opposite. Finally Jardine broke the spell and slapped a fist into his palm.

"Thank you, Frank."

"For what? You knew all this without coming to see me."

Jardine bent and picked up his glass, placed it on the coffee table next to the diagram. As he straightened he smiled broadly, an expression new to Foster.

"You know," he said, "you ought to try and get a job on a newspaper. Come out and cover the series. I think you'd enjoy it."

"I haven't enjoyed cricket since 1914," he replied, and his voice hardened. "Go out there and win, Douglas. Beat them any way you can. I think you will, as a matter of fact. But don't talk about enjoyment. If you want that, stick with the Harlequins or a pleasant afternoon on the village green. Where you're going, and with what you're intending to do, enjoyment is the last thing you'll find."

Voce and Larwood reached the Piccadilly Hotel shortly before 7.30 and waited in the foyer for Arthur Carr to arrive. After ten minutes, he still hadn't come and Larwood was conscious of some strange looks zeroing in from the receptionist and a particularly frosty doorman who glared at them as if they wore striped jerseys and had a sack over their shoulders marked "swag".

"Sod this for a game o' sodjers," Voce muttered, "let's go and find t'bar. Skipper's always late, any road."

"What if he comes and we're not here?" Larwood asked anxiously. He secretly admired Tangy's casual treatment of people it was wiser to show respect to, but thought in the long run it might work against him. But when Voce strode off towards the lounge bar he followed, looking back at the main doors, hoping the skipper would suddenly appear and so avoid apologies later. After all, he had said to meet him in the foyer. Lord knows why. They were playing the last game of the season and they couldn't make head nor tail of the message left in their pigeon hole at the hotel: "Meet me at the Piccadilly, 7.30 sharp. Skipper."

"7.30 sharp means eight o'bloody clock to our Arthur," Voce grumbled as they stood at the bar behind a row of people trying to be served. A gap finally opened up and after several tries, Voce caught the barman's eye.

"Two pints of Shippos, squire, when you're ready."

The barman looked blank.

"Two what?" he said, clearing an ear sarcastically with a finger. Two men in dinner jackets nearby turned their heads and grinned at one another.

68

"I see we have the hicks from the sticks in tonight," one remarked.

Voce took his attention from the barman and settled his gaze on the fellow who had spoken.

"You talking to me, son?"

The grin died on the man's lips and he coughed, embarrassed. "No, no, just—I was just chatting to my friend here—"

Larwood held his breath. It wouldn't be the first time that Tangy had started a rumpus and he had a mental flash of a wild fight here in this fancy hotel, feet and bottles flying, the two of them in the thick of it, only to have Carr wander in and wanting to know who started it—

With relief he saw his friend turn back to the barman: "We want two pints of Shipstone's Ale, lad," he repeated slowly. And getting another look as vacant as the last, went on: "It's a Nottingham brew. Ship—stones—beers."

The barman shrugged.

"Never heard of it," he sniffed. "You're not in Nottingham now, you're in London."

"Don't remind me," Voce replied. "All right then, give us whatever you've got."

"We don't sell ale in this bar," the man said, standing well back from the counter before smiling at the big man. Then he turned to serve someone else.

"Don't serve bloody ale—?" gasped Voce, making the most of his astonishment. "What you mean you don't serve ale?"

"Look out, here's skipper!" Larwood said, never happier to see Carr. He tugged Voce's sleeve and led him from the counter towards the door where their captain stood. He saw them and raised a hand.

"Sorry, skip," Larwood began, "We were keeping an eye out for you—"

It was then he realized Jardine was also beside the door.

"Hello, Mr Jardine," he said with some surprise. "Didn't know you was coming an'all."

"Evenin' Mr Jardine," Voce nodded and received a brief signal from the England skipper.

"I've booked a table," Jardine said matter-of-factly, "Let's go and find it, shall we?"

Knowing his way round the hotel, he led them out of the bar and along a corridor until they reached the dining-room. Trailing behind, Larwood put his mouth close to Carr's ear:

"Heyup, skip, what's this all about, then?" he whispered.

"Haven't the foggiest. Wait and see is my advice to you," came the reply.

Jardine was speaking to the headwaiter who nodded and pointed to the corner. As they caught up with him they heard him say, "It *is* in the corner, like I said?"

"Indeed, Mr Jardine," the headwaiter answered, picking up a pile of menus as they followed him through the crowded tables. "You won't be disturbed there, I promise."

Won't be disturbed? thought Larwood. What's going on? He felt like a spy.

Jardine pointed to various chairs and they sat round the table. Larwood and Voce on either side, Carr facing. When the headwaiter started to hand round the menus, Jardine held up his hand.

"Wait a moment, Pierre, don't go, this won't take long. Anyone any preferences?"

Larwood and Voce glanced at each other and shook their heads.

"You order, Douglas," said Carr. "This is your stamping ground. You must know what's decent."

"They do a passable steak and kidney. Anyone like that? Good. Four steak and kidneys, Pierre, please. Some soup to start—"

"We have a very nice *bisque d'homard*, sir—"

"Splendid. The usual veg—and who wants wine, beer? A bottle of Pomerol, I think."

"Yes sir, very good, right away Mr Jardine." The headwaiter scribbled on his pad, gathered up the menus and hurried off.

With the formalities out of the way, Jardine slapped his hands together briskly, presented a broad grin to both the fast bowlers.

"Look," he said, "sorry to intrude on your evening—"

"That's all right, Mr Jardine," said Voce. His place secure on the tour, he was keen to show his enthusiasm and would have talked about Australia all night anyway, even had he been elsewhere. As it was, he felt honoured. There was an air of subterfuge about them sitting in this corner of a posh London restaurant talking to the captain of England. It seemed as if this remote figure had chosen just the two of them to confide in.

"—but Mr Carr said he thought he could get you to come along," Jardine went on, "and, well, here you are."

Small talk and chattiness were not his strong suits and they sat waiting for him to get to the point. He turned to Larwood.

"Harold, I want to ask you one very simple question."

"Oh aye?" Larwood replied. Harold? By gum, he *was* being friendly. He had never called him that on the entire trip last time.

"How do you feel about bowling fast leg theory?" Jardine asked.

"Fast leg theory?" he repeated, knowing he sounded slow and stupid, but the question came out of the blue.

"Yes," Jardine nodded impatiently, glancing at Carr.

"Mr Carr tells me he's had you two doing it once or twice."

Larwood looked at his skipper who kept his eyes down on his wine glass.

"Not me, Mr Jardine," he replied. "I don't think I've ever set a leg theory field, not a proper one, any road."

Voce grinned and leaned forward.

"Is this how we're gonta do Bradman, Mr Jardine?" he muttered, excited. Jardine turned to him for less than a second.

"I'm talking to Larwood for the moment," he said, silencing the big man abruptly. Then: "You didn't answer my question, Harold."

The Nottinghamshire hero looked anxiously at Carr who remained transfixed by the empty glass in front of him. Tangy wasn't going to say anything more either after the last snub. Jardine waited.

"You ask me how I feel bowling fast leg theory, Mr Jardine," he began slowly. "Well, I'll be honest. I don't feel very good about it, to tell you the truth."

"Why not?"

"For a start, I've never had to. I've managed to gerrenough wickets wi'out it."

Jardine folded his arms on the edge of the table, each hand cradling an elbow.

71

"I asked you how you felt about bowling to this theory," he continued slowly, showing a patience that Arthur Carr thought was unusual. If you didn't grasp what Duggie was driving at first time, you more often than not received that tilted nose and a stone expression of pure scorn. He was handling Larwood quite well, seeing that this was probably the first time the two men had spoken to each other for more than a couple of sentences.

"Whether you have *had* to or not in the past is neither here nor there. Suppose you were out in the field and I threw you the ball and told you to do it. What would you say?"

You canny bastard, thought Carr and he peered briefly at his star bowler who fiddled with a spoon.

"Well, what could I say?" he answered unhappily. "You're t'boss, I'm a pro. I'd have to say yes, wouldn't I?"

"But you wouldn't be happy—"

"No."

"Why not?"

Tangy was grinning behind his hand when he looked over at his mate.

"Because at my speed," Larwood said, choosing his words carefully, "it's bloody dangerous, that's why."

There was a pause and Jardine leaned back in his chair.

"I'm surprised to hear you say that, Harold," he continued, now using an informal, almost chatty tone. "On the field, there isn't a more intimidating, aggressive chap in English cricket. What have the papers called you? The batsman-hater, the Notts terror, the Wild Man of the North?"

"That's newspaper talk," he said, flushing with embarrassment.

"But now you say that all the time you've been worried about your opponent's state of health. I'm astonished, frankly. You certainly hid your concern successfully on the odd occasions that you hit *me* in the ribs."

He pulled his face into a grin and the others followed suit.

"Mr Jardine." Larwood emphasized his words by prodding the end of the spoon into the tablecloth. "I'm not saying I don't let the ball fly now and then. 'Course I do, there's nowt wrong in that. It keeps the batsman hopping about, makes it hard for him to settle down. But leg theory is different, and we all know it is. Leg theory, you put the ball down over and over on the same spot. Legside, short and coming into the batsman. O.K., nowt wrong in that if you're medium pace. Even if he misses wi' his bat, all he gets is a bit of a thump. But wi' me, it's different. Some bloke could get badly hurt. I mean, really badly hurt, Mr Jardine, wi' the speed I can rustle up, and I don't care what t'bloody papers call me, I'd feel rotten if I did that to anybody."

Voce chuckled.

"Loll's gorra soft spot deep down, Mr Jardine. I keep telling him about it. Me, I reckon if t'batsman's gorra bat in his hand, then he should use it. If he can't and gets thumped in t'chest, then it's his own bloody fault, not t'bowlers."

To his surprise, Jardine gave him a beaming smile.

"My sentiments exactly." Turning back to Larwood: "Don't you agree, Harold?"

"Aye, I suppose so," he answered reluctantly. "But whether it's his fault or not, the bloke still ends up wi' a cracked head and very likely in hospital."

"Which he could do were he facing you, leg theory or not," Arthur Carr intervened. "I've seen men carted off walking into one of your deliveries outside the off stump or straight up and down. It's not your fault, it's not particularly theirs. Accidents are nobody's fault, Loll, old son. They just happen."

The wine waiter appeared, showed the bottle to Jardine who nodded brusquely. They stopped speaking until the wine had been opened, tasted by Jardine and approved, then poured round. After the waiter moved away, Larwood, having had time to marshal his thoughts, looked across at the England captain.

"Mr Jardine," he said slowly, "let me just say this: I've never bowled leg theory, not properly. I mean, there's been times where Mr Carr has tode me to let 'em fly a bit and shoved some fielders over on t'leg side, but I've never done it for more'n a few overs, now and again. But I'm a professional. I'm bound by law to obey t'orders of me skipper. So, if you tell me to bowl leg theory, then I've no option, have I? I'm just saying I'm not keen, that's all."

There was a pause, then Jardine nodded slowly, understandingly. "Thank you, Harold," he said. "I think that answers the question."

He turned to Voce.

"Now let's take up your point, Bill—"

Voce glowed as this austere, distant figure used his first name. He was really in—

"You asked if this was the way we're going to deal with Bradman. The answer, of course, is yes. Harold, you'll recall catching him on a damp wicket at the Oval, him and Jackson."

"Aye, he didn't know whether he were coming or going."

"He just could not handle those short deliveries on his legs. Well, you know how you can make the ball kick up on the Australian wickets—"

"That's right."

"There is every chance you can reproduce that Oval spell out there."

"Reckon I could, aye," Larwood said thoughtfully. Now he was getting to the point of this fancy dinner, finally. He had remembered the overs in the last Test very well. Right at the end of the Aussie tour, he had Bradman in trouble. Too late to do anything then, but at least he knew the little bloke wasn't God Almighty. However, until a few minutes ago, he had no idea that the answer was fast leg theory. He had often wondered if it hadn't been just a case of Bradman tiring, of the shower that had sparked the pitch—conditions unlikely to be repeated. Now here was Jardine, one of the canniest skippers in England, telling him he could tame Bradman once and for all—it was worth a try, surely.

He looked down to find Jardine had moved the salt and pepper pots into the centre of the table, bringing out a box of matches and placing six in a semi-circle round the salt:

"The salt is Bradman," he murmured, then traced a line from the pepper towards it. "The pepper is you, Harold. My finger is the ball. Down it comes, hits the ground, rises up, up—"

He described an arc with his fingertip and ended with it down among the matches.

"—a hasty stroke and there it goes, snapped up by one of the close-in chaps."

He leaned back.

"I'm not saying it's guaranteed to work," he declared. "What I am saying is, it's worth a try. Don't you agree, Harold?"

Larwood looked down at the condiments and the matches. A waiter suddenly appeared and placed down their bowls of soup. As he did he knocked over the salt. Larwood instinctively picked up some of the spilled grains and threw them over his left shoulder.

"Aye," he said, replacing the salt cellar upright. "It's worth a try."

Chapter Seven

The platform at St Pancras railway station teemed with a noisy, bustling, cheerful, weeping crowd as the team assembled to board the boat train to Tilbury. Every few seconds a photographer's flash exploded, giving some of the older men present an uneasy reminder of the war, making them duck instinctively.

Generally, however, there were more cheers than tears. A group of young men, all wearing sports blazers of the same club, stood in a tight knot holding up a banner that read: "ASHES TO ASHES, DUST TO DUST, IF VOCE DON'T GET YOU LARWOOD MUST!" Reporters pushed forward to reach Jardine who stood self-consciously, trying to carry off the final formalities with an ease he didn't feel.

"What are you going to do about Bradman, Mr Jardine?"

"Get him out quickly and often."

The reporters laughed but wouldn't be palmed off so easily.

"Do you have any special plan to get him out quickly and often?"

"None."

"But surely he's the one Australian you fear most?"

"We don't *fear* anyone. He is one of several fine Australian players. But we have just as good cricketers on our side. We feel confident that we shall prevail."

"You're taking four fast bowlers—is that any indication of how you intend to fight Bradman?"

"Gentlemen, why do you concentrate on talking about Bradman all the time?" Jardine smiled. "We are taking four fast bowlers because they happen to be the best chaps available, along with Verity and Tate and Mitchell and Hammond—really, I don't know why you're placing so much emphasis on our speed attack.

As I've just mentioned, we have as many spinners."

"Where is Maurice Tate?"

"He will join us later. At present he is unwell."

When the reporters looked at the team they were also unable to see Larwood. While the last questions were being asked, he had side-stepped into the crowd and was saying his final goodbyes to Lois.

"You behave yousen while I'm away," he said, trying to grin and dry her tears. She hugged him closely and sniffed hard.

"Fat chance of doing owt else in Kirkby," she replied.

"I've tode Alf to keep an eye on you."

She looked at him closely and tried a shaky smile. "Well, if you have to go, you have to," she whispered. "June'n I'll miss you all right, there's no getting round that. But if you go off for six months and come back without winning, it'll seem like a lot of wasted time."

"We'll win," he promised.

He heard the guard blow the first warning blast on his whistle and held her tightly, knowing these last few moments were going to have to do him for a long time.

The players climbed aboard, waving and blowing kisses to the wildly cheering well-wishers, grinning at the mascots thrust high above in the air and the banners telling them to win or else. The guards came down the platform, easing the people back and closing the doors. Larwood kept his eyes fixed on Lois who held a handkerchief to her cheek and waved frantically with the other arm. Then the train gave a shudder and a series of grunts and squeaks as the wheels began to turn. The funnel emitted a tall plume of smoke and the coaches clanked together.

The crowds waved and shouted and cheered, and not until the guard's van was a long way down the tracks did they quieten and start to disperse. Lois was one of the last to go. A reporter asked her how she felt: she smiled, shook her head and said nothing, turning away and walking slowly up the stairs to the exit.

At Tilbury Docks the scene was smaller but as exuberant as at St Pancras. Jardine answered a few more questions from the press who spotted Jack Hobbs, recently signed up by the *Star* to cover the series. When they asked him how he felt, he replied "seasick already" and explained that he was not boarding here, but going overland to Toulon.

"If there is a worse sailor than me," he told them, "I have yet to meet him."

The R.M.S. *Orontes* lay in dock and the other passengers stood along the rails watching the parting ceremonies. Most of them had not realized they would have the M.C.C. team in their company for the next four weeks, and the sight of the young, fit men trooping in line up the gangplank led to more than a few interested looks.

Two women in their early twenties watched them come aboard. They spoke in Australian accents, softened by an expensive English finishing school. One of them, Alice, a petite brunette with a birdlike way of holding her head slightly tilted to one side smiled.

"Well, at least they lower the average age a bit," she said, watching them step on to the deck where Jardine, the last aboard, shook hands with a senior officer.

Her friend Mary was taller and a few pounds overweight. She looked like the kind of girl who tries to swim the English Channel.

"I wish I knew a bit more about cricket," she muttered. "Do you know anything?"

"Only what my brother has told me," Alice replied.

"What did he tell you?" Mary asked. "I don't want to sound silly if they talk to me."

"All you have to remember," Alice whispered as the team filed past them, "is that there are bowlers and batters. The bowlers, my brother says, rub their balls on their trousers, while the batters stroke theirs along the grass."

Mary cackled loudly and Freddy Brown looked round, catching her eye. She put up a hand to her mouth but her eyes continued to laugh. He grinned back and gave her a broad wink.

"Who said a four-week boat trip would be boring?" he murmured to the man behind him. Wally Hammond glanced at the girl and understood the message.

"Life is what you make it," he said. "And I fancy those two little dears are thinking very much the same thing."

The routine on the ship soon took hold and the days and nights followed one another in a round of morning exercise periods, afternoon deck games and evening dances. Brown was, everyone agreed, only second to Valentino as a hoofer and attended to Mary while Hammond took care of Alice. The nights grew rowdier and the conga lines snaked over the decks when they left the Bay of Biscay and found warmer evening breezes down the coast of Spain and through the Straits of Gibraltar.

Jardine kept to himself, mostly reading in his cabin, but when he did appear at mealtimes he maintained a good-humoured attitude, enabling them to relax and enjoy what was, he had said early on the voyage, a bloody good holiday at public expense before they would be required to put their backs into the job. Occasionally he would have a chat with Larwood, sometimes with Voce, and the others would see them strolling round the decks deep in conversation. The Nottingham men had been asked by him the night they met at the Piccadilly Hotel to keep quiet for the time being about the leg theory idea.

"No point in letting Bradman know what we're up to. He'd only go and practise twenty-four hours a day—"

The ban on discussing tactics extended even to the other members of the side. Jardine had told them that the fewer who knew about it, the less likely the secret would leak out.

"I want Bradman to be so surprised when we try it out for the first time," Jardine had said, "that he won't have time to do anything about it. All right, you two?"

"You two" continued to make Voce and Larwood feel they were something special, a secret weapon, set apart from the others. There were times on the voyage when Larwood thought that Bowes was in on the plan. Jack Hobbs joined the ship at Toulon and there was a moment when he and Bowes came together one dinnertime. In August, Bowes had sent down a few bouncers at the older man and Hobbs had made it clear what he thought of it, going down the pitch to prod the wicket, glaring at the tall Yorkshireman and ducking more than he had to when the next ball flew over his head. Pelham Warner had condemned the incident in the *Morning Post*, writing curtly about Bowes and recommending that such tactics ought to be banned.

Now here were the three of them trapped on a month-long sea voyage. But Hobbs was a kindly man and, prompted by Warner, was soon able to joke about the affair, all hostilities forgotten.

However, it didn't stop Bowes saying to Larwood one day, "I may have got a bollocking for it, but I wouldn't mind betting that's why I'm here."

The ship moved beyond Port Said into the stifling heat of the Red Sea. By common consent the physical exercises were abandoned and the team, along with a great number of the other passengers, kept cool by staying up to their necks in the deck pool.

Gubby Allen noticed Jardine seated in a deck chair with the inevitable Chaucer in his hand. Allen never felt comfortable talking to his captain, convinced that the Wykehamist was usually trying to put him down. He wasn't unique in feeling this, but it irritated him nonetheless. There was no doubt that Jardine was more widely read than he was, but Allen had never understood why a person who read should regard himself as superior to someone who found pleasure in other pursuits. As an Etonian he felt their education had been pretty much the same: he had gone to Cambridge while Jardine attended Oxford. Why then, did it always sound as if he were being talked down to?

"Morning, Douglas."

Jardine squinted up and nodded.

"Hello, Gubby."

"Mind if I sit down?"

"Of course not. Take a pew."

He lowered himself into a deck chair and wiped his brow with the sleeve of his shirt.

"You shouldn't be feeling the heat," Jardine remarked, carefully inserting a bookmark into the Chaucer and putting it under his seat. "Weren't you born around here?"

"Australia isn't exactly 'around here' in the Red Sea," Allen pointed out.

"Well, you know what I mean," Jardine sniffed. "This part of the world's all the same to me. Like Clapham and Chiswick."

If that is meant to be a joke, Allen thought, I don't get it. "And anyway, I was only seven when I left," he added.

Jardine lifted his face to the sun. "I do find these journeys an awful bore," he said, closing his eyes. "Don't you?"

Allen shrugged. "As a matter of fact," he said, "I'm having rather a good time."

"Oh, good," Jardine murmured, yawning. Was the bloody man going to *sleep*?

"Douglas—"

"Mmm?"

"Douglas, aren't we going to talk about tactics?" Allen pressed. He had noticed Jardine speaking animatedly to Voce and Larwood on various occasions during the past two weeks. Since there was little likelihood they were discussing Chaucer or Trollope, he had assumed they must be talking about cricket. Then why hadn't he been brought in? He was aware that his surprise selection had probably been encouraged by Jardine, and for this he was grateful. But since the day the team had been announced, he had not been approached once to deal with his proposed role in the series. It was extremely odd.

"Plenty of time for that later," came the lazy reply.

"I would have said there was plenty of time for it now," Allen protested mildly. "It might even make the trip less boring for you."

Jardine didn't open his eyes. Once again Allen was irritated at being made to sound a nuisance, annoying a fellow who wanted to have a nap.

After a long pause, Jardine said, his eyes remaining closed tight against the glare of the sun, "You know, Gubby, there's only one way we're going to beat the Australians."

"Really?" he reacted, surprised. Jardine was coming right to the point. "How?"

"We have to hate them."

He emphasized the word "hate" and Allen started even more at the vehemence in his voice.

"*Hate* them?"

"Yes."

81

"Oh, Douglas, come along, really—!"

Jardine opened his eyes, turned his head and looked steadily at him.

"Don't tell me to 'come along, really'. I mean what I say." He spoke quietly but with an intensity Allen had not heard before.

"Do you imagine for one moment that we are coming all this way to play a few genial games of cricket, to be followed by a sing-song in the pub?"

"No, but I—"

"If you do, then discard the thought here and now."

Allen started to bristle indignantly.

"I know this is my first tour down under, Douglas," he said evenly. "I know you have far greater experience than I have. But believe me, I know the difference between a match between Eton and Harrow and one between England and Australia. I do not expect sing-songs or anything else."

"Oh, good, well done—"

"But equally, I don't expect to have to hate *anyone* while playing a game I happen to love."

Jardine closed his eyes again and turned his face upwards to meet the burning glare of the sky.

"I see," he remarked blandly. "And when did you decide that?"

"The day I was born," Allen replied. "As a matter of fact, I think I can say that I have never hated anyone in my life."

"I'm very pleased to hear it," Jardine responded. "However, if you cannot bring yourself to regard the Australian team as anything more than friendly rivals, don't expect to play in any of the Tests, will you?"

The clipped dismissal infuriated Allen and he opened his mouth to reply. But the words wouldn't form. He stood, pondered a moment to find a parting shot, changed his mind and walked quickly away.

Jardine opened an eye and watched him go. He smiled and settled deeper into the deck chair, folding his arms contentedly. That should keep Gubby churning over for a while. Good chap, but he does need bringing up to scratch. . . .

The days slipped by and the heat drained everyone of energy.

Mary and Freddy Brown became inseparable, and she grew used to the secret grins and the whispered asides as they passed by, or sat alone at a table in the dining-room. The others had started a running joke whereby whenever they appeared, someone would invite Brown to do something else. "Fancy a dip, Freddy?" "Game of deck quoits, old son?" "Any good at chess, Freddy. . . ."

"Am I keeping you from your friends?" Mary asked. He grinned and squeezed her hand.

"Yes," he replied. "Thank God."

The professionals and amateurs retained their polite separation from each other without embarrassment. Each evening the pros would find a large dining-room table and gather round, ordering the drinks and keeping up a noisy, cheerful banter. Pataudi would join them in Colombo, and of the other amateurs Jardine stayed apart for most of the day, occasionally exchanging a few words about the need to keep fit, to watch the drink in this climate, to make sure they got enough sleep and so on. Freddy Brown was ensconced with Mary while Bob Wyatt and Gubby Allen both kept very much to themselves.

They were almost across the Indian Ocean. Wyatt and Allen were dining together. Behind them at a long table, Maurice Leyland was keeping up a fund of funny yarns—three weeks out and he still knew plenty of new ones, while the other joker in the pack, Tommy Mitchell, added dead-pan comments, his eyes glinting behind his spectacles, the only sign of enjoying his own wit. Gales of laughter greeted Leyland as he mimicked his way through an argument on some long-ago cricket field; Wyatt identified Jardine and Jack Hobbs in his repertoire. He and Allen smiled and said how good it was to have someone like Leyland in the side to keep the chaps' spirits up.

Jardine entered and looked around, the ever-present book tucked under his arm. But tonight, it seemed, he was not interested in finding a single table. Seeing them, he came across and put a hand on a spare chair.

"May I?"

"Evening, Douglas. Yes, of course," Wyatt said and waved to a waiter. "Another glass, please," he ordered and then looked at the inch or so of wine left in their bottle. "Better have another bottle too, while you're at it."

A roar of glee erupted from the pros' table and Jardine half-twisted in his seat.

"They're a bloody marvellous bunch of chaps, you know," he said.

The other two glanced at him in surprise. He sounded almost maudlin.

"I don't know how they manage to stay so bloody cheerful," Allen remarked. "In this heat."

"I'll tell you something," Jardine went on, "I'll never have a finer side to lead anywhere. Perhaps we'll lose every single game. I don't care. Right now I feel damned proud to be in charge of this lot."

He glanced at a menu and when the waiter returned with a glass and a new bottle of wine said he would have the lamb curry. Each time the men behind guffawed he turned to look at them, nodding with approval.

"Do you know," he said, spreading a napkin over his knees, "It's a sobering thought, but if those men didn't have a talent for cricket, most of them would be standing in a dole queue."

Neither Wyatt nor Allen could find much to say to this.

"Very likely," Allen nodded. Presently, Jardine's meal arrived and they watched him attack the curry, scooping it up with a fork and chewing vigorously. The man had an appetite in weather that had stopped either of them eating anything for two days except bread rolls, a little salad and cheese.

"That's why we're going to win," he announced, before taking another forkful. "That's why we're going to thrash the buggers."

The connection was lost on the other two.

"How do you mean, Douglas?" Wyatt asked, frowning.

They waited for him to swallow, take a long draught of wine and pat his mouth.

"Because yapping at their heels", he went on, jerking a thumb over his shoulder, "is the prospect of unemployment. They know if they don't produce the goods, they're out of cricket. Oh, it's all right for us, we can go and do something else. No labour exchange for you, I'll bet, Gubby, or you, Bob. But them—they only know cricket. Some of them kicked off down a mine or somewhere, but none of them have a trade to speak of. No cricket, no job. No job, no food. The last time I came on this tour, we didn't have any feeling that the world was about to collapse. There'd be Percy Chapman leading the congas, lots of fun and games and no thought about tomorrow. It's different now. Everything is different."

Another round of laughter came wafting across.

"It doesn't sound to me that they are worrying about being out of work," observed Wyatt.

Jardine snorted.

"Oh yes, they are laughing fit to bust," he said. "That's just it. There's too much noise. It's forced. Can't you detect a desperation in their voices? Well, I can. It's there, all right. Some people whistle in the dark, others laugh loudly. I'm glad to hear it. It gives us an edge, don't you see? The Australians are all amateurs. None of them get paid to play. They all have other jobs to keep them going."

He turned and surprised everyone at the other table by waving. Allen glanced at Wyatt and raised his eyebrows, nonplussed.

Then he cleared his face as Jardine turned back and finished his wine in a gulp.

"Yes," he said. "We have the edge."

Chapter Eight

Jack Fingleton jolted awake as the train gave a lurch to one side and his shoulder fell against the window. His head throbbed and his mouth felt like dried leather. Outside the view was the same as when he had fallen asleep; in fact it was no different from this time yesterday. Or should it be this time four days, or four weeks ago?

The Nullarbor Plain derives its name from its principal feature, which is the lack of a single tree for over 500 miles. It occupies almost one third of the 1600 miles between Adelaide and Perth. Not that anyone would notice, even if they cared, when the Nullarbor ended and the remainder of the journey resumed, since the view was roughly the same; mile after mile of baked earth scattered with rocks and sparsely covered by short, brown grass. The railway runs arrow-straight across for almost 300 miles before a bend is encountered, and it was the slight change of direction which caused Fingleton to fall against the window.

He muttered a curse and licked his lips, tasting the fine red dust which seeped in from outside, powdering their skin and clothes. One leg had gone to sleep, and he pummelled it back to life before he was able to stand and stretch painfully.

Stan McCabe, at 22 a couple of years younger than Fingleton, sat opposite, his eyes half-closed against the glare of the cloudless sky. He watched his companion wince as he flung his arms outwards.

"How long was I asleep?" Fingleton asked, rubbing his face vigorously to try and refresh himself.

"I dunno," McCabe replied. "Who's counting?"

"I only hope the Poms will appreciate the fact that we're coming nearly 2000 miles just to say hello," he sighed. Every inch of his body itched and he began to wonder if the train had been invaded by some virulent strain of minute flying ants.

"They won't give it two thoughts," McCabe answered. "They don't have any idea of distance. I've heard them complain about going from London to Nottingham. Three hours at the most. Tell them you can take a train for three days out here and you're still less than half-way across the country and you may as well talk to them about life on Mars."

Fingleton laughed to himself.

"Well, they've got to do this bloody trip going back to Adelaide. That should teach them a thing or two."

Despite projecting an air of bored indifference, Fingleton was actually brimming with excitement. Having only come into Test cricket the year before against the South Africans, he was aching to walk out on to a field to play an England side. He, Bradman and McCabe had been chosen from New South Wales to join Lonergan and Richardson from South Australia to play in a Combined XI against the M.C.C. tourists when they arrived at Fremantle on 18 October. Apart from the honour and the enormous boost to his driving ambition to be a Test player, the trip gave him a welcome rest from his regular job of chasing ambulances for a Sydney newspaper.

"Seen Don lately?" he asked after a while. He couldn't stop yawning and had a nightmare thought that he would dislocate his jaw and miss the games. McCabe shook his head.

"He's probably sitting somewhere planning his second innings," he answered, bringing a smile to Fingleton's face. McCabe went on, imitating Bradman's high-pitched voice, "I think after I've got 50, I'll turn a few down to fine leg, then work the ball as much as possible between mid-wicket and mid-on. After 100, I'll concentrate on the offside, give them one or two square cuts. Probably save the pullshot for my third century."

Bradman was deeply respected by the two men but not much liked. The reasons were hardly his fault. After the 1930 England tour and two fine seasons in Australia, Braddles was a public hero, an idol to grown men and schoolboys alike. He was to Australia what Lindbergh had recently been to America and the idolatry was the envy of everyone in the game. Nobody hitherto had gained from cricket a reputation like it. Politicians flocked to be photographed shaking hands with the 24-year-old country boy from Bowral. Newspapers sold twice as many copies if they could bring his name into a front-page headline. "Bradman Takes a Leak" Fingleton had once suggested to a colleague in Sydney when they were looking for a crowd-pulling article.

Wherever the train stopped crowds of men and boys flocked on to the platform, each holding an autograph book. While Fingleton and McCabe looked on, the guard would delay the departure until Bradman had signed every one of them and made a short speech about how one day he would like to return to this lovely little town and play some cricket. In the days of the Hollywood star, he outshone them all among the Australian public. Even in places where, as the train waited to be refuelled and watered, all the passengers could see were shifting groups of aborigines holding up pathetic souvenirs to the windows, where the desolate landscape beyond suggested that they were passing through a part of the world entirely cut off from the modern age, like some setting from a Conan Doyle story of lost continents, even here among the silent wilderness they came with a book, a sheet of paper, a cricket bat for him to sign. "Bradman! Bradman! Bradman!"

And so it went, through Coolgardie and Kalgoorlie where the gold-mining sites produced huge crowds at the stations: men who yelled and banged on the train windows shouting for Don to come on out and show himself, and where Richardson had to warn him not to stray too far into the crowd lest their enthusiasm got out of control.

"He's treated like royalty," McCabe muttered as once again they waited for Bradman to get back in the train.

"Yeah, well," Fingleton drawled, smiling at him, "one day Stan, you'll be out there, giving away your autograph, having them all bow and scrape at your feet. Think you can handle it?"

"Sure," McCabe laughed. "Success won't change me."

"Reckon not," Fingleton said. "You'll still be the same poisonous little bastard you always were."

At Perth the crowds were larger than anyone had ever seen at the station, and a police guard was needed to bring Bradman through to a waiting motor car. Throughout, he accepted the attention in a patient, unhurried, good-natured manner that belied his years. He expected people to be there waiting for him, but without appearing conceited. Fingleton saw him once straightening his clothes and combing his hair when the train slowed down for a station and jokingly asked how he knew anyone would be waiting for him.

"Want to bet, Fingo?" was all he replied.

And, of course, there had been. Bradman simply stated the obvious. When his followers crowded round, he did what was expected of him. It was the performance of a level-headed man who knew exactly where he was going in life, and this ability to shape events into an orderly pattern, handle situations few men expected to face in an undemonstrative and sensible way, this facility to be famous without appearing ever to be overawed by the fame, brought him more enemies than friends.

Fingleton found his room at the Palace Hotel, and after knocking back a few beers and eating a huge beefsteak, went to bed and slept for twelve hours, despite the constant buzz of voices outside in the street where the locals waited to catch a glimpse of the Boy Wonder. The next morning they met in the foyer where a driver waited to take them down to Fremantle docks and join in the traditional welcome extended to the England side as they disembarked.

The *Orontes* was already in sight, having anchored offshore for the final night, waiting for the tide to take her into the harbour. The quayside was full of the welcoming committee which stretched to several hundred people, including a brass band, the Mayor of Perth and a phalanx of reporters and photographers representing the Australian press corps. In addition there were the cranks. Standing on a step-ladder a large, pot-bellied man dressed as John Bull, complete with a stove-pipe hat, was waving a banner that read: "WELCOME GENTLEMEN OF ALBION". In the face of fierce, good-humoured heckling he was laying odds on the series: "100 to 1 on England! England for the Ashes, a 100 to 1 on! Do I hear any bids?"

In the harbour, dinghies and power boats criss-crossed the

entrance, some with banners saying: "POMS GO HOME!" "WE'LL KILL YER, ENGLAND!" Others had men standing in the sterns blowing post-horns, bugles, banging tambourines or simply shouting at the tops of their voices. The recent harsh times allowed few carnivals, and nobody was going to pass up this one. Each time the M.C.C. had arrived at Fremantle for as long as anyone could remember, the inhabitants of Perth turned out in force to give them the usual backhanded welcome, a simultaneous handshake and raspberry.

Richardson, Lonergan, Bradman, McCabe and Fingleton mingled with the bustling group standing with the Mayor and gradually introduced themselves. They were allotted a space in the front rank, the Mayor asking specifically if Bradman would stand next to him, ensuring that his face would be spread over the nation's press the following day. The photographers popped bulbs in Bradman's face and he grinned and nodded patiently until a long blast of the *Orontes*'s funnel brought them round to face the arrival of the liner into dock.

Aboard, Brown and Mary stood on the rail watching the shore activity with something approaching disbelief.

"Is this all for you?" she asked, squeezing his hand.

"I suppose it is," he said, "unless your Prime Minister slipped aboard at Colombo."

Now the brass band started up as the ship gently slewed round to bring her port side level with the quay. "Land of Hope and Glory" was followed by "Colonel Bogey", and by the time the gangplank was hauled into place they were going through a quickfire selection from "Chu Chin Chow".

Some of the old hands—Sutcliffe, Jack Hobbs and Hammond —had spotted a familiar face below and were happily waving.

"Is it always like this?" Voce asked Larwood.

"Oh aye," he replied happily. "Aussies always gi'us a good welcome. You mind what you drink here, son. They'll try and get you blotto by t'time you reach the hotel. I'm warning you—"

"S'all right by me," Voce said and began to wave at anyone, not wanting to look like a novice.

"When will you be coming to Sydney?" Mary asked.

"End of November," Brown replied, turning to look at her. "You *are* going to be there then, I hope."

She shrugged.

"You'll probably be far too busy playing cricket," she said. "I suppose you have to go to bed early, stay fit and things like that—"

"Yes."

"Well then," she pulled a face, "you won't have much time for me."

"There's only one way I'm able to get an early night," he said, looking away down at the sea of faces below. "And that is by having someone to give me a helping hand."

She punched his chest and laughed. Brown took her in his arms and gave her a long, affectionate embrace.

"You know," she murmured in his ear, "I never did discover if you were a batsman or a bowler."

Jardine waited by the top of the gangplank. He was dressed smartly in a suit and looked nervous, correcting his tie and running the flat of his hand along the side of his head to keep his hair in place. Then the rope was removed and the passengers began to disembark.

The team were allowed off first and with Jardine and Warner in front, they trooped down the gangplank as the band struck up with "For They Are Jolly Good Fellows". The crowds went wild, pressing forward, men yelling each other's names and reaching out to clasp hands. The Mayor of Perth held a piece of paper, the contents of a short speech, but he lost it in the jostling as the welcome became more boisterous. He gave a despairing look at the bandmaster and the song ended raggedly to be replaced a few seconds later by the National Anthem. This had the effect of bringing everyone to a halt and as the last chord died away, the Mayor stepped sharply forward, holding out a hand to Jardine before the rowdiness could start again.

"Mr Jardine," he bawled, "on behalf of the people of the fair city of Perth, I would like to extend the hand of friendship to you and the M.C.C. team who have come to engage in what we all hope will be a keenly fought and enjoyable series of cricket. We would like—"

"Here, Charlie," a voice boomed from the crowd, "don't make it too friendly, they're only bloody Poms—"

The Mayor grinned self-consciously as everyone else roared with laughter, and he waited for them to quieten down before he went on.

"We would like to say that although you won't be playing an actual Test match in Western Australia, that one day we shall be able to provide you with a contest here in this fair city of—"

"You've said that once, Charlie! Get on with it—"

The Mayor gave in as the crowds whooped and yelled and shouted for him to resign.

"Thank you, thank you," Jardine shouted above the din. "Speaking on behalf of my team and everyone associated with the tour, I would like to say how pleased we all are to be back in Australia and how much we are looking forward to renewing old acquaintances."

Richardson pushed his way to the front, bringing the other Australian players in his wake.

"Douglas, nice to see you again," he said, holding out a hand.

Jardine nodded and smiled and shook it. "Hello," he replied, then glanced at the others. "I know Bradman and I think I once met this chap—"

"Stan McCabe," Richardson helped him and then added, "This is Jack Fingleton and Ray Lonergan—"

Jardine shook hands with all of them, repeating their names as he did so.

"How kind of you to come all this way," he said. "I'm sure you must know our manager, Pelham Warner—" He held out an arm to bring Warner into the introductions. "He's been coming here since the year dot."

The formalities over, the rest of the England team now began to be absorbed into the crowd, some to shake hands with Bradman, McCabe and Richardson, others to be introduced, others to be buttonholed by reporters. The band struck up with a second rendering of "Colonel Bogey" until Fingleton sidled over to the bandmaster and whispered in his ear. A few minutes later they heard the first plangent chords of "Waltzing Matilda" and the crowd yelled their approval.

Suddenly they parted as two men pushed their way through and dropped a crate of bottles noisily at Jardine's feet.

One held up his arms and announced, "On behalf of the Perth Wine and Spirits Company, I would like you to accept our traditional gift of a case of Scotch whisky. Seeing how it is one of the *few* really good things to come out of Britain—"

Cries of "shame" and "Boooo!" erupted from the laughing England side.

"—we thought you might like a reminder of home and also have something with which to drown your sorrows when you get beaten by our vastly superior cricketers."

More catcalls and whistles went on for a while before Jardine could reply. Without looking down at the crate, he said, "I thank you for your gift, but my men have got to remain fit on this trip and therefore I must regretfully decline your generous offer."

This time the crowd remained silent when he finished. Warner shot a glance his way, sensing the shock felt by the audience. They had been given a crate of whisky on their arrival for as long as he could recall.

However, Jardine hardly paused before he continued.

"And now, ladies and gentlemen, if we are to do battle in a few days' time against what I'm sure will be a formidable Combined Eleven—I hardly think Messrs Bradman, McCabe and Richardson have come along merely to watch—I hope you will permit us to find our hotel and commence a much-needed training programme after four weeks at sea."

One of the reporters, Claude Corbett of the *Sydney Sun*, came forward, tugged a pencil from behind an ear and held it over a notepad.

"What's your team for the first game?" he demanded.

Jardine glanced at the man, then snorted; a half-laugh, half-dismissive contempt. "Wait and see," he replied.

Corbett pulled a face.

"Aw, come on, Duggie," he complained. "The eastern papers go to bed in a couple of hours. Do us a favour!"

"I am here to play cricket," Jardine snapped. "Not merely to provide scoops for your bloody newspapers."

93

"Douglas!" Warner hissed behind him. "For God's sake! We're going to *need* the press—"

But Jardine turned his back and returned to a senior naval officer standing by the foot of the gangplank. He shook his hand and made a short farewell speech of thanks for all the kindness they had received on board. It was quite clear that, as far as he was concerned, the reception was over.

Warner looked around in alarm at the reporters who were muttering as they scribbled in their pads. He pasted a broad smile on his face and walked across.

"Gentlemen," he announced, "please forgive us if we have not yet found our land legs. If there are any other questions you wish to ask, please feel free to do so."

"Yeah," someone piped up from the back, "I've got a question for Mr Jardine—"

Warner cocked his head. "Very well, let's hear it," he said.

"Jardine," the voice called, "why don't you piss off?"

The reporters chuckled while Warner reddened and lost his smile.

"Oh, please, gentlemen," he protested, "can we not keep this on a higher plane?"

He saw Jardine walking away, following someone to a line of motor cars. Giving a cough to hide his embarrassment, he nodded briefly to everyone he could see—the Mayor, Fingleton, Lonergan, Richardson and McCabe, even the forlorn wine merchants and their crate of whisky—before hurrying after the rest of the side as they straggled behind their captain.

Fingleton called to the bandmaster as "Waltzing Matilda" finished. "Looks like you're done for the day, boys."

"Bit of a contrast to the last time," Richardson observed.

"When Percy Chapman was in charge. He'd have had the top off one of those bottles and passed it round before you could say 'Cheers'."

"What's wrong with this bloke Jardine?" asked Fingleton.

"He's too English," said McCabe.

"You mean like a fish is too wet?" Fingleton replied and McCabe nodded. They looked round for Bradman but he was nowhere to be seen.

The quayside was rapidly emptying. The band began to dismantle their instruments and the banner bearers tossed their welcome signs into the water.

*　*　*

Rain caused the first game of the tour against Western Australia to fizzle out into a draw. Jardine told Voce that he couldn't take part because of a sprained ankle he had suffered in the Colombo game played en route—a sprain that was news to the Nottingham man. He put Larwood on for six overs, instructing him to bowl on the middle and off and well pitched-up. Bradman watched some of the third day's play and was not surprised to find Larwood trundling down at half pace. He wondered why Voce wasn't out there until someone mentioned the ankle, news that made him grin.

For the second game against the Combined XI which included Bradman, Jardine played neither Larwood nor Voce. "Your ankle is still giving you some stick, Bill, and you, Harold, have a slight head cold."

Bradman was out for 3 in the first innings and 10 in the second and the spectators wondered if what they had read of the Boy Wonder back east was poetic licence. As if to compensate, he bowled nineteen overs and took 2 for 106, England scoring almost 600 in the first innings. Meanwhile Voce limped and Larwood coughed whenever they saw a reporter and both wondered if they were ever going to get a game.

"Plenty of time," Jardine said when Larwood cornered him in the hotel.

"When d'you reckon my cough's gonta get better then, skipper?"

Jardine detected the petulance in his voice.

"When I say so," he replied crisply. "And that goes for your friend's ankle."

He offered no explanations, leaving Larwood hurt and baffled. *So he wants to play silly buggers. He might lerrus in on it. I mean, it's nor as if it were a state bloody secret wi' Tangy 'n me, like wi' the rest. . . .*

After another draw they crossed the Nullarbor to Adelaide to play South Australia. There, on one of the most beautiful grounds in the world, the weather brightened after the rain and clouds of Perth. Voce was still told to hobble about the pavilion while Larwood scored 81 in a first innings total of 634; Sutcliffe, Leyland and Jardine all made centuries. However, when he came on to bowl, attacking the off stump to order, Jardine advised him to slow down.

"I'm not bowling fast, skipper," he protested. "Just warming up, as a matter of fact."

"Listen," warned Jardine under his breath, "do as you're told. Except for Richardson, they are second rate. I don't want you wasting your sweetness on the desert air—"

"You what?"

"Just keep them well pitched-up and don't go straining anything."

"You mean like Tangy—"

"Please do as I say," Jardine snapped and went back to mid-off.

"Sod this," Larwood muttered as he walked to his mark. "How do I get any exercise bowling no faster than Wally Hammond? I'll send down a tweaker. That'll gerrim going. No berrer not. Like as not he'll ban me from t'bloody series. Could do owt when he's in one of his daft moods, ode Sardine. Sod him, though. What's he think I am, anyway? Bloody novice on his first tour?"

Turning round he loped into the characteristic gliding run which brought him racing to the crease like a long jumper. Throwing his left arm high, he leaped in the air, rammed his left foot stiffly into the ground and let the ball go as fast as he could, following through 10 yards up the pitch. Nitschke, the opening bat, jumped backwards as the delivery hit the track 5 yards in front of him and came flying up past his face. Ames had to leave the ground in his jump to reach the ball and even then only managed to deflect it for one of the slips to retrieve.

Larwood felt better. For the first time he had geared himself up for a quick one and it cleared the tubes. He turned back from his follow through, and saw Jardine glaring at him. Here we go, he said, wait for it. But when he returned to his mark Jardine said nothing. Over was called by the umpire. At the end of the over he retrieved his sweater from the umpire and ambled down to fine leg.

"Gubby," he heard Jardine call, "take Larwood's end next over, will you?"

He spun round, furious. Taken off after five overs? What's going on—what the bloody hell will the press make of this? The first major game of the tour and he goes off after five overs?

Unable to catch Jardine's eye for the rest of the session, he remained seething until they reached the dressing-rooms.

"Skipper," he demanded when the other players had left. "Can I have a word, please? I'd just like a word, if I may, if you've gorra minute—"

"Well?" Jardine gave him the eyes-down-the-nose treatment. "Hurry up, I'd rather like my lunch."

"What's the bloody idea of tekking me off after five sodding overs?" he shouted. "I mean, what'll t'press say? They're gonta wonder why, you know."

Jardine shook off a boot and replaced it with a shoe.

"Unfortunately you skinned some of your toes in the first couple of overs and asked me if you could have a rest."

"Skinned a few toes—?"

"I agreed at once, of course," Jardine put on the other shoe and headed for the door.

"It seems," Larwood yelled unhappily, "that I'm just one big bloody disaster area, don't it? Fust a cold, then me toes—what happens next?"

Jardine turned and the Nottingham man was furious to see he was actually smiling.

"That's entirely up to you, Larwood," he replied quietly and with a friendly lilt to his voice. "Do as you're told and I'm sure we'll have you fit as a fiddle in no time. Don't do as you're told and goodness knows, you might even get bitten by one of those poisonous Australian spiders one reads about."

M.C.C. won the game by an innings and 128 runs. The commentators remarked how the spinners Verity and Brown took fourteen of the Australian wickets and hazarded guesses that although the tourists brought over four fast bowlers, so far they had shown themselves either to be injury-prone or ineffective on these early season wickets. In any event, against South Australia they weren't needed, although a great number of the spectators had come mainly to see Larwood in action, and he hardly bowled at all.

Three days later after an all-night train journey to Melbourne, they played Victoria. Larwood was dropped because his toes had still not properly healed although Voce took part, his ankle having cleared up nicely.

Against a team that contained almost half the Australian Test side, M.C.C. won by an innings and 83 runs. A combination of cold winds, rain and the exclusion of Larwood reduced the crowds in the huge Melbourne stadium who hoped they would receive better value for money the following week when Bradman was due to arrive to play for another combined Australian XI.

The night before the game Jardine called Voce and Larwood to his room.

"How are you feeling?" he asked and took pleasure in the looks he received. "Fighting fit, I hope—"

The two Nottingham men exchanged glances but said nothing. They grew restless as Jardine took his time lighting a pipe. What was it to be this time? Malaria, perhaps?

"This game tomorrow," Jardine said, wafting a cloud of smoke from his face, "Mr Wyatt will skipper. I'm off to do a spot of fishing."

That's nice, thought Voce. But why's he telling us?

"But you two are in the side. And as you're back in good health, I want you to bowl the way we talked about. All right?"

Larwood was the first to respond.

"At Bradman?"

"Well, not at the bloody umpire," Jardine replied with a harsh chuckle. "Of course at Bradman. You fellows have been belly-aching ever since we got here about not being allowed to have a go at the little bastard. Well, here's your chance. Not in some poky little hole in the back of beyond. But here, in the biggest ground in the country and with every newspaper poised to send the word out that we are ready to do business. The spectators are aching to see you in action, Harold. And their appetites have been sharpened by all these skinned toes and colds and what have you. Now, my friend, you are going to show them the reason I brought you."

Chapter Nine

The Melbourne Cricket Ground held something in excess of 70,000 spectators. Playing there, cricketers say, is like playing in a vast Valhalla surrounded by a tidal wave of faces. It is so large that seating is provided for all the spectators, with enough cloakrooms and refreshment areas for everyone. Echoes rebound and when the sun shines in summer, the heat in the middle of this enormous bowl is usually 20° higher than outside.

Jardine kept his relations with the press as sour as they became on the first day at Fremantle by a number of calculated devices. One which particularly annoyed reporters was his habit of announcing the England team only at the last minute. Not even the players knew who was in the side until he came in, half an hour before the start and pinned the names up on the dressing-room notice board. Those who were omitted would then change back into civilian clothes. His explanation was that he saw no value in announcing in advance to the likes of Bradman which bowlers they would be facing, giving them time to work out a strategy. In fact, this was only half true; he derived more pleasure from frustrating the Australian press and spectators—who also wanted to know whom they were paying to see—than "the likes of Bradman". It was a pity they never caught on to it; each time Jardine heard a frosty remark or read a hostile sentence about his unwillingness to show even the basic courtesies to his hosts, his resolve strengthened, his satisfaction glowed. Nothing is gained by teasing someone who won't be provoked.

The side he pinned up included, besides the Nottingham pair, Sutcliffe, Pataudi, Leyland, Allen, Paynter, Brown, Duckworth and Bowes.

"Forget Freddy Brown," he told Wyatt outside the dressing-room. "Larwood and Voce know what to do. Keep them alternating with Bowes and Gubby. It's not going to be particularly hot so they should be able to keep going all day, if need be. Oh, er, if Larwood wants to pack his legside field, let him. Bill Woodfull's notoriously suspect on his leg stump, so I told him and Voce to plug away at it. I'm off to the Snowy mountains for some fishing, but I'll be back Sunday and I'll come in to watch the Monday morning session. That's if you haven't won by then."

Thirty thousand watched Sutcliffe and Wyatt come out to open the England innings. The Australian XI included, besides Bradman and Woodfull, O'Brien, Darling, Oxenham and Ironmonger, all of whom were tipped to play in the Tests, along with a young unknown called Lisle Nagel from Victoria. Six feet 6 inches tall, he even outstretched Bowes. Only Bradman and Oxenham came from other states.

The England openers put on 56 before Wyatt was lbw to Oxenham. The crowd grew restless at the painfully slow scoring rate; only 7 runs were scored off Nagel in seventy minutes. Sutcliffe could not find his strokes, cobbling together a laborious 89 before he was caught by Bradman off Ironmonger. The sluggish pace continued with Pataudi and Leyland and by the end of the day a great many spectators had left before England came in with a little over 200 runs.

However, they all returned the following morning, a Saturday, knowing that if the rain held off, they would finally see the long-postponed Bradman–Larwood confrontation. The cricket sparked up at once: Allen and Brown threw the bat at everything and England finished before lunch with 282.

"I gather Mr Jardine has had a word with you," Wyatt said to Larwood as they prepared to go out.

"Aye."

"This business about Woodfull's leg stump and all that."

Larwood frowned as he tightened his bootlace.

"Worrabout it, skipper?"

It was Wyatt's turn to frown. "He told me you and he had realized Woodfull was weak on the leg stump. Something about him moving across, leaving it exposed."

100

Fust I heard of it, Larwood thought, but nodded.

"Oh aye, that's right," he said.

"Bill," Wyatt called across the room. Voce and Bowes answered. "Sorry, Bill Bowes," he corrected. "You take the second over. The other Bill and Gubby be ready to take over. I think short sharp spells from all of you is the order of the day."

Jardine's order of the day, Allen thought as they went downstairs. Odd he chose this game to stand down.

To prolonged cheering Woodfull and Leo O'Brien clattered down the pavilion steps. The captain glanced up at a threatening sky and felt the strong crosswind that had risen since the start of play.

"No hurry," he told O'Brien. "Wait and see what this wind does before you try anything bold. Don't try to drive until your eye's in. Since it looks like an all-speed attack, let the ball do the work."

Larwood took the new ball from the umpire and stepped out seventeen paces, drawing his toe studs across the turf to mark his run. Wyatt was setting his usual field: three slips, a cover, extra, mid-off, mid-on, forward short leg and deep fine. Larwood waved an arm at cover and extra, signalling them to move over on to the short legside. Nothing happened for a moment and Wyatt walked up the pitch.

"You're leaving the offside wide open," he murmured.

"S'all right, skipper," Larwood replied with a grin, "I'm not bowling any on t'off. Also, can you move over one of t'slips?"

Woodfull watched the fielders cross and shrugged. In the press box Jack Hobbs noted: "Larwood starts with heavily patrolled leg field."

Pelham Warner sat in front of the pavilion. He was feeling pleased. Glancing up at the flagpole he watched the tattered M.C.C. banner he had run up flutter in the breeze. He had been given it in 1902 and had flown it wherever he had watched a Test match. The truth was that it had rarely seen an England defeat. His thoughts were drawn back to the game by a babble of voices. Larwood had placed five men on the leg and was coming in to bowl the first over to Woodfull. He saw the ball skim down the pitch, land and catapult high past Woodfull's back as he moved swiftly inwards to avoid being hit. A murmur like wind in a tunnel went round the enormous stadium. Men looked at their companions and leaned forward in their seats. Most of them had seen Larwood before, in 1928, but rumours of his increasing pace in the last few years had reached them. Now they were able to see if they were true. The first ball produced everywhere a thrill of expectancy, Duckworth had to leap high to take it and the thwack as it hit the gloves resounded like a pistol shot.

Woodfull went forward and tapped the pitch, trying to hide his concern. He had not seen the delivery at all. Only vaguely was he aware of something travelling down the legside and when it bounced he had moved across in alarm without even trying to play a stroke.

At the other end, O'Brien felt the hair on his neck bristle. The ball had missed Woodfull by a fraction, ricocheting off the pitch faster, it seemed, than when it struck.

Larwood bowled again, hitting exactly the same spot, but this time Woodfull went on to the back foot and held his bat out to play it down to forward short leg. But he was far too slow and once again Duckworth raised his arms and pulled it down from rising 6 feet.

The third delivery Woodfull played in the middle of the bat back to the bowler. The fourth he let pass and the crowd at the bowler's end roared. What they could see was the ball shaving the leg stump. He stopped the fifth, pushing away to Allen at forward short leg, while the sixth and seventh skimmed over his head.

His relief at the end of the over was almost tangible to the close fielders, but he kept a schoolmaster's calm and camouflaged his nervousness by slipping off his gloves and tightening a strap on his pads.

Bowes came on at the other end and flung the ball down from a height of over 7 feet. Even if he was nowhere as menacing, he kept both Victorians in a constant state of unease. Then back came Larwood. By now the crowd had caught on to England's tactics and a wave of hostile barracking developed.

Warner counted the first three overs and was shocked to realize that every single delivery was on the line of the leg stump. What the devil was Wyatt playing at? Turning his head, he heard the rising anger in the conversation around him. So far the score had advanced by three byes, two no-balls and a snick from Woodfull that crossed the stumps and ran through the slips.

On the field, Wyatt gazed round at the crowds, listened to the increasing irritation until he could feel fear touch his spine. Perhaps the bowlers should ration the legside stuff. Although, heaven knows, it was working. Neither batsman had played one confident stroke since they came out. Let it go on a little longer, then if the objections persist, rearrange the field. Mind you, if Jardine were here, he wouldn't change anything. But Jardine is a man apart; he thrived on aggravation.

Woodfull tapped the crease, waiting as Larwood raced in. This time the ball was an inch over towards middle and leg. He went back and showing both shoulders, brought the bat up to play a conventional defensive shot. But again the speed deceived him. His stroke was only half-completed when the ball shot through and thudded into his chest just below the heart. He felt the seam tattoo the skin, followed by a pain so excruciating that he dropped his bat and fell away from the wicket, choking. The blow pounded the air from his stomach, and as he fell to his knees he panicked when he found he was unable to suck anything back into his lungs. A forest of white-flannelled legs surrounded him and a pair of hands grasped his armpits. Through watering eyes he could dimly make out concerned faces as the players bent over, shocked at the blue tinge to his lips and the hoarse noises in his throat.

Larwood waited at the other end, worried, but determined not to go down the wicket and show the sympathy he felt. Out of the crowd came a few strident voices.

"Happy now, Larwood?"

"Whyncha go down and give him a kick to finish him off, you bastard?"

"Take him off, take him off!"

Allen waited, holding Woodfull's bat as the Victorian captain rose shakily to his feet, helped by Pataudi and Brown. Leo O'Brien was telling him to bend and straighten as much as he could to restore his breathing.

"I'm—I'm all right, I'm all right," he whispered.

"Go off for a bit, Bill," O'Brien urged, but Woodfull shook his head.

"I'm all right," he repeated, looking round for his bat.

Allen stepped forward and handed it to him.

"Dreadfully sorry," he sympathized, but Woodfull ignored the remark and returned to the crease aided by a huge cheer from the crowd.

Wyatt lobbed the ball back to Larwood. He desperately wanted to tell him to go easy but knew that in his present mood the fast bowler listened to no one. There was a Jekyll and Hyde quality about the man. With the catcalls and the insults, with a batsman who could hardly hold his bat, and with a track perfectly suited to his needs, he would hear no words of caution, much less heed them. This was the fifth match of the tour and so far he had bowled under a dozen overs. And anyway, Jardine had told him that this was the game they had been waiting for.

In some parts of the stands they began to count as he raced in but he hardly heard them. He was looking down at the spot between middle and leg. Keep it short, keep it short—

He bowled and Woodfull found himself facing exactly the same delivery. This time he reacted a fraction more quickly, pushing it away towards leg slip. However, his stroke was a carbon copy of the one which had failed the ball before and this set the spectators off in a renewed storm of booing.

Warner wondered what on earth was happening. Woodfull was a quiet, intelligent man whom everyone admired; a captain of sterling qualities who, as Kipling urged, treated winning and losing in the same way. This kind of brutal treatment was doing us no good at all. Why doesn't Wyatt put a stop to it? Surely it can't simply be the state of the wicket. No, it can't be. They had started off from the very first ball with a packed legside field. It was as if they were following some preconceived plan. If they were, nobody had informed him about it. Why, he hadn't seen a field like this since the pre-war days of Frank Foster.

At the end of a long over, which included the five minutes it had taken Woodfull to recover, Wyatt suggested to Larwood it might be better to revert to a normal field for a while.

"Mr Jardine said to keep the pressure on," he muttered. "Seeing how Bradman must be watching every ball."

He gave a quick grin which failed to reassure the captain.

Up in the Australian dressing-rooms Bradman was indeed

watching the game intently. Three weeks ago here in a New South Wales game against Victoria, he had scored 238 in 200 minutes. Twenty-five thousand people had watched an effortless display of superiority in awed admiration. They had seen Woodfull fail to set any kind of field that checked his scoring rate, and had said to each other that with the Boy Wonder on this kind of form, nothing could stop Australia from keeping the Ashes. Many had come up after the game and told him so. He thanked them for their kind words, but he knew that there was nothing to compare the Victorian bowling with the crop of speed merchants England had brought.

His concentration was caused less by apprehension than by a need to see how much the pitch was helping Larwood. In 1930 he had scored hundreds of runs off him. So many, in fact, that the Notts man had been dropped from the Fourth Test. But the Australian wickets, especially early in the season, were far more unpredictable than in England. The ball came through at different heights and it was imperative to have a good "reading" of the pitch before coming in, or the first ball could easily be the last. He watched Woodfull and O'Brien vainly struggling to tame the England opening attack and he knew he would be out there before long.

Fear wasn't part of his make-up. He wouldn't like to take one in the chest like poor old Woodfull, but he realized without conceit that he wasn't likely to. Bill was always slow on his feet. Over the years he had seen him hit many times, walking ponderously into the ball instead of darting out of the way.

They were putting them all down on the line of the leg stump. Of course they would, knowing Woodfull's weakness in that area. But would they continue to do so to him? His eyes travelled to the enormous gap on the off; nobody between cover and the bowler. Step backwards a pace and cut it—there was a chance. He would get 20 or so, settle in, and have a go. Then they would have to get rid of some of the short legs to plug the hole.

He came out of his trance of concentration to say something and discovered everyone else had either fallen completely silent or were muttering in undertones. During the early part of an innings, the rest of the players usually performed various chores, or played cards or dozed; few actually watched the game. But today no one took their eyes off the field. A stunned reaction had settled over the dressing-room and Bradman could see the sapping effect of the England tactics on the players' morale.

Wyatt rung the changes with his men and replaced Larwood and Bowes with Voce, who continued with the leg-trap, and Brown. He noticed Allen had a tight-lipped expression which didn't alter when he explained he was keeping him in reserve for later. At one moment as they changed over, Allen hissed:

"For God's sake, Bob, tell them to pitch it up!"

But he knew Wyatt was powerless. Larwood and Voce were answering to another voice, and Bowes, seeing the success of the leg-trap, was equally not about to yield the advantage. So the game went on, the spectators becoming more and more unrestrained, the players, especially those in the deep field, ever more anxious about their safety—a few bottles appeared on the grass—and at what they would read about themselves the next day. And the batsmen discovering that, until now, they had learned nothing about the tourists which gave them the slightest indication of what to expect.

Woodfull went when the score reached 51, lbw to Bowes. The crowds leaned forward with one accord and greeted Bradman as he came out and ambled to the wicket. Despite the drama of the first two hours, he wore his customary broad smile and the people cheered more loudly when they saw he was refusing to be intimidated.

Bradman stopped the first ball from Bowes and swung at the second, scattering the forward short legs who turned and covered their heads as it sped through to the boundary. The spectators reacted like a soccer crowd applauding a home goal. They stood and shouted, "Good on yer, Don!" jumping up and down with the relief of seeing a positive response after two hours of indecisive dithering from Woodfull and O'Brien.

At the other end, O'Brien played out a maiden from Voce, without offering a single stroke. Eight times he moved across and bent low to avoid bouncers that flew like a tennis ball off tarmac. Poor Duckworth behind the stumps leaped in all directions, mostly upwards, and felt the sting worsen across the palms of his hands inside the inadequately padded gloves.

In the next over from Bowes, Bradman swung at the first ball and missed, pulled the next for 4, the third for 2, the fourth for another 4, let the fifth go past and pulled the sixth for 3. Whether Bowes was tiring now and dropping them too short, or whether Bradman realized that this kind of bowling was perfect for his favourite shot, the spectators were unable to agree. The following over, Bradman let the first two Voce deliveries go by, hooked the third down hard on the ground for 2, played a yorker past the bowler for another couple and let the rest of the over pass by contemptuously refusing a stroke at balls that went sailing 2 yards over his head.

The crowds lost their antagonism and settled back to enjoy seeing England receive their come-uppance. Bradman's footwork began to make an inroad into the bowling, allowing him to get right out of the way or leap into position to push the ball where there were no fielders. Soon the leg-trap began to move back, a yard at a time. When he reached 20, he cut a Voce bouncer, using a forehand tennis shot, into the emptiness of the offside. This brought the spectators to their feet. The audacity of the man!

Wyatt took Bowes off and brought Larwood back. The din in the stadium steadied. This was what they had been waiting for. Larwood felt the occasion—how could he fail to when 30,000 voices lowered in unison? He strode briskly to his mark, examining the ball, now battered and dull. Just right for leg theory. No fancy swerves: down the line, on the spot and let it go with the arm. Bradman took a fresh guard, saw the forward short legs return and gave them a broad grin.

Larwood flung the ball down short of a length on the leg stump. Bradman stepped two paces back and square cut it for 4 through the covers. The spectators yelled with delight. The Boy Wonder proved it wasn't only possible to do this to Voce and Bowes—he was even square-cutting Larwood! Moving into position while the ball hurtled down at 100 miles an hour!

For a moment not even Larwood could believe what happened. One of his fastest deliveries and the sod *cuts* it through the covers! He sent down the same thing again. Bradman ducked and the ball

107

screamed over his head to reach Duckworth still rising 20 yards behind. The third one was no different, except faster, but it didn't come up as high and Bradman hooked it for 4. The next he let go, leaning inwards and letting it skim his thigh. The next he ducked and the sixth he smothered down to one of the short legs.

The crowds sat back and beamed. In the press box the reporters were wondering if this was the Great Event they had waited for— why, Bradman was playing the same as always. With plenty of time, feet in the right place. Always in control. Larwood may be the Poms' secret weapon, but he was being made to look quite ordinary. The Run Machine was putting everything into a proper perspective.

There were only two men in the Melbourne ground that day who didn't share this view. One was Bradman. From the moment he received Larwood's first ball, he knew that he was faster than in '30. Faster and far more dangerous. He had cut and hooked in the first over, but knew they were lucky shots. The ball was coming through at all heights as he had feared. But what he hadn't grasped, looking on from the pavilion, was the deadly speed of this man, or his pinpoint accuracy. Not a single ball had varied a fraction from the line of the body, slightly short of a length. Only the level at which it came through had allowed him to cut and hook those two. He was in deep trouble. And if he was, the rest of the side didn't stand a chance. They would lose unless he could do something, and do it quickly. The crowds would soon begin to twig the fact that he was unhappy out there. The press would jump on it in a second. All he had to do was make a few false shots.

The other dissenter from the complacency of the press room and the stands was replacing his sweater and moving down to fine leg, pleased with himself.

"Hey, Larwood," someone shouted, "whyn't you change to tweakers? Our Don's not impressed by your quick'un, is he?"

Just you wait, you daft bugger, he thought, smiling. Your Don's worried. I know he is. Why, there was one moment when he even stopped grinning.

For weeks the papers had been full of the approaching "Bradman–Larwood" duel, but now it was taking place, scarcely a viewer present, pressman or schoolboy, expert or layman, appreciated what was happening right under their noses. There may have been faster bowling before, but none so fast and at the same time so devastatingly accurate. Larwood knew that his fast leg theory was less physically dangerous to the batsman than it appeared because it was predictable. If the batsman felt assured he would know the precise direction of every delivery, and be able to take evasive action in good time. But here, on this blustery Melbourne spring day, the incalculable factor was the pitch. The ball would not come through at a predictable height and therefore any batsman who remained doggedly at his post was likely to be hit over and over again. And there had to come a time when such punishment affected his performance, no matter who he was.

Very, very belatedly, the spectators caught on. The following over, Bradman let five consecutive deliveries from Larwood go past, brushing him high on the hip as he moved inside them, each one pitched on the line of the leg stump. His previous attempts to push the close field back, to collar the ball any way he could, had failed and now the press and the crowd began to have second thoughts. The scoring rate dwindled as runs became harder to get. There was one moment, facing Voce, when a ball popped and Bradman lost his balance, and fell over backwards.

Even when Bowes returned, Bradman could not regain his momentum. He mixed bad strokes with good ones, jabbing one through the short legs while looking to the off, expecting his shot to have gone in a different direction. And he was no longer smiling.

Larwood finally trapped him lbw for 36. The middle order of the Australian XI disintegrated with only a spirited piece of slogging towards the end giving them a score of 218 in reply to M.C.C.'s 282.

Jardine returned from his fishing weekend on Sunday and listened to an account of the play with a delight that not even he could disguise. He had Larwood tell him over and over again how Bradman was tied up, how he fell over, and about the shots that didn't go where he intended.

"What did the little bastard *look* like?" he demanded, gloating at the vision of Bradman losing that damned smug smile, of actually *falling over*!

"You were right about t'wicket, Mr Jardine," said Larwood as they strolled round the Botanical Gardens. "T'ball comes through different height each time. That's what gorrim worried. I mean, I gorra be fair about Bradman, he don't scare easy. He don't scare at all, as a matter of fact. I sent five quick 'uns down on t'spot each time. If any one of 'em had hit him, he'd a been carried off. But he were like one of them whaddoyacallits, them as fight bulls in Spain. He just leaned across and lerrem go by, sometimes not half an inch in it, skimming past his body."

Jardine beamed.

"Well, you never can tell, Harold," he remarked. "One day you'll score a direct hit. The main thing is, you got him out for 36. That means, do you realize, that in four innings against us, Bradman has scored precisely 62 runs. He's bound to feel that. The main thing now is not to let up. Give him a breather and we'll lose the initiative. He's on the ropes. Don't let him off. Go for the knockout. I know you can do it, Harold. I know *we* can win this series. We're half-way there already."

With Warner, the conversation was less exuberant. Returning from his walk Jardine found a note in his pigeon-hole asking him to go and see the manager in his room.

He found the older man seated by the window with a selection of the Sunday newspapers scattered over the table. There was a chilliness in the air and after calling out, "Come in", in response to the knock on the door, Warner said nothing further until Jardine was standing in front of him.

"Your note said you wanted to see me," Jardine said, keeping up a briskness designed to take the wind out of what he knew was coming. He recalled an old adage his father taught him: "When you know you are to be attacked, that is the time to go on the offensive. Never complain, explain or apologize."

Warner waved a hand at the newspapers.

"Have you seen what they have said about the game?" he demanded.

110

Jardine cast a deliberately casual eye over the headlines: "ENGLAND SAY IF YOU CAN'T BOWL 'EM OUT, LAY 'EM OUT!", "DANGEROUS PLAY AT MCG", "ENGLAND BOWLERS UNREPENTANT", "IT'S NOT CRICKET — AND IT AIN'T!"

"Yes," he sighed. "Bloody squealers."

Warner stood up quickly. Jardine had rarely seen him so agitated.

"Douglas," he snapped, "you weren't there. You have no idea of the resentment felt at the way our chaps bowled. I was sitting in the middle of it and I can tell you, things were being said I wish I hadn't heard."

"What kind of things?" asked Jardine, genuinely interested but also knowing this would make Warner bristle all the more. Spot on.

"That is neither here nor there!"

"Well, I don't see how I can help," Jardine said with a shrug. "I wasn't in charge. I wasn't anywhere near the place."

Warner looked at the man for a moment and forced himself to rein in his temper.

"Douglas." He spoke quietly, feeling for the words carefully like a lawyer drawing up a watertight document. "Is it or is it not true that you instructed Larwood and Voce to bowl short on the leg stump?"

Jardine thought about that for a while, with a mocking gravity.

"That is—ah—true," he replied.

"Might I ask why?"

"Because Woodfull is suspect on his legs," he explained. "He's an offside player who tries to work everything onto that side. It doesn't take a genius to suggest the bowlers plug away at his weakness."

"Bradman isn't weak on the legs," Warner broke in, ticking off his fingers. "Nor is O'Brien, nor were Rigg, Darling or Oxenham. And yet each batsman who came in yesterday was subjected to a barrage of short balls aimed directly at their bodies. Poor Woodfull got a terrible blow in his chest, Rigg was hit repeatedly on his thighs and Darling very nearly caught one in the head. In view of the fact that Larwood, Bowes and Voce bowled forty-three of the fifty overs, the suggestion is inescapable that you instructed Wyatt to keep them on and to let them bowl exclusively to leg-traps. Do you know at one time Voce had *six* men on the leg? *Six!* No one has ever *seen* such a field before!"

"I notice we have a 70-run lead," Jardine observed mildly. "It seems our tactics paid off."

"They most certainly did *not* do anything of the kind!" Warner shouted, thumping the papers with his fist. "Do you call *that* kind of press 'paying off'? Do you call 30,000 spectators, all furious at the way we played, 'paying off'? Do you, even in your most obtuse moments, Douglas, really and truly believe that it is better to play cricket in this kind of atmosphere than in one where opponents occasionally applaud each other's performances?"

"Did you ask me up here to talk about philosophy or the way the game is progressing?" Jardine asked, presenting Warner with his profile and including a world-weary sigh to underline his boredom with either matter.

"I asked you here," Warner said slowly, deliberately, "to make it clear that I abhor the tactics we used yesterday. I abhor them and I implore you to stop it. I want to win this series just as much as you do, but I want to do it within the rules. You may call that old-fashioned, antediluvian—I don't particularly care. But I have been associated with this game too long to allow it to devolve into some—some all-in wrestling bout."

There was a longer pause than had been usual up to now.

"Plum," Jardine replied, giving the impression he had considered the other man's words very carefully, "You say you want to win as much as I do—"

"Yes."

"Would it be true to say then, that victory in sport is gained fairly when two teams agree to a set of rules, play by them, and eventually one of the teams emerges as a winner."

"Ah—well, yes—"

Warner felt himself drowning in quicksand. Jardine had forced him to say yes, when a single word answer wasn't sufficient. The whole question of morality in sport required a much more qualified response—

"Then show me, please," said Jardine, "a rule in the laws of cricket that forbids a bowler from adopting the tactics that Larwood and co. used yesterday."

"That isn't the point!" Warner exclaimed, knowing this would be Jardine's counter-thrust but helpless to prevent it. "The rules are only part of it! What about the *conventions*? Cricket is a complicated and deeply complex mixture of rules and generally accepted traditions. It is a game that is ruined by too many written regulations. Do you suppose it is necessary to specify in a rule that a batsman shall not go down the wicket and strike the bowler over the head with his bat? But it isn't done. Or that the umpire shall not be argued with. Yet it isn't done. A hundred, a thousand things are not done simply because of the players' basic civilized behaviour, Douglas! The conventions we observe in cricket are the conventions we observe in living our lives—that is the wonderful part about this marvellous game! It doesn't apply anywhere else. Have you ever seen one rugger side applaud a try scored against them? Or soccer teams shaking their opponents' hand for a clever goal? But when a man scores a century, *everyone* congratulates him, as they should."

An urge gripped Jardine to argue with the older man. An anger rose in his gorge that was difficult to suppress. How dare this fellow lecture him on ethics! How dare he make his gnomic observations on life and lay them out as a way to win at sport! How dare he presume to order him to regard his foolish old Victorian ways as a guide to living in the twentieth century. Had he never heard of the Somme, or Ypres, or Passchendaele? Had he never read a newspaper since 1910? Had he never noticed that the Edwardian sun had set, that a new world had grown up which regarded Britain as just one more dot on the map? Did he really think that England could still proselytize the natives by showing them what sportsmanship was, by giving them a few bibles and sending them a missionary trained at one of the better Anglican colleges?

While Warner continued, Jardine grasped the urge and forced it down. Why waste breath? The thirty years that separated them was the largest generation gap there had ever been since the one which had straddled the Norman Conquest. Warner was no different

113

from most men of his era. It would be both unkind and a waste of time to try and persuade him the world was a different place now. A different and, for Englishmen, a crueller, colder place.

"—and so," Warner was saying, the effort turning his cheeks red, "I am going to insist, Douglas, that your whole approach both to the press and the public over here, and your approach to the games must be changed. And immediately. I don't know why you have this antipathy to these people and frankly I don't very much care. But let me remind you we are their guests and as such we are obliged to follow some fairly basic rules of hospitality. Now about this game going on at present. I am sure you regard this legside bowling, this short stuff, as a perfectly justifiable tactic to use against men like Bradman and Woodfull and so on. Yes, we have contained Bradman in the innings he has played against us so far, and yes, I am pleased no end about that. But I must reiterate that if tactics, any tactics, become by their very nature dangerous, then they must *not* be used. It isn't simply seeing these kind of articles in the newspapers, or listening to angry spectators at the ground, although God knows that's unpleasant enough. It is recognizing that there are some conventions which *must* be observed if the game is not to disintegrate into chaos. You will recall I said so in print this past summer when Bowes let them fly against Hobbs in the Surrey–Yorkshire match. Well, I repeat what I said then now. Please stop it, Douglas. At once."

The following day the ambling giant Nagel wrote himself into the history books by taking 8 wickets for 32 runs in 10 overs. M.C.C. were all out for 60 and during the rain that followed immediately the last wicket fell, Jardine listened silently as Warner discussed the crisis with Wyatt. The Australian XI required 125 to win and all the M.C.C. could hope for was rain. When they asked him his view, he passed, much to Warner's displeasure.

"Douglas, you have a responsibility to give us your opinion—"

But he remained silent, although Wyatt noticed him chatting to Voce and Larwood later on as the rain pelted down outside.

The following day it stopped and the wicket rolled out quite well, but remained damp. Larwood didn't ask for a leg-trap, nor did Allen with whom he opened. However, his first over was of a pace

114

and such lethal accuracy that except for the wicket-keeper, fielders were unnecessary. He pitched each delivery five yards in front of both Woodfull and O'Brien, neither of whom came anywhere near touching it. The dampness on the surface of the track made it springy, like a rubber mattress, and no matter what attempt the batsmen made to measure up, they were left either bent double to avoid the ball screaming a yard over their heads, or desperately scrambling towards the off to avoid being hit. Not one came up at a height to be parried by the bat.

Woodfull swung despairingly at one from Larwood in the third over and was caught by Duckworth behind. The crowds, larger than ever, expecting an easy home victory, roared as Bradman made his way to the wicket. Off Allen, he put one between second slip and gully, a lucky shot. Three balls later the ball flew off his glove to Duckworth who knocked it up with his hand above his head, but Sutcliffe failed to reach it in time. He cut the eighth ball of Allen's over to third man for a single, bringing him up to face Larwood.

By now the clouds had rolled across the stadium and there was a general movement in the crowds as they put on raincoats and stood by with their umbrellas, cursing the weather, knowing it was likely now to stop them watching the first defeat, and a crushing one at that, of these aggressive and hostile Poms who, it seemed, had come down to Australia with but a single purpose, to kill a few of their best players.

Larwood waited until Bradman had taken guard and performed the preliminary routine with his gloves and cap, then ran in. The rain was going to stop this very soon, so he would put all his energy into every ball. He had to show Bradman that the Larwood of old, the man who was hit all over the ground back at Leeds two years ago, was no more. He had to show him that he was faster and more devastating than anything he had ever faced in his life. He was 28 years old and a fast bowler could expect only a limited career. Perhaps he would have two more Test series against Australia but after that it was a gradual but unavoidable decline into retirement. Right here, right now, if he didn't make his name ring round the world, he might as well get ready to sign on again back at the pit. Even blokes like Percy Chapman make one mistake and they're never heard of again—

He released the ball with an explosion of air from his lungs. His follow through was so fierce that the knuckles of his right hand brushed the ground. The ball was short. Bradman drew back to cut, but miscalculated the height as it came through. He played over the top and it hit the top of the off stump.

The crowd was as still as if someone had called for the two minute silence on Armistice Day. Bradman was scared! Disguised as an attempt to cut, he had pulled back, out of the way, and let himself be bowled all ends up! Duckworth watched a bail spin past, as he jumped high in the air along with the three slip fielders. Bradman was out for 13.

The rain began to fall before he reached the pavilion and the game was abandoned as a draw.

"Pity," Jardine said as they came in. "I doubt if they would have made a 100. Well bowled Harold. Well skippered, Bob," he said to Wyatt. "I think you read the game splendidly."

Pelham Warner stood behind him and he half turned as he added: "Don't let anyone tell you differently."

Chapter Ten

The team left Melbourne at 4.30 Tuesday afternoon and arrived in Sydney at 9.15 the following morning after changing trains. For a few fleeting seconds they were able to glimpse through the sleeper windows the recently completed new bridge across the harbour.

The game against New South Wales commenced on Thursday. Bradman played although the newspapers had announced that he was feeling ill. Returning from Melbourne he had complained of a sore throat and a temperature and gone straight to bed. Jardine toyed with the temptation to produce Larwood again, if only to show the Sydneysiders what Melbourne already knew—that the Boy Wonder had his limitations. But something held him back: the way the Nottingham man was throwing everything into his game, he risked injury each time he played, and the first Test was only a week away. And there was another consideration, one he could not ignore: Voce and Bowes were showing a mild jealousy at the attention he was lavishing on his star. He had to be careful. Professionals were different animals: they thought differently. They measured their worth only in performances, and worth meant money. Well, a certain amount of provocation never did any fast bowler harm. Pretending to fawn over Larwood might make Voce bowl all the more aggressively. But there was a danger of overdoing it. When a player becomes truculent, his game suffers.

So he would rest Larwood and play Voce—hadn't the big fellow knocked Bradman over at Melbourne? Voce and Allen, although Gubby was being rather tedious lately. On the train he had heard him going on about the short fast bowling tactics.

"There is a limit to the number of times you can go over to an injured batsman," he told Wyatt, "and convince him how sorry you are."

Nothing wrong in giving Gubby the idea that he had better do something in this game or he might be out of the Test. Voce and Allen, Hammond and Brown, with Verity and the newly arrived Maurice Tate. Six bowlers, although Tate still looked pale, following his recent breakdown.

Since their collision at Melbourne, he and Warner had not spoken much, although he knew the old man had been desperately worried when the side was skittled out. He wondered how far Warner's generous spirit extended. If England were to face overwhelming defeat in a Test, if he were told their only hope was leg theory—how would he jump?

He lost the toss and New South Wales opened with Fingleton and Bill on a wicket that displayed some alarming bare brown patches. Once again, the tone of the game was set from the first ball. Voce pitched it nearer himself than the batsman and it hummed past Fingleton's chin. Fingleton went all the way down the wicket to prod the mark, smiling at his partner:

"Nothing half-hearted about that," he called, more for the bowler's benefit.

The next ball was exactly the same and Fingleton held up play by sauntering the length of the pitch again, this time sarcastically prodding down Voce's footmark.

"From the other end," a wag yelled from the crowd, "that'd be a yorker!" Fingleton returned to his crease to a ripple of uneasy laughter.

At the end of the over, Allen approached Jardine.

"Can't you do anything about this, Douglas?" he demanded.

"About what?"

"You know perfectly well what," Allen persisted, pointing to the divots in the ground all less than 10 yards from Voce's end.

"Did you see them score any runs?" Jardine asked, catching the ball from Ames.

"Score?" Allen scoffed. "They couldn't get anywhere near the bloody thing."

"Precisely."

"Douglas," Allen went on, lowering his voice as Fingleton and Bill conferred, "would you tell me how we can expect to get a wicket if the ball flies 6 feet over the stumps, and the batsman cannot reach it with his bat?"

"You'll see," was all he received by way of an answer. Then, "Now do you want to bowl or not?"

While Allen measured out his run Jardine moved over extra cover and a slip to the leg. Seeing his offside field virtually disappear, Allen called "I'd rather like extra cover to come back."

Jardine behaved as if he didn't hear. All right, thought Allen as he rolled up his sleeves, let's play silly buggers.

The first three balls were well pitched-up on the middle stump. Fingleton, renowned for his offside play, scored a two and a single, driving them into the gap between mid-off and cover. Jardine glared up the wicket, but Allen continued to bowl on the middle and off stumps. His first over cost 11 runs. However, when he came on for the second, his extra had been restored.

The home side made 273. Fingleton carried his bat for 119 and his fourth wicket partnership with Stan McCabe, taking them from 90 for 3 to 208 for 4, was the only highpoint of the New South Wales innings. Tate took the first four wickets, including Bradman's, Allen ended up with 5 for 69, albeit mostly tail-enders, while Voce only got one wicket in nineteen overs, giving away 53 runs.

If the batting was unspectacular, the bowling was not, especially that from Voce to Jack Fingleton—a contest that would have made more sense inside a boxing ring. When the Australian opener walked in at the end, the crowd gave him the first standing ovation of his career. In the dressing-room, surrounded by a grateful team, he gingerly removed his pads, shirt and trousers. The others looked in dismay at the pattern of bruises reaching from his shoulders to his knees.

"You tell me I played some pretty shots," Fingleton grunted, lying back in agony. "Well I'll tell you I don't remember one of them. All I *can* remember is that bloody ball hitting the ground and coming up at my head. All I remember is it crunching into my ribs or my legs, Jesus! All I remember is the sound as it went past my ear at Christ knows how many miles an hour. Just my luck. Carry my bat, make a ton, have them all on their feet. And all I'll ever recall is that bloody great gorilla coming up to bowl with his eyes trained on my cap."

Warner watched the M.C.C. side follow Fingleton and the last man Howell off the pitch, and heard the cheers for the century-maker change into a roar of booing. He watched Jardine behave as if he were on some village green at home, standing back to applaud the wicket-takers Allen and Tate, then grasp Voce by the elbow and thrust him in ahead of the others as well, patting him on the back for everyone to see. He watched appalled, but more than that, he was in a kind of despair. The tour was hardly a month old, yet it was clear already that no matter what he might say, Jardine had no intention of listening to him. A short while later he heard the England captain describe how Bradman went:

"We had him playing back to everything. We've got him, we've got the little bastard!"

Is that what the game was deteriorating into? A childish gloating over one man's wicket? And Bradman was not fit, any one could see that by looking at his face, the sweat on his temples. Did no one think to mention this in the general euphoria of getting him out?

The following day a full-page drawing of Fingleton appeared on the front page of a newspaper. Superimposed on a dozen parts of his body from thighs to shoulders were drawings of speeding cricket balls to show the punishment he had suffered. Peppered around the diagram were vitriolic headlines, and one reporter debated the possibility of prosecuting for assault and battery a sportsman who played in a brutal and dangerous manner.

M.C.C. made over 500 runs and won by an innings, making New South Wales the third state to be thrashed in this manner by the visitors. Voce increased his leg-trap to six men in the second innings and took five for 85. With these results there seemed no reason to stop at six, people said. Why not have ten? There was nothing for anyone to do elsewhere on the field, with every ball going in exactly the same place every over, hour after hour.

Included among his victims was Bradman. He was clean bowled

by a delivery that pitched absurdly short yet failed to rise as he anticipated. He made no attempt to play a stroke, moving away to the off and turning his back on the ball. He looked shocked, but worse, inept, as he glanced disbelievingly back as the stumps were shattered. He may have left his bed to play; there may have only been 2000 spectators present, since it was clear the night before that England would win. There may have been a dozen reasons why he had left the ball alone. But the facts were that despite all the excuses, he had been made to look incompetent. England had revealed their plan of campaign when they selected four fast bowlers; now they had put it into action and were proving that it worked.

As he started the long walk back to the pavilion, he was sure of one thing: he would always remember this dismissal.

After the game Jardine went to a cable office and despatched a wire to London: "Everything going according to plan stop you have every reason to be pleased stop Bradman contained ends."

He read the message through twice, wondered if he should say anything further, decided against it and wrote down the name and address of the recipient.

Fingleton went round to see Bradman to be told by his wife that he had gone straight to bed. The doctor had taken a temperature that read over 106°. As they were speaking, Bradman called out from the bedroom, "Who's there?"

Promising to be only a few minutes, Fingleton went up to the bedroom.

Bradman was lying back on the pillows without a trace of colour in his normally ruddy complexion.

"I won't ask how you feel," Fingleton grinned, "because I can see."

"Thanks for coming, Fingo."

"Seen the papers?"

"No, and I don't want to."

"Oh, you're all right," Fingleton assured him. "They're saying you deserve a medal for even going out there in your state."

Bradman didn't look consoled by this.

121

"Don," Fingleton said hesitantly, after a while, "what's to be done with the Poms?"

"How do you mean?"

Fingleton spread his hands, pleading. "The first Test's next week and they've hammered us, Victoria and South Australia, each time by an innings. I've got no idea how to handle Larwood or Voce. No one has except you, and frankly, after yesterday, I'm starting to wonder even about you—"

"You want an answer here and now, just like that?" His voice cracked hoarsely and he broke into a prolonged coughing fit.

"No answers, Don," Fingleton replied, "just ideas."

"Getting nervous about next week?"

"Wouldn't you?"

The patient blew his nose and lay back, breathing through his mouth.

"Don't be," he whispered. "You'll do all right. Hell, you just hit a ton. What more can I say?"

"But not against Larwood."

"Larwood's only human," Bradman murmured, sounding sleepy. "Don't make him out to be something he's not. He's 28 and he's bowling less often. All right, I grant you, when he does, he's fast. But he's got to be answered, Jack. It's no good saying we're helpless, unless you want to cede the bloody series. We're not helpless, not by a long chalk."

"Don," Fingleton said, lowering his voice, "I guess I have to ask you this."

"Ask away."

He tried to order his thoughts.

"This leg theory stuff," he stammered. "I know there are people who say it's justifiable. But be honest with me. Do you reckon they're deliberately trying to crook us?"

Bradman looked on, but said nothing. Fingleton pointed a finger from his shoulders to his knees.

"I'm black and blue, all over," he said. "O.K. I've been hit before, I'm not squealing. But never before have I been convinced that the bowler has no interest in hitting my wickets, or getting me caught, not even by all those blokes breathing down my neck.

Each time Voce came to bowl, I could see it in his eyes. They were trained on *me*, not the pitch. He looked like he was saying: 'Right, mate, the next is coming for your teeth.' I'm not the only one who thinks this way. A couple of the blokes said they felt like coconuts in a fairground. Don, tell me straight, do you think any side, any cricket side, would play with the sole purpose of laying the other team out?"

For several moments Bradman looked up at the ceiling, his breathing growing harsh through his open mouth. Then he shrugged.

"I don't know, Jack," he said. "I don't know and that's the truth. Jardine's a cold fish. I get the impression he doesn't like us very much. But whether he'd go as far as that, I can't say. In the end, nobody will be able to say for certain what the idea is behind fast leg theory. I mean, there *is* a theory. Packed legside field to mop up the catches. It goes without saying that there'll be more batsmen hurt facing this kind of stuff because it's aimed directly at them. But it'll take a good lawyer to prove the idea is to lay the fellow out, rather than force him into giving away his wicket. I don't know the answer to your question. Ask me at the end of the season. If I'm still able to walk."

"Do you have any idea what to do against it?" Fingleton said after a pause. Bradman gave a wan smile and wiped his forehead with the sleeve of his pyjamas.

"Yes," he said.

"What?"

"Practise."

123

Chapter Eleven

"Heddie!"

Marsh chuckled and put down his fountain pen. Sounds as if Jimmy has reached the Governor-General's letter. Closing the report he was annotating, or rather underlining the relevant passages for his boss, he stood and walked through the interconnecting door into the Minister's room.

Sure enough, Thomas was holding the letter from Canberra, leaning back in his chair and scratching his head in the exaggerated way Harry Langdon did in the cinema when he wanted to show how incomprehensible life was.

"Have you seen this?" he rasped, flapping the letter to and fro.

"I cast an eye over it, yes, sir."

"Well, cast another and tell me what I'm supposed to do about it," Thomas growled, spinning the paper across the desk. Marsh skipped through the paragraphs.

"If I might suggest, sir," he began.

"Heddie," Thomas barked, "I've no time for all your social niceties. Don't ask if you *might* suggest, go on and bloody *suggest*."

"Don't do anything," Marsh announced. His boss leaned forward and closed his hands over the desk.

"You mean pretend I never got the letter?"

"Oh, no, sir, not that, of course. I'll draft a reply, if you wish."

"But 'e sounds as if the buggers are up in arms. I can't simply ignore it, can I?"

Go carefully, Marsh told himself. He knew this ploy well. Crafty old Jim would give the impression he had no clue how to act, ask his advice, and then do the opposite. It was a way senior politicians had of preserving some sense of independence from their civil servants. Whether the outcome was successful or not didn't matter. It was important to be seen to be one's own man.

"The Australian newspapers are notoriously sensational," Marsh offered. "They are, after all, principally designed for people who can't read."

"I'll tell the Guv you said so," Thomas grunted, taking back the letter. "Then send you on a commission to Horstralia explaining what you meant."

"I'm not putting the Australians down, sir, I'm merely offering the view that their sporting journalists tend to overstate their case in somewhat riper language than they would use if, say, they were attempting to explain the mysteries of the universe. If the Governor-General is nervous at the kind of articles appearing about our chaps, all I would do, since you asked me for an opinion, would be to advise him to wait and see whether we win the First Test or not. If we lose, the press will stop complaining about our infamous tactics, and start waxing lyrical about how they fought toe to toe and beat the dreaded Goliath by sheer guts and determination."

Thomas gnawed his lip for a few moments, studying the letter, but Marsh knew his mind was a long way off.

"You think we could lose, do you?" he muttered.

"One can never tell with cricket," Marsh observed, 'It's—"

"—a funny game," Thomas finished the sentence, adding an irritated glare over the top of his spectacles. "Heddie, I don't need to 'ear that again. That's all you cricket lovers hever say. 'It's a funny game, cricket.' It's about as funny as earache."

"I was using the word more in the sense of 'peculiar', sir—"

"I know, I know!" Thomas shouted. He noticed Marsh was smiling. Supercilious sod!

"All right, joke's over. Draft me a letter to Canberra," he ordered. Marsh picked up the letter and headed for the door.

"Oh, and Heddie?"

"Sir?"

"Send a cable to Jardine." Thomas stared for a moment at the desk top, thinking.

"Tell him we're delighted at the way he's playing and say he 'as my every good wish for the First Test. Tell him to pass on my best to

Larwood and say I'll give him a quid for each cap he can knock off their flaming 'eads."

"A cable is rather, well, a rather *public* way to send such sentiments," Marsh cautioned. "Perhaps a letter might do instead—"

Thomas gave a mischievous grin and looked up again over the rims of his ridiculous glasses.

"Heddie," he said, "how many times must I have to tell you, in this game, it's a case of nothing ventured, nothing gained."

"Very good, sir," Marsh nodded and returned to his room. He would, of course, send a letter rather than a telegram, just as Thomas would wish, even if he wanted to indulge in a little daydreaming.

* * *

"Excuse me, sir, there's a young lady downstairs asked me to give you this."

The bellboy came in as Brown was thinking about getting up, but convincing himself he didn't need breakfast after all. And it was Sunday. And Saturday night had been energetic. The press might be gunning for the England players, but it hadn't stopped the social invitations from pouring in from *le tout Sydney*. His head felt like a ton weight.

He took a piece of paper from the bellboy. It read: 'From the Purser of R.M.S. *Orontes*. We would like to see you *re* a matter concerning some missing silverware. M. Sinclair."

For a moment he felt a cold hand clutch his heart. Missing silverware? What on earth? Then he peered again at the name. Sinclair—

"Would you give the young lady my compliments," he smiled, "and ask her to wait. I'll be five minutes."

As he came down the stairs she noticed his pallor and the way he held on to the bannister.

"You've been playing too much cricket," Mary said as they embraced. "You need a break, get away from it all."

Outside, a Daimler roadster stood by the entrance. The day was hot and clear and the sun was already burning the pavement, although it was not yet ten o'clock. Brown shielded his eyes.

"Is that yours?" he asked, impressed.

"No," she answered, "but we Sydneysiders are a generous lot. We share everything. Get in."

"Do you mind if I get a hat?" Brown asked, squinting up at the sky. "Last night gave me severe brain damage. I can do without adding sunstroke."

Mary edged in behind the steering wheel and felt under the back seat. She pulled out a battered hat with a wide brim and a ribbon. "Try this for size," she said.

He climbed in beside her and looked quizzically at the hat. Tutting, she leaned across, took it and jammed it on his head, then tied the ribbon in a bow under his chin.

"There," she exclaimed, studying the effect for a moment. "You look fine."

"I look ridiculous," he protested.

"Well, at least," she remarked, pressing the starter, "no one will recognize you as a Pommy cricket player. From what I hear, that's not such a bad thing—"

The car lurched forward and he rammed a hand onto the top of the hat as they joined the main road.

"Where are we going?" he shouted.

She didn't answer. Handling the wheel as if she were at a race track, she edged into the traffic. Skimming round a bend, Brown caught a glimpse of Sydney harbour. Hundreds of small dots were heading for the open sea, the sun glinting off the sparkling white-painted bows. Around the scalloped coast, hundreds more were moored like rows of pearl necklaces. And overshadowing them all hung the magnificent Harbour Bridge. He had never seen anything like it in his life and his loss of speech was all Mary required.

They drove round the harbour, stopping often so he cold enjoy yet another magnificent view of the city, past Double Bay, Rose Bay and into Vaucluse, a fashionable peninsula in the Eastern Suburbs where, Mary explained, her family kept a summer house.

"You never told me you were rich," Brown remarked. She had a disconcerting habit of taking her eyes off the road to look at him when she spoke.

"Does it make any difference?" she asked.

127

He beamed with pleasure. "Oh yes."

The Sinclairs were old money. That is, they had made it around sixty years ago farming, transferring to road construction when Sydney began to expand outwards and the combustion engine took people beyond the rim of the nearby hills. Their children were sent to England for an education which ill-suited them when they returned home. Mary explained as they drove along the winding road towards Vaucluse that Australians do not pigeonhole humanity according to accent. A millionaire publisher might talk the same way as his gardener: like Americans, they had trouble understanding the deeper themes of Shaw's *Pygmalion*.

The only accent that presented a problem was an English one, and Mary and her elder brother came back speaking like BBC announcers. In their own exclusive circle of acquaintances who lived in fashionable suburbs, this mattered less than when they travelled beyond these stifling confines and attempted to meet Australia at large. Then they met opposition. They could, of course, revert to the voice of their childhood, but as educated people, she said with a trace of bitterness, this was unacceptable. Her younger brother Robert was only 12 and was attending a private school in South Australia, an hour out of Adelaide. He had yet, she said, to be disorientated by the statutory mincing machine of a good English public school.

"I have to say," Brown observed, "that in the five weeks I've been here, I haven't come across one serious example of anti-Pomism."

"From what I read in the papers," she laughed, "you won't have much longer to wait."

The car growled and strained as Mary took it through a series of bends until they swept into a gravel path of a huge stucco mansion perched on the edge of a cliff. For a heady moment Brown believed the house was empty, but the idea faded when the doors opened and a handsome woman, tall and erect, came out to greet them. Why do all Australian women look like life-guards, he thought as Mary waved, explaining out of the side of her mouth:

"My mother. Don't talk about the boat—"

Mrs Sinclair strode to the car as they stepped out and her daughter introduced Brown.

"How do you do, Mr Brown," she said, taking his hand in a grip he had never felt from a lady of quality at home. "Mary tells me you took care of her on the ship. You must tell me all about it—"

Inside, out of the midday heat, a maid brought in drinks, and shortly afterwards Mary's father appeared dressed in tennis clothes, his face purple and beaded with sweat.

"Do you play tennis, Mr Brown?" he asked, towelling his face. In *this* heat? Brown thought. Actually he was pretty good, but the prospect of going outside even to sit, let alone run round a tennis court, encouraged his modesty.

"Afraid not, sir," he replied. "Sorry."

"Just as well," Sinclair remarked, sinking a half pint of lemonade in three gulps. "If you fellows play tennis like you play cricket, you'd probably take my head off with your service."

"Jack," his wife cautioned, "go and change and we shall have lunch."

Neither parent spoke with the Roedean flavour of their daughter and Brown warmed to them immediately. He had always been used to people of means speaking in a different way, illustrating the English definition of good breeding as an ability to talk about any subject—politics, the weather, sin, sport, sex, religion—without imparting the merest hint of passion.

They ate lunch and at the end of three bottles of Australian rosé were laughing at anything anyone said. Sinclair was keen to know what Jardine was *really* like, what Larwood was *really* like, what Hammond was *really* like. So he told them. Then he wanted to know what Bradman was *really* like, and McCabe, and Richardson and Fingo, so he told them that too. He explained the psychology behind the England tactics, and added that, confidentially, there was a rift in the camp about the rights and wrongs of leg theory. Some of the players were all for it, especially Voce and Jardine and Larwood, but there were others who didn't like the things said about them in the newspapers.

"Like what?" Mary's father demanded. He was rattling a drawer in a sideboard and eventually pulled out a box of Havanas.

"Well, things like we're a bunch of thugs who go about hitting people on the head."

"Do you believe 'em?" Sinclair asked, passing the cigar cutter.

"No," Brown replied. He carefully sliced off the end of his cigar and took a box of matches from Mary after she lit a cigarette.

"Then what does it matter what they say?" her father snorted.

He lit up, twisting the end of his cigar round and round in the flame, creating clouds of smoke about his head.

"It just isn't very pleasant," Brown said lamely.

The old man brayed with laughter.

"The British are wonderful," he shouted. "Bloody marvellous. For generations you've been ordering us about, telling the Colonies what to do, how to do it, and warning them of the consequences of failure. You send us experts, advisers, all manner of men with but a single manifesto—'Go out and show them how it's done.' You cut down forests, lay a million miles of railway lines, take a savage out of the jungle, civilize him enough to sign an X on a deed that deprives him of his land. You dream up all sorts of games, teach others how to play them and organize competitions which, on the whole, you win because you make up the rules, and can therefore change them when you want to. And now, suddenly, out of the blue you hear somebody dare to question your motives. And you're shocked. Shocked! You have what the Jews call *chutzpah*, and what I call a bloody nerve!"

The cigar was making Brown's throat dry and the wine was finished.

"I don't think it's as simple as that—" he began, then dissolved into a paroxysm of coughing.

"Cigar too strong?" Sinclair asked mildly.

He shook his head and tried to stop Mary pounding him on the back.

"If—if I could—could have some water—!"

The reception the previous evening had not ended until four o'clock and had left him with an unslakable thirst. Once or twice he had noticed Mrs. Sinclair looking at him oddly as he drank glass after glass of water. The maid had her work cut out refilling the pitcher. He had explained that he was unused to the heat, and

130

resolved not to reach for his tumbler more than twice in a minute, but the resolution had crumbled.

"You got a thing about water?" Sinclair asked, pointing to the pitcher as the maid came in. The girl stared at Brown before taking it out once more.

The tickle in his throat persisted and when the jug returned full he resisted the temptation to drink straight from it.

"I don't think I agree with everything you said, sir," he croaked, sipping carefully.

"I never agree with *any*thing he says," Mrs. Sinclair smiled.

"What do you dispute, lad?" her husband demanded. He smoked the cigar like a cigarette, with rapid, deep draws, inhaling deeply.

"I don't think *everything* the British have done abroad can be labelled as exploitation."

"Name me one example where you fellows have performed a service out of pure charity," Sinclair challenged, pointing the soggy end of the cigar across the table. "Where the basic motive was not self-interest."

Silence. Oh Christ, Brown thought, there has to be *something*! "Q.E.D.," Sinclair grinned.

"I saved your daughter from drowning," he blurted out. Mary gave him a look of utter blankness.

Sinclair slowly withdrew the cigar from his mouth.

"What?"

"On the ship," Brown said. In for a penny—

"I might remind you, if you don't already know," Sinclair remarked, "that Mary was the runner-up in the all-Sydney swimming championships of 1928."

"Nevertheless," Brown pressed on, his fingers tightly crossed under the table, trying to reach Mary by telepathy to tell her not to contradict him, "she was in the deck pool. She got cramp and started to go under for the third time. I saw her, dived in and fished her out."

Mary's father turned and stared at her through the smoke.

"Did he?" he asked, astounded.

"Yes," she answered. "I had the most frightful cramp. I would have drowned. Freddy pulled me out, gave me a bit of the old

131

artificial respiration and that was that. And what's more, he never asked for a penny in payment."

I could marry this girl, Brown thought as he watched her father go quiet.

"Well, I'm very pleased you did, Mr Brown," Mrs Sinclair said, standing and moving to the door leading out to the patio. "The place wouldn't be the same without our Mary."

She knows I'm lying even if the old man doesn't, Brown decided as they followed her.

In the garden the cicadas hummed and the air became still and heavy. Gradually, the sun moved down behind a line of trees. The wine made him sleepy and for a while he dozed in a deck chair before Mary squeezed his hand and asked if he wanted to go down to the beach for a swim. She went inside and found him a swimsuit. By the time he had changed she was already in the car waiting.

"Don't get cramp," her mother called as the car turned, the wheels spitting gravel.

"You have no principles, do you?" she laughed as she turned off the engine and they freewheeled down towards the beach. "Saved my life!"

"I had to say something," Brown protested. "Your old man was wiping the floor with me!"

"Perfidious bloody Albion!" she shouted over the slipstream, holding onto the wheel like a bull wrangler as the car snaked silently round the sharp bends.

Later in the evening, when dinner had been cleared away, he and Sinclair went outside to smoke a cigar.

"Do you like Mary?" he asked.

"What do you think?"

Sinclair grunted.

"Correct," he growled. "Bloody daft question."

"So far," Brown went on, "I like everything about this country. It began on the boat when I met your daughter, and so far I've had no cause to change my mind."

They wandered round the edge of the lawn. A full moon was casting a sword of shimmering silver across the water below.

"I went on a bit at lunch, didn't I?" the older man said.

"So did I."

"No, you were very gracious. If you had attacked me and my country under your roof, I wouldn't have been half as discreet. I'd probably have thrown the bloody fruit bowl at you."

"Mr Sinclair," Brown said quietly, "I think you're making a mountain out of a molehill about the way the British treat the Australians. Seriously. You seem to have a bee in your bonnet about us looking down our noses at the Colonies, cheating them and generally behaving like a nation of bandits. That may be true of some people, but it's not true of everyone. I prefer to take people and places as I find them, make up my own mind."

They approached the house.

"Very noble of you, son," Sinclair said, "but we'll talk again after a few weeks. From what I read in the papers, there's a war blowing up, with battlefields clearly marked out with by lines and boundary ropes. Maybe you won't be so tolerant when the shooting starts."

Brown grinned.

"We'll see, sir," he answered, stepping through the main doors into the cool of the hallway.

Mary came out of the drawing-room.

"Mary," her father called, "try and get this young chap to come and spend Christmas with us." He turned to Brown who looked surprised. "You'll like an Aussie Christmas. Eating turkey and plum duff and mince pies in 110°. All very civilized."

Chapter Twelve

Pelham Warner came up personally to relay the news to Jardine in his room where he sat reading *Barchester Towers*.

"Bradman isn't playing tomorrow," he announced.

Jardine laid the book aside. Warner could hardly contain his excitement.

"I mean, it's bad luck and all that," he added, "but it's nothing serious, I'm glad to say. However, his doctor has prescribed complete rest. Frankly, I thought he looked awful at Melbourne and shouldn't have played in the New South Wales game. Still, there it is."

Jardine tried to straighten his thoughts. For a moment the news had thrown them into a heap. Of course, it was tremendous news that Bradman had pulled out. Apart from McCabe and Fingleton, the rest of their batting didn't worry him in the slightest. But *why* had he withdrawn? What were his motives in waiting until the very eve of the game before announcing he wasn't fit? He could have said so days ago—the rumours were he had hardly left his bed in a week. Why wait until now?

"At least," Warner was saying, "we can look forward to a damn good game played fair and square. Wouldn't you say?"

Jardine hardly heard him.

"Sorry?"

"I said we don't need any of the—ah—the leg theory stuff now, do we, with Bradman out of the game," Warner repeated uncertainly.

"I think he's scared," Jardine announced. "Oh, he's got a bit of a chill, I'm sure, but the truth is, he's scared of Larwood, and he's scared of Voce. He wants time to think about leg theory. I'll bet

134

right at this moment he's in the nets having them bowl short."

He slapped his hands together and grinned.

"Well," Warner said, unsure if Jardine had heard him say anything after the initial announcement, "I thought you'd care to be one of the first to hear. It might be worth thinking about playing Maurice Tate, you know. He always did marvellously well on the S.C.G."

Despite the obvious advantage of having Bradman out of the opposition, Jardine felt a twinge of disappointment. The way he had brought Larwood and Voce up to peak form, with Allen and Bowes giving good support, he had been looking forward to watching them contain the Don on his home ground. To have seen the press grub around for excuses, heard the crowd's disappointment. The thought that Bradman could have come off never entered his head. After the last two games he was certain the man had been cut down to size.

"Tate?" he queried, raising an eyebrow.

"Yes," Warner nodded. "And Verity could be useful. You saw the brown patches on the wicket—they surely won't have disappeared by tomorrow."

Jardine laughed briefly.

"Come along, Plum," he scoffed, "Bradman or no Bradman, the bowling has to be Larwood, Voce, Allen, Bowes and Hammond."

Warner's jaw hung.

"*Five* fast bowlers?" he gasped. "*Five?* I've never *heard* of such a thing!"

Jardine continued to smile. Warner had never seen him look so buoyant.

"Bradman may have the vapours," he said, "but you can bet your life the little bastard will be watching every ball. It was Voce who knocked him off his feet at Melbourne, who bowled him at Sydney when he didn't even play a shot. It was Larwood showed him fast bowling such as he's never had to face in his life. Do you think for a moment that I'd fritter away our advantages just because he's not on the field? I want him to see what's waiting for him the rest of the series. And I want those buggers in the press box to see the same thing."

As it happened, while a crowd of 30,000 watched Woodfull win the toss, Jardine inspected the wicket and dropped Bowes, bringing in Verity, whose ability to exploit worn pitches was well known. As they prepared to field, Jardine brought Larwood, Voce and Allen together.

"I'll tell you now," he said, "I'm expecting the three of you with Wally as a back-up, to do most of the work. Apparently the amount of rain they had in September has played hell with the top dressing. And they've changed the soil. It comes from Newcastle now, not Bulli. My spies predict it will be lively and the breeze will help the swing. If you lot can't get wickets today, you never will."

The Nottingham men grinned, winked at each other and left in high spirits. Allen, on the other hand, looked solemn and held back.

"Douglas," he said nervously. Jardine glanced round.

"What is it?"

A deep breath:

"Douglas," he repeated, then plunged in, choosing his words with great care. "I must make one thing clear."

"Well go on, then," said Jardine impatiently, a hand on the door. "Out with it, Gubby."

"Douglas, I'm sorry, but if you ask me to bowl leg theory, I shall refuse."

He waited for the expected reaction, the pursed lips, the close-set eyes narrowing on him. But instead, Jardine folded his arms and looked down at his feet.

"Your mind is made up, is it?" he said.

"Yes, it is," Allen replied. "I won't play in a manner I think is contrary to the spirit of the game."

Jardine opened the door, paused and replied with his back to Allen:

"Very well," he snapped. "Then I won't ask you."

The wicket was less lively than Jardine had hoped, but this didn't prevent England from winning in four days by a margin of ten wickets. Larwood bowled flat out from his very first ball but only the very short ones lifted. Voce succeeded in hitting Kippax hard in the chest, ruining his concentration so that he was soon out lbw to Larwood. McCabe was the only batsman to rise above the terrifying intimidation of the Nottingham pair and scored 187 not out. The beating he took to his thighs and body didn't prevent him, as it did the other batsmen, from going for his shots, pulling and hooking gloriously. But apart from this, the rest of the Australian side looked sadly demoralized. Afterwards Ponsford admitted he just could not pick up the flight of Larwood's fastest deliveries. He didn't see them until they struck either his bat or, more often, his body.

Fingleton, battered and bruised after three innings against concentrated leg theory, went out wearing an elaborate body armour under his flannels and needed it in Australia's second innings when Voce, who had been the main target from the barrackers on the Hill, flung down over after over to a legside field of six men.

"Come on, Voce, you're not playing baseball!"

"Wrap your bat round the bugger's head, Fingo!"

The booing swelled to a prolonged roar each time a batsman was struck, but for most of the second innings, Larwood had not been the butt of the spectators' fury. However, when McCabe came in, Jardine took his time instructing his star bowler and the crowds began to shout and catcall when they saw the fielders cross over to pack the leg. Until this moment, Larwood had bowled a good length on the stumps and taken five wickets in the first innings. Now the balls pitched half-way down the track and skimmed McCabe's head, forcing him to duck and to decide against playing any kind of stroke at all.

The leg theory which had been designed for Woodfull and Bradman was now extended to cover all the recognized Australian batsmen. Exposed to its full fury, Fingleton and McCabe soon fell and the famous tail—"Six out, all out!" as the papers derided their team—collapsed. England were compelled to come out on the fifth day to make a single run for victory. Any thought that the pitch and not the bowling was the reason for their débâcle was scotched by the three centuries scored for England by Sutcliffe (194), Hammond (112), and Pataudi (102).

As the sprinkling of spectators drifted away after the final run was made, Hugh Buggy, a veteran journalist, gloomily picked up a telephone in the press box to cable a report to his paper, the *Melbourne Herald*. He dictated his notes and ended by adding some random comments:

"England tactics," he said slowly into the receiver, "continue to cause anger and controversy. But Jardine will not abandon line of body bowling which is likely to be a major factor in the series."

He paused and made an alteration on his notepad, ringing the word "body" and drawing an arrow to place it before "line". "Hello, dear," he said to the operator, "look—ah—delete 'line of body' and insert 'bodyline'. It saves a word, doesn't it? Text now reads: 'Bodyline bowling, which is likely to be a major factor in the series'. . . ."

After changing, Jardine found Warner and took him to lunch. He was in an expansive mood, laughed frequently for no apparent reason, and ordered a bottle of champagne.

"Plum," he said, "we have the bastards on the run."

His voice carried over the restaurant and Warner huddled forward, mutely encouraging him to speak more softly.

"They are certainly lost without Bradman," he agreed. "Apart from McCabe—"

Jardine shook his finger like a schoolmaster.

"Forget McCabe, or Fingleton," he advised. "They don't like being hit any more than the rest of them. They thought all the stick we're getting from their bloody reporters would make us tone it down, and they were horrified when they realized that we're not."

"The crowd didn't like the amount of times play was held up," Warner remarked.

"No?"

"No. You heard the Hill, they went quite mad, especially against Voce. I wish you could get him to pitch them a little further down the wicket, Douglas. Good God, some of them landed at his feet! It made a mockery of the game."

But Jardine wasn't paying attention. He was fishing for

138

something in his inside jacket pocket, pulling out a folded sheet of paper.

"You think the crowd don't like our tactics," he repeated.

Warner looked suspiciously at the paper as Jardine opened it out and started to read: "'Total attendance on the four days, 158,125.' Perhaps you can explain, if the crowds so passionately hate us, that on the second day they were only 400 under the ground capacity record. 'Receipts, £15,000'."

He held the paper up.

"And this was without the pull of Bradman *versus* Larwood. I'll lay odds we break records at Melbourne."

Warner glanced at the figures unhappily while Jardine attacked his roast beef with a boyish vigour.

"That may be so," Warner conceded, "but I hear that Warwick Armstrong cabled the *London Evening News* and said he forecast trouble if our bowlers go for the body and not the wicket. He said in Australia such tactics were considered unsportsmanlike."

Jardine lowered his fork.

"Armstrong said that? He's got a nerve. I didn't notice him restraining Gregory and MacDonald in '21 against us."

"Nevertheless he's a respected name and people listen to him."

Jardine's smile returned.

"You know," he said. Warner's heart began to sink. What now? "I rather hope they *do* squeal."

"It isn't a question of 'squealing'," Warner protested.

"It can only make the crowds bigger," Jardine exclaimed. "The more the newspapers write about us, the more they accuse us of being unsportsmanlike, the more people will come and see us. Half this bloody country's on the dole, Plum. We'll pack them in. Let them use every kind of dirty name. What does it matter? We'll go home knowing we pulled in more spectators than any other side in history!"

The older man sighed. How he wished he had stayed at home and made do with the newspaper reports. Why, oh why had he come? How different everything was from the old days! He recalled Bismarck's weary admission at the end of his life that he was unable to understand or care about the new world that had grown up around him. And he sympathized.

Chapter Thirteen

It was hard for the newcomers on the tour to get used to Christmas at the height of summer. They watched with blank surprise the cotton wool placed in the corners of the shop windows, the paper holly and rubber mistletoe hung from the ceilings and breathless Santa Clauses trying their best to look avuncular and jolly as they sweated under arctic suits in the heat of the day.

Larwood received a batch of letters from Lois, with a drawing by June of a Christmas tree and two angels. There had been some early snow in Kirkby, and a neighbour had slipped and broken a hip. More men were laid off and a number were thinking of moving south to look for work. It all seemed another world as he lay on the sands at Bondi, taking it in turns with Tangy and Tommy Mitchell to buy ice creams from the shop up on the road.

Jardine let him off games at Wagga Wagga and one of two fixtures in Tasmania over the Christmas holiday.

"Just see you are in trim for the thirtieth," he was ordered.

There were continuing doubts about Bradman's fitness to appear in the Second Test, not only because of his recent illness but also because it was said that he had flouted the rules of the Australian Cricket Board by writing articles for the newspapers while continuing as a player. The Australians were all classified as amateurs, and to make money in a related field, in his case sports writing, offended some in their efforts to keep the game unsullied by profit.

Jardine followed the sometimes hysterical accounts of Bradman's battle with the authorities, but was certain that his usefulness to the side would steam-roller the objections. The only real question concerned his physical fitness. Rumours abounded he was suffering from anaemia.

Pelham Warner travelled to Ballarat in Victoria to spend Christmas with old friends of his, Sir Alan and Lady Currie, who lived in nearby Ercildoun. The side had gone to Tasmania and he was glad of the break. On the train across the hot plains, he wondered whether he was making too much of what the newspapers were now calling "bodyline". True, the crowds at Sydney had resented the England fast bowling, particularly by Voce, who was introducing an element of farce into the game, pitching balls almost on his toes. On the other hand, Jardine had a point about the gate receipts. It was an unhappy reflection on the human race that they could never resist the scent of blood. If public hangings were still allowed, he was sure that a large segment of society would turn out for them.

People who came to watch cricket were no different from any other spectators anywhere. They came to see excitement—why else attend?—and if this was created by the spice of physical danger, then so be it. He desperately wanted to meet Jardine half-way. It was a matter of record that he had denounced dangerous bowling in England, and would do so again without hesitation. Granted, as one of the managers of the touring side, it would be much more difficult to do so here, and so far he had not felt the need. Some of the Australians had been hit, but not enough to make a fuss about. No one had had to leave the field, go to hospital, or needed stitches. And if this spectacle satisfied the Australian crowds, brought in revenue, and if, too, the methods enabled us to wipe out the ignominy of 1930. . . .

If only Jardine would tone it down, just a little! But the man seemed intent on causing a major row. All one can do is to pray that no one gets seriously hurt by this "bodyline" business. And yet there was a long way to go: four more Tests. Perhaps if we take the first three, when the Ashes are won, Jardine will put a stop to it. . . .

He was dozing when the train pulled into Ballarat station. Alan Currie met him and they drove over the dusty roads to Ercildoun, catching up on the years of gossip since they had last met.

The large house resounded to the sounds of a lively party, ages ranging from grandchildren to grandparents. Warner had been to

141

many parties given by the Curries in England: full of gaiety and laughter, tennis, swimming and hiking expeditions, half a dozen dogs yapping at everyone's heels. They seemed to have reproduced them at Ercildoun, even down to a squad of Australian terriers who created a perpetual high-pitched protest as the guests raced back and forth.

Christmas Day passed in a heat wave that reached 105° at three o'clock, although this didn't prevent everyone from demolishing two turkeys and platters full of mince pies. The children shrieked and fought over their presents, then shrieked and fought further when they were forbidden to go in the pool for at least two hours after lunch.

Warner settled back in a chair beneath a fan and for the first time in weeks let himself relax until the thoughts that had buzzed around his brain during the train journey yielded to the opiate of the surrounding comforts and a glass of port. Occasionally he struck up a dilatory conversation with a guest—the balance appeared to be half British, half Australian—and some referred to cricket, expressing their delight at the win at Sydney and the need to keep the momentum going next week in Melbourne. Only one appeared to disapprove, a middle-aged man introduced as Bartram. While a group had been gossiping about the results to date, Warner noticed him look at each speaker, but remain silent. It was obvious the subject interested him, since he stayed throughout the conversation, drifting away only when the others went off in search of tea.

After dinner Sir Alan rose and a hush descended on the long, merry table.

"Ladies and gentlemen," he called, "I know Christmas is not the time to spend making long, pompous speeches. I have the rest of the year to do that—"

When the laughter subsided he went on:

"But it would be churlish of me if I were not to give a special welcome to my dear friend Plum Warner—"

The clapping was prolonged and noisy.

"—whose team is doing so well in restoring the morale of the Poms out here."

Some cries of "shame" were yelled good-naturedly amongst the applause.

"In a world where Great Britain is constantly being told she is making a terrible mess of things, Plum and his friends are providing a much-needed boost to her fortunes. So I would ask you all to raise your glasses. To you, Plum. It's darned nice to see you, and the very best of luck."

Beaming with pleasure, Warner watched them drink. Except Bartram.

The servants cleared a space in the drawing-room, pushing the furniture to one end, and teams were chosen to play charades. Warner borrowed Currie's army uniform and with a young lady, Miss Macpherson, played out a scene from the currently popular film *Shanghai Express*. He took the part of Clive Brook while she vamped a passable imitation of Marlene Dietrich. They chose the train corridor sequence when the two ex-lovers meet after a long absence.

She: "What have you been doing all these years?"
He: "The usual routine for a soldier. Couple of years in the Sudan, three in India, six months in Egypt."
She: "And did you ever think of me?"
He: "Every second of every minute of every hour. What did that fellow call you just now?"
She: "Shanghai Lil."
He: "And how did you come by that title?"
She: "Oh, it took a lot of men to earn the name of Shanghai Lil."

At midnight, they huddled around the wireless and heard the frail voice of George V give the Christmas broadcast, stood as the National Anthem followed, after which Sir Alan proposed a toast to the King.

While the younger guests went to the games room to play table tennis now the temperature had dropped a few degrees, Warner followed his host and the other men out on to the verandah where they smoked cigars and looked over the peaceful quiet of the dark, flat countryside. A gentle breeze drifted over them.

143

"I shall always treasure this day, Alan," Warner murmured from the depths of his chair.

Currie laughed.

"And I shall always treasure your impersonation of Clive Brook."

Bartram came out and stood by the balustrade, smoking a cigarette.

"This house of yours," Warner went on, "the atmosphere, the relaxed ease you manage to create. Reminds me so much of England. Everything here does, as a matter of fact. Except the weather, of course. That is one thing we could well import from Australia."

Bartram flicked the ash from his cigarette and when nobody else spoke turned and said quietly, "Apart from the sunshine, Mr Warner, don't you find any other differences between your country and mine?"

Warner cast a wary glance over at the silhouette.

"No, not really."

"I find that rather strange," Bartram replied.

"Why? We're the same people. We're from the same stock," Warner said. Bartram gave a wry look and shrugged.

"We used to be."

"Surely, we always *shall* be," Warner insisted.

Currie saw Bartram turn away and chuckled.

"You are unconvinced, Tim," he said.

"It doesn't matter," Bartram muttered, staring into the darkness.

"Oh, come on, old son," Currie exclaimed. "If you've got something to say, let's hear it."

After a long pause, Bartram turned back to Warner and came forward a few steps so that the verandah light fell across his face.

"Mr Warner," he said softly, "why don't you do something about bodyline?"

An uncomfortable shuffle went around the other men and one muttered: "Oh no, not that!"

Warner himself was half-expecting something of the sort and replied with an awkward gesture.

144

"Mr—?"

"Bartram."

"Mr Bartram, the idea was not mine, I am not the captain of the side and I am not consulted on policy. Given all that, tell me what I *can* do!"

"Well, for a start, you can climb down off the fence," Bartram replied.

"I hardly think Plum is sitting on a fence, Tim," Currie retorted.

"Well," Bartram said, never losing his mild-mannered voice, "I've seen no public announcement from the management condemning it."

Warner toyed with his cigar, unaware it had gone out. He wasn't angry. Bartram wasn't a club bore, thrusting his views at him. He knew the man had spent most of the day winding himself up to mention the subject. He deserved an answer, but for the moment he could not put one together.

Bartram sat on the balustrade.

"Sir," he said, "I can't play cricket, but the game has always meant a great deal to me."

"And to me," Warner murmured.

"It's like any other great institution," Bartram continued. "If it isn't properly cared for, if it isn't nurtured and constantly attended, it will fall apart. The vandals will invade, they'll loot and plunder, they'll turn it into a travesty until there is nothing left of the original ideals at all."

"I agree with you."

"I was in England a few months ago. I saw the game between Yorkshire and Surrey. The one where Bowes let fly some bouncers at Jack Hobbs. I was very gratified the next day when I picked up the *Morning Post* and read what you had to say about the matter. 'Short-pitched bowling,' you wrote, 'aimed at the batsman's head, is not bowling. Indeed,' you went on, 'it isn't even cricket. And if the practice continues then laws should be introduced to ban it.' Do you remember writing that, Mr Warner?"

The older man nodded unhappily. "I remember."

Currie saw his guest's shoulders slump a little.

"I hardly feel this is the time or place—" he began, but Warner looked across sharply.

"Let him finish," he ordered, then to Bartram: "Go on, sir."

"You said just now, that there is no difference between us and the British. If that's the case, how is it you can condemn a certain kind of behaviour in one country, but not in the other?"

Warner made no attempt to answer.

"Sir, you remind me of how Aldous Huxley once described a certain type of Englishman. The kind who behaves abroad in a way which would be unthinkable at home."

Still Warner remained silent. There was nothing, absolutely nothing he could say and he wisely did not try.

Bartram threw his cigarette over the balustrade and gave a short nod to Currie.

"Good night," he muttered, and walked inside.

Currie looked across at his guest and noticed the rims of his eyes were glistening. He drew on his cigar and gazed over the land beyond.

*   *   *

Between the end of the First Test on 7 December until Christmas Day, Bradman had a busy, frustrating, anxious three weeks. He watched every ball of the game and afterwards examined the bruises that covered McCabe's body following his 187 knock.

"Think you can bowl looking like Gene Tunney?" he had asked.

McCabe had bowled and done so respectably, fifteen overs for only 42 runs, but for Bradman the English methods were thrown into doubt, not because they were likely to injure the batsman—he had always subscribed to the idea that cricket was a contest between bat and ball and if one prevailed the other must find a way to reply— but because they were used against a man who was also a bowler, and whose performance as such would be seriously affected by the constant bombardment. Just as the Englishmen did not bounce them head high at the tail-enders, so they should be restrained from doing so at those players who had other roles than simply batsmen.

When he took this idea to the Board of Control, they wouldn't listen. He would, they implied, have to take bodyline in his stride.

Perhaps if he had not already been at loggerheads with them over the "player-writer" question, they might have lent a more sympathetic ear. But there it was; for the time being, as Australians flocked to the turnstiles, the Board were not about to rock the boat.

The doctor had eased his mind just before the match when his blood tests revealed he was not suffering from anaemia as feared. He was ordered to take a complete rest, and he and his wife Jessie took off for a holiday along the south coast. They found a spot accessible only by foot at the base of a steep mountain path, and settled in for two weeks of uninterrupted relaxation.

It was not to be. Instead of press reporters, wireless interviews and the wearisome round of public engagements, the Bradmans faced a spate of forest and bush fires that at one time threatened their tent for twenty-four hours. A change of wind provided a temporary relief before the direction altered again, and they were eventually only able to salvage their belongings with the aid of some passing hikers.

The distraction, however, proved a tonic for Bradman. With his mind wonderfully concentrated elsewhere, the problems of his career were temporarily buried. When tranquillity returned to the beach, he saw the solution to bodyline as if suddenly struck with a vision. He could hardly wait to return to Sydney and talk it over with his old friend Johnny Moyes, the sports editor of the *Sun* and onetime selector for New South Wales.

"Listen, Johnny," he started, "I've got to make runs. I'm not going to be brained by bodyline, because I'm too fast on my feet. Equally, there's no percentage in staying out there all day just dodging the ball and hoping Larwood's going to get tired, because the wickets are going to fall at the other end. Right?"

"This is your vision, not mine," Moyes grinned. "Go on."

"O.K. I was wrong about Larwood. Before the Sydney game I said he was getting older and wouldn't be able to sustain his bowling as long as he used to. I'll say I was wrong! He proved he's *much* fitter than in '28. At one time he bowled eleven overs non-stop."

"So what shots *can* you play?" Moyes asked. "When they're bringing them up at you? The hook shot's no good, you're not tall enough to get on top of them."

147

"Right," Bradman agreed, ticking off his fingers, "nor is the pull. Larwood brings them in to the body all the time, I'm too cramped to play it and anyway I only have to miss one and he knocks my head off."

"So," Moyes asked, spreading his hands over his desk, "what's the answer?"

Bradman answered by showing him. He took up his batting stance on Moyes's office carpet.

"Six, seven men, who knows, maybe the whole side is over on the leg," he said, holding an invisible bat. "There's only one solution. Step backwards towards square leg and try to cut the ball through the offside field—".

He performed a reverse dance step and waved his arms in a cutting stroke, grinning broadly.

"Keep doing it until they *have* to take some men away and put them back on the off. Once they do that, I'll go back to batting normally."

"You've been out doing that," Moyes reminded him. "Remember Melbourne? You stepped away from Larwood, the ball didn't rise as much as you thought and you lost your off stump. The crowd thought you were scared."

Bradman nodded.

"That was before I started to practise," he said. "Now I'm sure I can do it."

"You're right about one thing," Moyes commented.

"That's nice of you to say so. What?"

"It's all you *can* do against these bastards."

A Sheffield Shield game against Victoria had been due to begin on 21 December and, desperate for match practice, Bradman drove to Melbourne to get a medical certificate from the Victorian Cricket Association proving his fitness to play. They gave it reluctantly. When the game finally got under way on Boxing Day following two days of rain, he handled a varied attack from Alexander and Nagel masterfully, ran into his best form of the season and scored 157, the last 50 coming with a furious burst in thirty minutes.

*   *   *

148

The second M.C.C. game against a Tasmanian side fizzled out into a draw and Jardine snatched a few hours fishing in the mountains. The side had been on the island almost two weeks and the conversation invariably crept round to the bodyline question. As a matter of fact, he found himself surrounded by well-wishers in Launceston and Hobart. The traditional coolness between Tasmanians and Australians meant that on the question of tactics, England could do no wrong. "Show the squealers" was the advice given to Jardine, and he replied that he would certainly do his best. But after a while, the constant support of his hosts bored him. He couldn't wait to return to the mainland where the press were sharpening their pens, ready for the next round.

The next round. As he sat in the fresh mountain air and watched the bubbles rise around his line, he recalled the fierce English-woman who had grasped his arm at one party in Launceston, her fingers like the claws of an eagle round its prey, and demanded to know what on earth was wrong in wanting to knock the batsman's block off?

"I mean to say, they do it in boxing, and *that's* a sport, isn't it? Well then—"

There were times when he disliked those who were on his side more than those who hurled abuse. Women like that made him feel that he and they were part of some evangelical mission against the barbarians, and the connection horrified him. It was like sitting in a crowded restaurant with someone who, either through too much wine or too little breeding, brayed at the top of his voice. Those around them would assume, since they were seated at the same table, that he was just as awful: guilt by association. So too, when buttonholed by idiots like that dreadful woman, he sensed that all the others within earshot would place him on an equal footing. He seemed to spend a greater part of his life disengaging himself from his peers, he mused, reeling in a small rainbow trout. Well, too bad. He had always told them he was not clubbable. Why should they assume he didn't mean it?

The serenity of the surroundings calmed his thoughts and motoring back to Launceston he put his position into an acceptable perspective. No, he didn't loathe Australians. He

149

merely didn't regard them as worthy of his serious attention. No, he didn't despise Pelham Warner: he considered him a genial old codger who was thirty years out of date. No, he would not seek to win this series at all costs. He would always observe the rules. But his job *was* to win; that was the reason he came. He had a responsibility to those who appointed him. And so far he was doing well. His strategy had already won one of the five Tests. The man they feared most was contained. There was no reason, given an absence of injuries, why this state of affairs which *he* had created, *he* had maintained by hard work and rigid discipline, should not continue.

Arriving at his hotel, he bought a newspaper at the reception desk and took it to his room. On the back page was a large photograph of Bradman in a balletic pirouette, pulling a ball in a Shield game against Victoria. And to one side was the headline which put an end to Jardine's euphoria: "BRADMAN SCORES 157 IN BRILLIANT RETURN TO FORM".

* * *

There was a dampness in the night air. The Melbourne curator felt it as he strolled out in the darkness to the pitch he had prepared for the following day. He shone a torch over the track, pressing his foot here and there into the soft green stretch to measure the strength of the topsoil. He was satisfied. His efforts over the past few weeks had been repaid. The wicket was exactly as he had promised.

A heavy cloud moved away to the north-east, and the enormous stadium became dimly lit by a ghostly silver light. Please Lord, the curator prayed, keep the rain off tomorrow. Let us get even. Give us a chance . . . .

Chapter Fourteen

Jardine announced his side an hour before the start of play and once again the reporters in the press box ran through the usual litany of complaints. Melbourne had woken up to a single headline in their papers: "BRADMAN PLAYING".

They arrived in their thousands, so that even before the teams tossed, the turnstiles were recording an unprecedented first day's gate of 64,000. The ground was a huge bowl of staring, excited, chattering faces. A roar greeted the appearance of Jardine and Woodfull and a greater one the news that Australia had won the toss and would bat.

It was then Jardine announced his line-up: himself, Sutcliffe, Leyland, Pataudi, Hammond, Ames, Wyatt, Allen, Larwood, Voce and Bowes.

The reporters looked at the names askance. *Five* fast bowlers? "I've never seen such a cock-eyed attack in my life," Arthur Mailey grunted. Mailey had retired two years before after a distinguished career as an Australian right-arm legbreak and googly bowler. Normally he was a man who would take any news, earthquake or the Second Coming, with a non-committal "Uh huh", but five quickies and no spin in a game that might very well be interrupted by rain seemed ludicrous.

The head groundsman saw the curator in his usual seat and they exchanged a confidential smile as the England team was read out over the loudspeakers.

Jardine led his side out. He was wearing the brightly coloured Harlequin cap which he had discovered four years earlier affected Australian spectators like a red rag to a bull. They had learned the background of the cap, who the Harlequins were, and during the First Test several letters appeared in the newspapers demanding to know why Jardine thought the wearing of an England cap was infra dig on these occasions. The other affectation they didn't like was his habit of wearing a white silk neck scarf.

Behind him trooped his battery of fast bowlers. Bowes was playing in his first Test against Australia and his expression, as he gazed around at the enormous expanse of stands filled to overflowing, was seen in the press room by Jack Hobbs, who scribbled a note: "Bowes appearing for the first time in a Test here, as I did. If it is anything like mine, he will never forget it since we won by a single wicket, last pair Barnes and Fielder having to make 20 runs. Look on his face as he comes out very much as I felt."

Larwood fired down the first over. From his second ball he knew something was wrong. The pitch was dead. Woodfull took first strike and even with his slow footwork, he was able to get behind each delivery and play it down with all the time in the world. Taking his sweater at the end of the over, he went across to Jardine.

"Did you see that, skipper?" he demanded. "Bloody pitch is like rice pudding. I can't gerrem to come up at all."

Yes, he had seen it. The Melbourne groundsmen had produced a strip that Verity and Tate would have given their eye teeth for. And he had picked five fast bowlers.

"All right, all right," he replied irritably. "Just bang them in as hard as you can."

At the other end Voce tried to find some life but his shortest balls bounced so slowly the crowds began to laugh. When Larwood returned, Jardine signalled his fielders to form the leg-trap. "Just with a nod of his head," Arthur Mailey noted in the press box, "Jardine signalled his men and they came across on the legside like a swarm of hungry sharks."

With leg theory operating at both ends, the run rate dwindled and the spectators wondered why they had bothered to get up so early. Jardine replaced Voce with Allen who struck quickly by bowling the hapless Woodfull. Then, an over later when Fingleton played to short leg and went for a single, O'Brien failed to send him back and tried for an impossible run. Pataudi's return was wide but Ames, dashing up to the wicket, scooped the ball up on the half-volley and shovelled it onto the stumps with O'Brien two yards adrift.

Then Bradman's name came onto the scoreboard and the disconsolate crowds suddenly revived. A huge roar of welcome greeted the familiar figure as he stepped out of the pavilion and strolled to the centre, walking slowly, in a wide semi-circle, almost like a lap of honour for the cheering throngs. The applause continued as he took guard, looked round the field and settled down to face Bowes.

The tall Yorkshireman started his run, but the continuing noise from the stands put him off and he pulled up short. Bradman straightened, touched his cap and his pads, grinning all the while, and waited. Bowes filled in the time by moving his mid-on up into silly. He began his run for the second time but the yelling resumed and he ground to a halt again. During this pause, Bowes waved an arm to have fine leg move down to the boundary. Bradman turned and eyed the change of position quizzically.

His look was caught by Bowes.

"Bloody hell," he thought, "He's expecting a bouncer. He hasn't twigged about the wicket yet. Can I fool him? Make it look as if it's coming up but send it through normal height? Can I, can I?"

Finally the crowd quietened and he ran in with the most threatening expression he could muster, a look that said, "I'm going to knock your bloody teeth out with this one!"

The ball flew down from a height of over 7 feet and followed a direct line towards the batsman's legs, short of a length. Bradman stepped across the wicket intending to hook it out of sight. But suddenly, as it hit the track, he realized it was not a bouncer at all. In a manner that only a really great batsman could achieve, he changed the elevation of his intended shot and got an edge, but it didn't work. He played the ball on to his leg stump.

The Melbourne crowd who had come to watch him, who had forgiven all his previous innings against the visitors, who twice had seen him slaughter the Victorian bowling and prayed that he could reproduce such form against England, fell into dead silence as he walked back to the pavilion. Out first ball playing a show-off shot that would have been a gamble had he already scored a hundred!

The spell was broken by a woman's solitary clapping, a feeble sound that stood out among the hushed throng.

An excited chatter followed this lone sound of sympathy—or was it a stranded England supporter? Nobody knew—and when Bowes gazed wondrously around he saw Jardine, hands above his head, doing an Indian war dance. Jardine! The sphinx, old granite face, was going berserk!

When Larwood took the ball for his next over, the lethargy that had subdued the vast crowd vanished. They counted in one accord as he strode to his mark, then became silent as he raced in. A tram could be heard clanking a long way away and the bowler's footsteps resounded around the stadium. His arm flashed over, the batsman played and missed and the ball thwacked loudly into Ames's gloves. The tension snapped and another earsplitting roar erupted.

Charged with this electric atmosphere, the game pursued a remarkable course. Australia recovered from the early disasters and went from 67 for 3 to a total of 228. O'Reilly and Wall then scattered the England batting for 169. Coming in to bat a second time, Australia lost four wickets for 81 before a record-breaking crowd of 68,188. Fingleton was out in the second over, caught off Allen by Ames, then three overs later Larwood sent O'Brien's off-stump cart-wheeling. When Bradman joined Woodfull they presented, for the first time, the two major targets for leg theory at the crease together.

Woodfull fell into the trap, Larwood forcing him to give an easy catch to Allen at forward short leg. But the truth was there for all to see: the wicket was totally unsuitable for bodyline. In the press box Hobbs remarked, watching Bradman and Woodfull, how much the Melbourne pitch had changed since his time. Never before had he known it favour spin, but here were England, back in the pavilion, because of O'Reilly, and now the terror of the England attack sweated and strained, unable to make the ball rise beyond the batsman's knees.

"I think they changed the soil," someone remarked. "It's from the Glenroy district now. Much drier."

When exactly did they change it? Hobbs wondered, but left the question out of his written notes.

Jardine varied his bowlers, giving each a proper rest. But as the third day continued and Bradman's strokes gained in confidence, he nursed the growing apprehension that he had not yet succeeded in containing the man. He had been out to a fluke in the first innings, but now, on a wicket dead to fast bowling, he could see the old arrogance return, the sureness of the footwork, the uncanny timing.

From the moment he came out, the Australian knew he was facing a great crisis in his career. Still, he presented his smile to the field and to the crowds who remained loyal in spite of the disaster of the first innings.

"Good on yer, Don," a voice yelled. "Everyone in Australia is behind you, except me, and I'm a Pom!" The joke relieved the tension for a moment, but then the stadium grew serious as he faced Larwood, who had strengthened his legside field. For an over or two he watched every ball with enormous care. Then, as Bowes sent a short one down he hooked it gloriously to the fence to open his scoring. What Larwood had feared from the very first ball of the match now became wretchedly apparent: the pitch simply failed to provide that extra two or three inches of bounce which would have made all the difference. The plan Bradman had discussed with Johnny Moyes was not required. Any ball pitched short on the line of the body let him move across and deflect it safely down through the field. As his confidence moved into top gear, he stepped back from a Larwood delivery and forced the ball back past the bowler, an amazing shot to play against such pace.

As the "six-out-all-out" prophecy of the Australian team once again came true, the only question was whether Bradman would reach his century before he ran out of partners. When the number eleven, Ironmonger, came out, he was still 2 runs short. Ironmonger survived the last two balls from Hammond, bringing Bradman up against Voce. Five deliveries came down but he couldn't get any of them away. As Voce returned to fire in the sixth, Bradman took a quick look around the ground, gripped the bat a little tighter and waited. Voce bowled and he clamped his teeth shut and swung. The ball went soaring over the leg fieldsmen for 3.

England needed only 251 to win, but Bradman's century had an incalculable effect on Australian morale and by three o'clock on the fourth day, when the weather turned the stadium into a Turkish bath, England were all out for 139, O'Reilly's deadly spin collaring a further five wickets. Woodfull, so nearly dropped from the side, pilloried by every newspaper in the land, was chaired off the field. The pitch was torn to pieces as the delirious spectators fought for souvenirs of a game that had restored national dignity. Nobody complained about England's tactics; bodyline was regarded as an outworn method of attack that would surely now be abandoned. That evening, Don and Jessie Bradman were presented with a piano bearing the inscription, "To Mrs Don Bradman, by numerous admirers of her husband in recognition of his not-out century score."

When the news of the defeat reached Thomas's desk he bellowed for Marsh.

"Well, 'ere's a nice to do, Heddie," he growled, "'ere's a nice state of affairs."

Marsh folded his arms and leaned against the door, restoring some equilibrium.

"There's an old saying, sir, how does it go—'One can't win them all'—"

Thomas trained his eyes over the wire rims.

"Oh? And why not?"

"I—ah—I don't know exactly," Marsh stammered, never having had to answer such a question before. "I—ah—think it has something to do with the law of averages."

"Law of averages?" Thomas exploded. "Where d'you think I'd be today if I'd believed in a law of averages? Born a bastard in a Welsh slum, went to work at nine—and 'ere we are, a Cabinet minister? Where's the law of averages in all that, heh?"

Marsh picked up the newspaper and read the headlines: "BRILLIANT BRADMAN CENTURY", "ENGLAND BOWLERS CONTAINED".

"We still have three more Tests to go, sir," he offered. "I'm sure this defeat will spur our chaps on."

"You can keep that kind of talk for the public, Heddie," Thomas muttered. "I want to know the odds on us winning. This Jardine bloke—not one for chucking in the sponge, I 'ope."

"Quite the contrary, sir."

Thomas's eyes narrowed.

"I've had a fellow on the blower just now from Horstralia 'Ouse. Laughing his bleeding head off."

"Somewhat juvenile, wouldn't you say, sir?"

"Not really. I bet him a tenner we'd win."

He raised his eyes gloomily to look at his languid companion.

"Tell me we *are* going to win, Heddie. It's so rare to 'ear good news these days. Feed me some words of comfort, there's a good chap. . . ."

Elsewhere in London, Miss Stevenson silently placed a cup of coffee before her employer, who was staring transfixed at the sports pages of *The Times*. She had almost returned to her own office before he came out of his thoughts to say:

"Oh, Miss Stevenson—"

"Yes, sir?"

"I'd like to send a cable to Australia."

She brought in her notepad and sat facing him, pencil poised.

"Who is it to, sir?" she asked.

"D. R. Jardine, Melbourne. Received your cable after Sydney. How did you guess it was me? Remember Adelaide is the liveliest wicket in the world."

Miss Stevenson copied down the message.

"Leave it unsigned," he instructed.

"Where is Mr Jardine staying, sir?" she asked.

"Find out from the M.C.C.," he told her, "but don't identify yourself. Just say you are a well-wisher."

"Very good, sir."

Chapter Fifteen

He blamed himself for the Melbourne defeat. He should have had
the wicket checked. There was no question it had been doctored.
Not one person he had talked to could recall a track like it in the
history of the M.C.G. He had spent so much time concentrating
on tactics, how to deal with Bradman, that he had quite forgotten
that the wicket's preparation was as important an ingredient in a
match as the starriest performers.

Their batting had, of course, let them down. Pataudi would
never play again, not under his captaincy at any rate. Refusing to
field in the leg-trap! Not even Allen and his pious objections to leg
theory had gone that far. But His Highness announced he was a
conscientious objector. How dare he try to teach him morality!
However, since he had only scored 15 and 5, there would be no
opposition to having him dropped. Let the little bastard object
from the pavilion.

He received the cable pointing out the liveliness of the Adelaide
wicket, and was consoled. They couldn't possibly sabotage
that one. It might be worth keeping the five-man pace attack,
although the other selectors, particularly Sutcliffe, were pushing
for Verity. Anyway, what did it matter? The game would belong
to Larwood.

Pity they had crossed swords at Melbourne. Early in the first
innings, Larwood's boot had split and he was off the field for over
an hour. Borrowing a pair from Duckworth, he had proceeded to
split these as well, and another hour elapsed while he scuttled
round the pavilion looking for others. The pitch had not been
giving him any help and Jardine had assumed Larwood was
malingering. He had told him so and had a go at Voce as well. He
had never seen Larwood so upset. For a moment, at the lunch

break, he had thought the man was going to hurl one of the broken boots at him. Then Voce had come across and said:

"Don't talk like that, skipper. It's not our fault t'bloody pitch is useless. Let me tell you here and now—I'll be led, but I won't be driven. D'ye hear?"

They still weren't speaking, he and Larwood. Bloody silly, the whole thing. Yes, yes, all right, so he *had* been angry when he realized the wicket was slow. Angry with himself, not with anyone else. And yes, he *had* taken it out on them. He hadn't meant to: it was just his temper. He had even been short with Leyland. And Wyatt. He'd been disagreeable with just about the entire side. So why was that little sod continuing to be so bloody-minded?

They had gone to Bendigo to play a country XI. Larwood had indicated that he would like a rest, so to show him who was running things, he had put him down as twelfth man. When he pinned the team up on the noticeboard, Larwood had had the nerve to cross his name off! In the end they agreed to play twelve a side and the bastard *had* to turn out. But the incident had only created a wider gap between them and he was reduced to transmitting orders to the fast bowler through Wyatt. If only he could apologize! But he couldn't, and that was that. He refused to toe the line just to please a bloody little prima donna upstart who thought he could dictate his own terms!

However, the Third Test was upon them and it would be fatal to go on the field to communicate with the one man who could win the match.

Finally, there was the question of his own performance. He had managed one run in two innings at Melbourne, put himself in first at Bendigo and still only scored 11. Perhaps he should stand down. That would solve two problems: it would strengthen their batting and enable Larwood to bowl in an atmosphere less riven with bad feeling.

When he put his suggestion to the other selectors, Warner, Sutcliffe, Wyatt and Hammond, they refused outright.

"There is only one captain who can win this series for us," Sutcliffe said, speaking for the entire team, "and that is you."

The only changes made were to replace Pataudi with Paynter

159

and, as a sop to Warner, who hated the notion of five fast bowlers, and to Sutcliffe who regarded his Yorkshire team-mate highly, Verity was recalled in place of his colleague Bowes.

Meanwhile, the Adelaide curator Albert Wright was preparing the fastest wicket the Oval had ever known. An unusually cold spring had left the middle almost bare of grass for the early season games so that when the couch finally did come through in late December, it was fine and closely-woven, the perfect surface for a fast bowler.

This time Jardine, remembering the London cable, kept himself fully informed on the state of the pitch. Nevertheless, when he won the toss for the first time in the series, he chose to bat.

The decision was disastrous. On a bright, clear morning in front of a crowd of 50,000 spectators, a larger crowd than any of the veterans in the press box had ever seen there before, he and Sutcliffe opened. An hour later, along with Hammond and Ames, they were back in the pavilion for a total of 30. A shower the previous day was causing the ball to kick and rear. By lunch, any advantage that should have come by winning the toss was lost and Jardine was left staring at the wall of the dressing-room trying to fathom the reason for his extraordinary blunder.

The conditions out there were absolutely *perfect* for Larwood! Even Ironmonger's medium pace was making everyone duck. Hammond caught behind, Sutcliffe caught as one from O'Reilly popped vertically. And neither he nor Ames saw the ball that fizzed through and scattered their wickets. For God's sake, why had he *batted*?

After lunch, when it looked as if the wicket was drying out, Jardine sat behind a pillar in the pavilion and except for the occasional tentative peek round the side, would not watch Wyatt and Leyland as they tried to stop the rot.

Which they did, enabling England to reach 341 by the middle of the second day. Jardine came out from behind the pillar and told Wyatt to send Larwood to meet him in the umpires' room.

"Come in—ah, come in, Harold," Jardine mumbled as the Nottingham man put his head round the door. "Close it, would you?"

160

"Mr Wyatt said you wanted to see me."

There remained a frosty tone in his voice which Jardine caught.

"Look here, this is bloody ridiculous," Jardine snapped. "We may have had our differences over the last few weeks, but it's quite pointless to carry on like this. We have a great deal of work to do, and it will not be completed if you and I have to constantly ferry messages to one another via a third party."

"I didn't start it," Larwood retorted hotly. "T'weren't my bloody fault them boots kep' splitting."

"I'm prepared to forget the boots affair if you are," Jardine said.

Larwood pulled a face and sucked his teeth before giving a curt nod. "Right, we'll say nowt more about it, then."

"Good," Jardine replied. "Now may we talk about what we have to do this afternoon?"

"Wicket's fast," Larwood commented. "Fast and tricky. We've 300 to bowl at. Shouldn't be too bad."

"I'd like you to dismiss any notion you might have that it's going to be a piece of bloody cake," Jardine ordered. "It's not. You remember the last tour. We started with 334 and only won by 12 runs—"

"Aye—"

"In '25, Australia made 469 and they only won by 11. There's a strange pattern in games here, and this one is starting off no differently."

"So what do we do?" Larwood asked, wondering why they were meeting in the umpires' room. Jardine stared at him until he grew self-conscious and started to fidget.

"You'll never have a better wicket to bowl leg theory," Jardine said. "It *has* to work this time. If we lose here, we'll never pull back. It just *has* to work, Harold."

"Well, I can only do me best, Mr Jardine."

"Bradman *has* to be knocked out," Jardine continued, lowering his voice. A cold hand settled on Larwood's chest.

"Knocked out?"

"I mean knocked out of the running," Jardine amended. "Removed."

"I suppose so."

161

"And as soon as possible," Jardine pressed on. His intense expression did nothing to relieve Larwood's growing unease at the weird conversation.

"Happen he'll cock one up," was all he could find to say and took a step backwards when Jardine came closer, a fierceness in his eyes he hadn't noticed before.

"Harold," he murmured so quietly he could hardly be heard. "You must bowl as you've never bowled before. You're in prime condition and the weather's not too hot. I want you firing on every cylinder. We'll alternate a regular field with the leg-trap, but throughout, I don't want any of those bastards to settle in."

The door rattled and George Hele, one of the umpires, came in. His eyebrows went up in surprise when he saw the two of them.

"What's this?" he grinned. "A plot to overthrow the government?"

While Freddy Brown waited for the Australian openers to appear, a ground steward handed him a message. It told him Mary's father and her younger brother Robert were outside the pavilion and he hurried out to greet them.

"Why didn't you tell me you were coming?" he called, shaking hands with the boy, a tall, athletic youth he had met at the Sinclairs' over Christmas. "I could have got you seats inside the pavilion."

"We didn't know we'd be here until two days ago," Sinclair said.

"I told my headmaster we were old mates of an England player," Robert grinned. "And he gave me a long weekend pass. The school's not far from here."

Brown took them inside and introduced them to as many of either side he could find, overcoming the boy's reserve by telling Herbert Sutcliffe, Eddie Paynter and Larwood to sign his programme.

"Sorry to hear you weren't picked," Sinclair said as they emerged into the sunlight again. Brown shrugged. The subject was a sore point, but he had become resigned to it. Jardine had made up his mind the only bowlers he wanted were quick ones. He and Tate would only be needed in places like Wagga Wagga and Bendigo.

"Oh, it's too hot for me," he laughed. "I much prefer to watch the others sweat, sitting inside with a beer in my hand. Did Mary come with you?"

"No, but she sends her love. The fact is, I had to come to Adelaide on business and when Robert said he could get out of school—well, pleasure before making money, I always say."

Brown had grown fond of the Sinclair family. They had been especially kind over Christmas, restructuring a number of engagements so as not to leave him out of things. He and Robert had knocked a ball around on the lawn and it was clear the lad was a promising cricket player; quite a good military medium pace and a lively middle-order batsman, he had reported to his father.

They had seats half-way along the west side of the ground and they squeezed up to let him sit with them for a while.

Woodfull and Fingleton came out just before 3.30 and were cheered all the way to the wicket. Larwood opened from the River end and in his first over struck Fingleton twice, on the hip and forearm. Brown fidgeted uneasily as the crowd around them began to boo, then catcall. The bodyline wound was reopening already, despite Larwood's offside field, although Sinclair said the opposition was created more by the sight of an opening batsman quickly becoming unnerved when what was needed was some aggressive stroke play.

Jardine ignored Voce and signalled Allen to start from the Cathedral end. Three balls into his over, he had Fingleton caught behind for nought, bringing Bradman to the wicket. As at Melbourne, the 60,000 spectators roared and cheered him all the way in, continued while he took guard and were still in full throttle when Allen came in and let fly a short ball outside the off stump that Bradman made to play but drew away from at the last second. Allen grinned. He had never felt better than in this first over, not in the whole tour. The wicket was spectacular, the finest he had known.

Larwood came back for his second over and tied up Woodfull completely, making him play shots far too late and hang his bat out to dry. After the third ball, Jardine came across.

"Bring the field over," he muttered, but the Nottingham man shook his head, breathing hard.

"Not yet, skip," he panted. "Please."

Jardine didn't like the idea but decided against an argument.

The next two balls shot past the off stump, tempting Woodfull to find an edge that caused a horrified "Aaah" from the crowd.

"Leave 'em alone, Bill, let 'em go!" someone yelled. Woodfull went down the wicket and tapped the turf, trying to compose his jangled nerves.

He returned to face the last ball of the over. Larwood fell into the rhythmic loping run which brought him racing to the crease like a dash sprinter: up went his arm, the stiff left foot jabbed down, the roll over the right hip and the follow through—the ball scorched along the pitch, banging into the turf short on the off.

Woodfull walked across to play defensively but missed. The ball struck him in exactly the same place as at Melbourne, just below the heart. But this time, the fearsome track brought the ball catapulting through at a far greater speed. Pushed backwards by the force, he doubled up and fell away, dropping his bat and clutching his chest.

The crowd went berserk. Having seen only three overs, a wicket fall, and their captain tied up in knots, this was the final insult. Standing in the deep, Leyland noticed a line of policemen run out and position themselves at intervals in front of the barrackers' section, from which beer bottles and fruit now came raining on to the outfield.

Larwood watched anxiously while the fielders surrounded Woodfull who was gasping and rubbing his chest, his face twisted in agony. He wanted to go down the wicket but saw Jardine, remaining at mid-on and tossing the ball from hand to hand, shake his head.

"Bastard, Larwood! Bastard! Bastard!"

"Go back to the jungle where you belong, Larwood!"

"Come over here, and we'll give you some of the same!"

In ordinary times there is no cricket ground in the world as attractive as the Adelaide Oval. There is no discordant note anywhere. From the members' enclosure the view is one of trees of various shades of green and brown reaching to the nearby rolling hills. The few visible rooftops melt gently into the picture and to the left, near the scoreboard, rise the spires of the cathedral.

But today, abuse poured in torrents across the field and the air became soaked with menace. The players grew uneasy, like people on a small boat watching black clouds roll towards them and the waves begin to swell.

Sinclair turned and berated a man behind them who had a nice line in swearing, telling him to remember there was a young boy present. Robert was enjoying everything but he could see his father was irritated and wisely hid his pleasure. Sinclair whispered to Brown: "You had better go back to the pavilion before someone recognizes you."

"Who's going to recognize me?" Brown answered. "Unless they come from the backwoods."

"Oblige me," Sinclair said and made it clear by his tone he was not in a bantering mood.

"Oh, they'll settle down," Brown persisted. "Look, I've heard this at every game we've played so far. It's only people working off steam—"

Someone pushed behind them and a spectator who had been returning to his seat was flung across their shoulders, his arms flailing to find a grip. Brown stood and helped him upright before a row erupted between the victim and the person who had done the shoving. Then a beer bottle smashed on the steps at the end of the row and a newly arrived policeman on the edge of the field turned and ran to stand by a nearby entrance, glaring at the group of men at the back of the stand who were doing most of the shouting in this part of the ground.

"Please go back to the pavilion, Fred," Sinclair urged quietly and when Brown hesitated, he dropped the pleading note in his voice and spoke quite sharply. "Listen, if they find out you're a Pom, there'll be a scrap and it's Robert I'm worried about."

Brown left quickly, alarmed that in twenty minutes the warm camaraderie between him and Mary's father had evaporated.

Woodfull recovered and declined to go off. The spectators mingled their abuse with applause for his bravery. The clapping continued for some time until the Australian captain returned to his crease. When quiet resumed, Jardine walked the length of the pitch and in full view of everyone slapped Larwood stagily on the back and grinned broadly, speaking loud enough for Bradman to hear: "Well bowled, Harold."

This brought the stands to their feet once more to produce a much louder flood of hooting and catcalls. Play was impossible. Jardine glanced at Bradman and noticed he was fiddling with his gloves, turning the bat round in his hands, unable to keep still. Good, he thought. The delay, the noise was rattling him. So too was the notion that the ball was being bowled in a deliberate attempt to hit the batsman. How else could Bradman interpret his remark to Larwood?

Sinclair peered nervously about him. Even the respectable spectators had assumed twisted, angry expressions and more than one bottle curved over their heads on to the grass, despite the presence of the policeman. He looked at his son, wondering how to suggest leaving or finding somewhere less dangerous. Robert was grinning excitedly, oblivious to any danger. Sinclair felt he was watching a boxing match. He asked Robert if he was all right and received no answer as the boy leaned forwards, elbows on his knees, waiting for play to restart.

When it did, Bradman hooked a 4, then a 2 off Allen. They were shots which in any other context might have seemed full of courage and nerve, but Jardine standing in close, noticed a hurried desperation in the strokes.

Larwood caught the ball for a new over but was stopped in his run up by Jardine who called out loudly: "Bring the men over for this batsman!"

The effect on the crowd was instantaneous. Here was a man who had just been hit a fearful blow now being subjected to bodyline the very next ball! It took a moment for the audacity of the move to sink in, but when it did all hell broke loose. A man slipped through the cordon of police and was brought down by a rugby tackle and frogmarched back. Bottles, cushions and oranges flew like scattershot from all sides, littering the outfield.

Larwood looked round at the furious scenes coming from every direction.

"Heyup, skip—" he started to say.

166

"Right. Now bowl!" Jardine snapped. "Do you hear me?"

Woodfull crouched to face the first ball. The shouting rose to a crescendo, and then died, giving him a chance. Larwood reached full speed and flung down the fastest ball of the game. Unerringly aimed at the leg stump, it forced Woodfull to jump back and ram the bat blindly in front, hoping for contact, any contact. The delivery was on a good length, but rose sharply and knocked the bat out of the Australian captain's hands.

If the savagery of the barracking that continued unabated until the tea interval was designed to put off the bowlers, it failed. Bradman was caught by Allen in the leg-trap off Larwood and shortly afterwards McCabe went in the same way. Woodfull was hit repeatedly, each time arousing the police on the ground to face the rage of the spectators and grimly wait for the inevitable charge. Larwood hit him often: Voce, before twisting his ankle and leaving the field, bounced several off his chest and shoulders. When the end came, playing on from Allen, the Australian captain quietly breathed a sigh of relief. His body shrieked pain from neck to thighs, and he had long ceased to believe he was taking part in a game he taught to his schoolboy charges as the epitome of the sporting ideal.

At the close of play Australia reached 109 for 4. Pelham Warner sat in the members' enclosure throughout the dreadful three hours when it looked as if the game might have to be abandoned by an invasion of the pitch. In all his years, he had never seen such scenes. Hitherto, he had always argued with those who claimed that the Australian barracker was motivated by a mean and callous temperament. They were noisier than in England certainly: less inhibited, he liked to call it. But over the years he had come to believe that they were basically fair-minded. Quick to see the merit in the opposition, to criticize their own team if they played poorly. It was simply that over here they said so at the tops of their voices. But today it was different. This afternoon he had felt unadulterated waves of hatred roll across the stadium. When Jardine, the damn fool, had ordered leg theory after Woodfull's crack on the chest, it was too much!

In this mood, he went round to the Australian dressing-room at the end of play. His knock was answered by McCabe who was surprised but stood aside to allow him to enter.

Woodfull was lying on a massage table having liniment carefully wiped over the ugly blue-black circles covering the left side of his body. Fingleton, Bradman, and one or two others were standing around, changing. Warner winced when he saw the injuries, and felt the coldness in the room which had fallen silent the moment he had come in.

"Hello, Bill," he said, approaching the table.

Woodfull looked away.

"I'm most dreadfully sorry for what happened," Warner stumbled through his rehearsed speech. "We all are—"

"I don't want to speak to you, Mr Warner," Woodfull replied.

The older man let a few moments pass.

"We most sincerely hope you aren't too badly hurt," he stammered.

"The bruises are coming out," Woodfull replied.

No one else said a word. Warner hesitated, tried to add something, then turned towards the door.

"Mr Warner," Woodfull called. He stopped and looked back.

"There are two teams out there. One is trying to play cricket. The other is not. The game is too great to be spoiled by the tactics your team are using. It's time some people got out of it. The matter is in your hands."

"I know you are justified in—" Warner started to say, but Woodfull cut him off:

"I have nothing further to say to you. Good afternoon."

It is time some people got out of the game! The idea that he should be told such a thing, hear an implication that it was he who should get out—this was inconceivable, yet it was happening. The world he had always taken for granted, the secure, immutable world of the gentlemanly athlete—it was now being suggested he was unfit to be a member of it!

A short while later Jardine knocked on the same door. This time it was opened by Richardson. "Look who's here," he called, and those behind him did.

"Where's Woodfull?

168

"Why, you want to finish him off?"

"It's come to my notice," Jardine snapped, "that one of your men called Larwood a bastard."

"Is that so?"

"I demand an immediate apology."

Richardson looked back at the others.

"Here," he demanded. "Which one of you bastards called Larwood a bastard instead of Jardine?"

The England captain waited for the laughter to subside.

"I want you all to be clear about one thing," he said, speaking with a simple clarity that banished ambiguity. "Whatever happens out on the field, whatever injuries occur as a result of the bowling or the state of the wicket, the responsibility is *mine*. The bowlers obey *my* orders. When they bowl leg theory, it is because I wish it. Therefore, if you have anything to say about the matter, say it to *me*. If you have any names to call, level them at *me*. Not them."

He turned on his heel and stalked away. Richardson pulled a face. "Well, now we know, don't we?" he sighed, and closed the door.

Sinclair pushed through the crowds towards the exit, keeping Robert firmly in front of him. He had never known behaviour like it at any game he had attended in his life. When they reached the quiet of the road outside he said to his son: "I don't believe what I've just seen!"

"I know !" Robert exclaimed. "Wasn't it terrific!"

The following day was Sunday. The newspapers were packed with scenes of the last three hours of Saturday's play, showing Woodfull doubled up, another with the bat flying from his hands. They also carried the full text of the confrontation between Warner and Woodfull in the dressing-room.

"Who the devil leaked that?" Jardine grunted.

Warner had never felt more wretched.

"Both Bradman and Fingleton were present," he said. "Both have their newspaper contacts. My bet is Fingleton. Bradman is a gentleman."

In another paper was a picture of Leyland fighting to make his

169

ground during an attempt to run him out. The photograph, Warner claimed indignantly, had only been included because of the position of Leyland's body: his head was buried in his chest, and he was twisting away from the direction of the ball as if afraid it was being hurled at him rather than the stumps.

On Monday, play was resumed. Ignoring Warner's pleas, Jardine set the leg-trap immediately. The wicket was easier but Larwood continued his bombardment of Ponsford and Richardson, soon bringing the boos and catcalls from the crowd up to the level they had reached the previous session.

Ponsford played Larwood simply by turning his back on all the short-pitched balls. He scored 85 and proved the only batsman whose play was untroubled by the pace. When he was finally out, bowled by Voce, he returned to the changing rooms where they counted eleven large bruises covering his shoulder to his hips.

After the sixth wicket fell, removing the last of the recognized batsmen, Bertie Oldfield, the popular veteran wicket-keeper, came out to join Grimmett, and Larwood dispensed with leg theory. Oldfield started well and soon rattled up 41 runs. Larwood, who classed Bertie as one of his closest friends, grew impatient. The batsman had played himself in and was seeing the ball well, so he dropped one short. Oldfield swung, going for the hook, but the ball came off the pitch more slowly than he expected. He had swung almost full circle when it caught the hump of the bat and rebounded back on to the right side of his head, felling him in his tracks.

Sinclair sat in the same stand as on Saturday. Robert was beside him. He had argued with some passion that he did not think it a good idea to return to the Oval for the resumption of play, but Robert had pleaded, begged, implored him to go. Had he not scrounged a long weekend pass from school which included Monday? And anyway, this was the best game he had ever seen! And everyone at school would think he was crackers if he didn't go on the Monday, when he had the time *and* the ticket! What was wrong with a bit of aggravation in the crowds? At Melbourne it had been quiet as a field of lambs, and even though we had won, the game had been almost *boring*! Larwood hadn't hit *anyone*!

"So that's what you want, is it?" Sinclair said in some distaste.

"That's what everyone wants, Dad," Robert had answered. "Why is every seat taken? Why are there thousands turned away outside? I've never seen so many people at one game in my life."

There being no immediate response to this, Sinclair had taken him along for the Monday start. A gnawing anxiety worried him from the first ball, when it was apparent England were not going to bow to public pressure. And when Oldfield toppled to the ground, he knew his doubts had been well founded.

The crowd gasped with one accord, then stood and roared with full-throated rage as the fieldsmen raced towards the stricken player. The police, already in position, with a squad of mounted officers keeping barely hidden outside the stands, moved into operation, linking arms to meet the wave of incensed spectators leaping over seats to get onto the field. Their line buckled and almost gave until more police raced in and formed a second line behind the first.

One was tugging at the leashes of two Alsatian dogs.

Oldfield lay on the ground shaking convulsively, a dark red mark swelling like an egg on his right temple. Slowly his eyes fluttered open and he looked about him, dazed and uncertain.

"What the hell—?"

Larwood pushed the others aside and knelt beside him.

"Oh God, Bertie! I'm sorry! I'm sorry!"

His eyes filled with tears of fright. Oldfield sighed.

"My fault!" he croaked. "It was my fault—"

Hammond squinted at the erupting stands and sidled over to Maurice Leyland who had walked quickly in from square leg.

"If this goes on," he muttered, "we're going to see a lynching before the day is out."

"*See* it?" Leyland exclaimed. "We'll bloody *be* it!"

The police lines were taking more and more of the strain as men sprinted round the edge of the field to help in the pushing. Throughout the stands came the chant of "Bastards, bastards, bastards!" in a rhythm that orchestrated the rage sweeping over the stadium, growing in ferocity the longer Oldfield remained prone on the ground.

Sinclair almost fell into the row in front when three men

171

charged over the top of the seats, knocking everyone aside in their pell-mell race to take on the police line.

"That's it!" he snapped to Robert and grabbed him by the lapel, pulling him to the aisle. "We're going!"

"Oh, but Dad, wait—!" the boy exclaimed but fell in behind his father as the older man fought against the tide of protesters to reach an exit tunnel. Neither spoke until they were outside, their ears ringing with the screams and cries of the spectators. Ground stewards were running back and forth; most of them, it seemed, trying to get out of the way rather than help.

"Dad," Robert panted, "we can't go now, not when it's all going on!"

His father stared at him in some astonishment.

"Don't you realize, you bloody idiot, we could have got trampled to death in there?" he shouted.

"But we have to see what'll happen!" Robert protested. "I can't go back to school saying we ran away in the middle!"

"You can and you bloody will!" was all Sinclair said as he pulled him towards the gates.

"Well, at least, let's go and see Mr Brown," the boy argued.

For a moment Sinclair stopped.

"Why?" he asked.

"Well—I don't know," Robert stammered. "Just to be polite, that's all—"

Sinclair paused and for a moment it seemed as if he was going to agree. But then he took hold of his son's coat and hauled him out into the road without speaking.

In the middle, Sutcliffe joined Hammond and Leyland and for a while they surveyed the stands, the yelling and high-pitched screams of men out of control. They watched the bottles, streamers, cushions rain on to the pitch and the punishment received by the line of policemen as they heaved like rugby forwards to keep back the tide of fury which threatened to engulf them all.

"If they get on to the field," Sutcliffe said, calm and level-headed as always, "they'll go for Loll and the skipper—"

Voce came across, bringing Paynter.

"—and it'll be up to us to stop them."

"You reckon," Leyland exclaimed. "There's 60,000 o' them an' there's eleven of us!"

Sutcliffe turned to Voce:

"I shouldn't think they'll forget you, either, Tangy."

"Lerrem try," Voce grunted. He was in his element.

"If the police line breaks," Sutcliffe murmured, "grab the stumps. You, Wally and Maurice, stand round Jardine. I'll take Loll. Now go and tell the others, half for skipper, half for Loll. Use owt you can get your hands on. Stumps, bats, anything—"

By now Oldfield was on his feet. Allen and Wyatt were each holding him under an arm and were starting towards the pavilion. They met Woodfull, who had run onto the pitch with Ironmonger. He pushed Wyatt aside:

"Leave him alone," he rapped. "I'll manage."

As the crowd roared, hurled abuse and anything they could lay their hands on, they hobbled off with the stricken batsman, who kept saying over and over "Not your fault, Loll. Stupid shot. Shouldn't have tried it. Not your fault—"

The umpires met and spoke to each other, calling Jardine over.

"I don't like this, don't like it at all, Mr Jardine," George Hele said, gazing round at the stands. "It's our feeling you should take your men off until things have cooled down."

"I'm sorry about Oldfield," Jardine replied crisply, "but it was nobody's fault but his own. He hooked the ball back on to his head. Neither Woodfull nor he was hit because of leg theory."

"I know that," Hele said grimly. "You know it. Even Oldfield knows it. But they're the ones—" pointing to the pandemonium, "who are making me nervous, and they *don't* know it."

"Unless you order us to," Jardine declared, "I will not leave the field. We have a crucial advantage, and I do not intend to go and sit in the pavilion and play cards."

And so the game resumed. Every time Larwood touched the ball, an earsplitting wave of jeering broke out. When he bowled, the crowd counted each step, trying to put him off:

"One, two, three, four, five-six-seven-eight—!"

173

Less than an hour later Australia were all out for 222. When Jardine led his men in, the police ringed the pavilion and faced the milling throngs who stood and chanted: "Bastards, bastards, bastards, bastards, BASTARDS!" Oranges and bottles were hurled and the team ducked and ran the last twenty yards. The crowds, ugly and dangerous, flocked round the pavilion until the police moved amongst them, two on horses, ordering them to go back to their seats or leave the ground. They grabbed a couple of the loudest protesters and bundled them away, and slowly the rest simmered down and dispersed.

Warner doubted that this game would ever be finished. How could England bat in such conditions? The crowd was still in a state of pandemonium. The noise was unbearable and the spectators, yelling and screaming obscenities, threatened to trample underfoot the young and old.

Larwood was left in the hospital corridor for an hour before a nurse appeared and said he could go in.

Oldfield lay propped up on pillows, his head swathed in bandages. The bruise from his temple had spread and filtered into his right eye, discolouring the top and lower rims. But he was awake and alert and when he saw Larwood enter with his face trailing on the ground he tried to say something, then winced.

"How are you, Bertie?"

"Only hurts when I laugh."

"I'm so sorry," Larwood said. "Honest, Bertie, I'd a give owt for it not to've happened—"

"I thought you'd come to give me the score, not cry all over my nice clean bedclothes."

"We're 85 for 1."

"Who's out?"

"Herbert. Went for 7."

"He's had a rotten game, hasn't he?" Oldfield grinned, willing him to cheer up.

"You'd never believe it," Larwood said.

"Believe what?"

"Jardine's got 45. T'crowds went mad, yelling and screaming

174

every time he played t'ball, burrit don't do any good. He's playing like it was Sat'day afternoon on t'recreation park."

Oldfield laughed, then rubbed his bandages.

"What do t'doctors say?"

"Aah, could be worse."

"I know that," Larwood retorted, "but what happened?"

"They call it a linear fracture of the right frontal bone."

"Oh Christ!"

"Oh, shut up, will you. You're making me cry. You saw what I did. Pulled the bloody thing back on to my head. It wasn't your bloody fault, so stop playing the big martyr."

"I shouldn't have dropped it short—"

"You know, if you go on like this, I'll have you thrown out," Oldfield said. "You're making me depressed. They said I could only see blokes who would prove to be therapeutic."

"What's that?"

"Well, you're not right now. Does that tell you anything?"

The game moved into the fourth day. Jardine made 56, Hammond 85, and England finished with 296 for 6, 400 ahead and all the time in the world to make as many as they liked, since these Test matches were all played to a finish.

Late in the afternoon a meeting was called by the Australian Board of Control in Sydney. None of the members was a first-class player nor, as Bradman had discovered, were they particularly concerned with the outcome of the games they arranged, whose sides they picked. They were only interested in administration: ensuring that players were properly registered, free from conflicting or mercenary interests, keeping to the rules.

The reason for the meeting had set them by the heels. They had heard of the disturbance in Adelaide, scenes which had been reported by more than one account as sinister and dangerous. The reason had been the insistence by the England captain on using the same bodyline tactics that had raised tempers in the Sydney Test and on many occasions during State games. Apparently Jardine was unmoved by pleas to desist. The Board had heard Bradman complain not on his own behalf, but on behalf of players who, battered by the ball, were then prevented from performing their other functions, such as bowling in the case of McCabe; and now they heard that the wicket-keeper, Oldfield, would take no further part in the Adelaide match and might be laid up for weeks, even months, with a fractured skull.

Something, it was plain, had to be done. Australia were going to lose the series unless an agreement was struck immediately curbing these violent tactics.

"Well now," said the Chairman as the members of the Board took their seats around the long table. "What do we do?"

They knew they could not arbitrarily alter the rules or give the umpires greater authority to caution sides that engaged in dangerous play. They knew they could not approach Pelham Warner or Palairet since it was well known they had no influence on Jardine. And they knew they could not approach Jardine, who despised them all. So, under great stress and in great haste, they drafted a cable to the M.C.C.:

> Bodyline bowling has assumed such proportions as to menace the best interests of the game, and to make protection of the body by the batsmen the main consideration. This is causing intensely bitter feeling between the players as well as injury. In our opinion it is unsportsmanlike. Unless it is stopped at once it is likely to upset the friendly relations existing between Australia and England.

When Australia went out to bat in the second innings they needed 532 runs to win. Larwood quickly removed Fingleton for another duck, and Ponsford, bringing in Bradman at 16 for 2. Never did Australia need the 'Run Machine' more than now. If England went one up in the series, the psychological pressure they were able to apply with the use of bodyline made it virtually certain they would regain the Ashes. He simply *had* to come off this time.

For a while Larwood kept his offside field and Bradman pulled, cut and drove him for three fours. Leaving the pitch to bind a chafed toe, he returned to the attack and was struck hard through the covers by Bradman who was also scoring freely at the other end off Verity. Larwood moved the fielders across.

The effect was instantaneous. Arthur Mailey, watching from the press box, wrote: "Bradman now swings wildly at every ball. The brilliant off-drives, back-cuts and leg glances have been killed by the introduction of the leg-field."

Maurice Leyland, down at deep fine leg, began to dodge the missiles which were now a permanent feature of the match, along with the jeering and the "counting out" when Larwood ran in to bowl whenever Jardine signalled his men to cross over. Like a familiar chorus of a popular song, the lilting refrain of "Bastards, bastards, bastards" returned, bringing out police reinforcements on cue.

At the end of the over Leyland approached Jardine.

"Hey, skipper," he declared, "I'm getting cheesed off dodging all the bloody nuts and oranges down there. I don't suppose there's anyone'd want to swap places for a bit?"

Verity bowled a maiden. Jardine signalled Leyland.

"Take my place," he snapped.

"Hold on, skipper," Leyland shouted. "*You* aren't going down there, are you?"

The barrackers saw Jardine walking towards them and their initial burst of abuse died. Unable to believe their eyes, they watched him march to the ropes, then turn his back.

"Hey there, *Sar*dine," a voice bawled, "Come another 10 yards and *we'll* give *you* some bodyline."

No reaction.

"Sardine, sardine, the biggest bastard I ever seen—"

"What rock they find you under, Jardine?"

A fly settled on Jardine's neck and he slapped it.

"Hey, Sardine," a stentorian voice called out, "you leave our flies alone."

At the end of Larwood's over, Bradman went up the pitch to meet Woodfull who had played three consecutive maidens against Verity. "We're not going to make it this way, Bill," Bradman murmured.

"Too right."

"We've got to change round. You take Larwood. I'll score off Verity."

He saw the captain nod unhappily.

177

"Sorry, Bill," said Bradman, "but it's the only way."

"It's all right," Woodfull smiled wanly. "I came prepared." He slapped the body protector that encased him from his neck to his knees.

For the next half dozen overs Woodfull avoided any stroke play and let the ball smash into him. Meanwhile Bradman tore into Verity. He hit 66 out of 88 in 73 minutes and finished by lofting a shot for 6, the first he had ever hit in a Test in Australia. Trying the same off the next ball he was caught and bowled.

He and Woodfull had taken the score to 186 but the impression among the dispirited crowd was that he had given his wicket away after going to pieces against Larwood's bodyline, exposing Woodfull at the fast end and leaving him there. Woodfull, hurt so often in the past, was forced to shield the Boy Wonder.

As the last Australian wicket fell for 103, Jardine, still down at fine leg, watched the spectators behind him make their way towards the exits. Several gave him a parting shot:

"You may have won, Sardine, but you're still a bastard!"

He looked fixedly towards them for several seconds. Then he hawked and spat loudly on to the ground.

One of the spectators watched him walk away and said with not a little awe, "He could have been killed, but he comes down here. Then he spits in our faces. He's either mad as a hatter or the bravest bastard in the world."

The reply to the Board's cable was not long arriving:

We, the Marylebone Cricket Club, deplore your cable. We deprecate the opinion that there has been unsportsmanlike play. We have the fullest confidence in the captain, the team and its managers, and are convinced that they would do nothing to infringe the laws of cricket and the spirit of the game. We have no evidence our confidence is misplaced. Much as we regret the accidents to Woodfull and Oldfield, we understand that in neither case was the bowler to blame.

If the Board wishes to propose a new law or rule it shall receive our careful consideration in due course. We hope the situation is

178

not now as serious as your cable appears to indicate but if it is such to jeopardize good relations between English and Australian cricketers, and you consider it desirable to cancel the remainder of the programme, we would consent with great reluctance.

The Chairman of the Australian Board of Control looked at the last sentence. It mesmerized him. Cancel the remainder of the programme? Cancel—? Sydney had a gate of 150,000. Melbourne 250,000—cancel?

"Those buggers," he breathed. "They got us by the short and curlies. What do we do now?"

"Feeling hungry?" one of the others asked.

"No, why?"

"You're going to have to eat a lot of words. . . ."

We, the Australian Board of Control, appreciate your difficulty in dealing with the matter raised in our cable without having seen the actual play. We unanimously regard bodyline bowling as adopted in some of the games of the present tour as being opposed to the spirit of cricket and as dangerous to players. We are deeply concerned that the ideals of the game shall be protected and have therefore appointed a committee to report on the action necessary to eliminate such bowling from all cricket in Australia as from the beginning of the 1933/34 season. We will forward a copy of the committee's recommendations for your consideration and, it is hoped, cooperation as to their application in all cricket.

We do not consider it necessary to cancel the remainder of the programme.

"Good God almighty!" exclaimed Warner in a rare moment of invective. "Let's hope that that is the end of this dreadful affair."

He had come to Jardine's room to show him a copy of the latest Board cable sent to London.

"Quite truthfully, I have never in my entire life been quite so frightened as I was at Adelaide," he went on. "It could hardly have been worse in the trenches."

"They haven't apologized for calling us unsporting," Jardine declared. He turned the paper over as if expecting more on the reverse side.

Warner blinked in surprise.

"What?"

"In their first cable," Jardine said, "did they or did they not accuse us of unsportsmanlike behaviour?"

"I—ah—yes, I believe the words they used—"

Jardine waved the paper. "There's nothing here that says they withdraw their remark."

"Oh, it's implied—"

"Implications aren't enough," Jardine announced flatly, handing the paper back. "They must apologize."

"*Apologize?*" The older man's heart shrivelled. "After all this— you want *them* to apologize? Douglas, are you feeling all right?"

The England captain smiled, reached for his pipe and began to fill it.

"You can go down and tell them this," he said calmly. "Until the Australian Board of Control state, in writing, that they withdraw their accusation of unsportsmanlike behaviour against us, I refuse to come out of this room."

"Whaaat—"

"Tell them that, Plum, if you please."

"Douglas, Douglas, for heaven's sake," Warner pleaded. "*Why?*"

"Oh, it's really quite simple," he replied breezily, filling the room with smoke as he kindled the tobacco. "Put yourself in their place. You are two one down. Your great white hope has been contained. Your Board has had to make representations on your behalf asking the opposition not to be so rough. But it didn't work because of the number of people who are paying to see the most exciting series there has ever been. And now, on top of all the humiliation and shame, you are required to say how sorry you are for calling them unsporting. My dear fellow, how could *anyone* play a decent game of cricket after all that?"

The room spun a little for Warner, but not because of the noxious smoke. He was listening to something he didn't fully understand, or ever would. Here was a man speaking about a game,

180

but using the kind of tactics he had only previously associated with psychological warfare.

"Is it—has it really come down to this?" he whispered, appalled and repelled. Jardine winked.

"We'll see," he grinned. . . .

We, the Australian Board of Control, do not regard the sportsmanship of your team as being in question. Our position was fully considered at a recent meeting in Sydney and is as indicated in our cable of January 30. It is the particular class of bowling referred to therein which we consider is not in the best interests of cricket and in this view we understand we are supported by many eminent English cricketers. We join heartily with you in hoping that the remaining Tests will be played with the traditional good feeling.

Fingleton received the news that he had been dropped from the Fourth Test at Brisbane without rancour.

"You know, Stan," he reflected as he walked with McCabe out of the S.C.G. after a Shield match, "I used to love this game. Couldn't wait to get togged up and go out there. Ever since I was 10, everything about it held a magic for me. The shine on a new ball, the smell of linseed oil. Nothing like it in the world. But I reckon, after this series is over, there won't be any of us who played in it will feel the same way ever again."

They passed a newsvendor. One of the billboards read:

BODYLINE—AUSTRALIA APOLOGIZES

"Here, mate," Fingleton said, pointing to the sign, "are you the local comedian around here, or what?"

They stood and read the text of the A.B.C. cable.

"Well what do you know, Stan," he breathed in awe as he read, "'We do not regard the sportsmanship of your team as being in question.'"

He gave a short laugh.

"First they are, then they're not. That's what I call nerve. Bloody old Jardine."

There was an undisguised admiration in his voice.

"You think Jardine is behind this?" McCabe asked.

"Well, it sure as hell wasn't old Warner," Fingleton said.

"You know he thinks it was me leaked the Woodfull story?"

"That was Braddles, wasn't it?"

"Yeah, but Warner thinks Don's a gent. He's too much of one himself to make the Board crawl like this though—" he slapped the paper.

"That's Duggie. 'Make the bastards eat dirt.' I can just hear him saying it. I tell you something."

"What?"

"I wish he was on our side. With him in charge, we'd have no problem."

"Got a feeling you don't mean that, Fingo," McCabe said warily. Fingleton screwed up the newspaper and threw it into a bin.

"Better get used to the Jardine approach," he grunted. "Because from now on, that's how it's going to be. When they discovered the bow and arrow, war was never the same again. Ditto the gun. Now someone's shown that cricket isn't about a way of life, that it's like any other sport, it's about winning. People aren't going to forget what happened here. Just the reverse. Jardine's laid down a new set of rules, and we'll all have to abide by them. Mark my words."

Chapter Sixteen

"Why, Mr Brown, this is a surprise." Mrs Sinclair opened the door and took a stagey step backwards when she saw who was calling, although she could not possibly have not heard the backfiring of the car he had borrowed to drive out to Vaucluse.

"I'm sorry to drop by without warning," Brown stammered. Something was wrong. He knew it the moment she opened the door. He was getting the cold shoulder in a royal way.

"I've been ringing for days, but your maid said you were out."

"We've been very busy," she said, allowing him in. He looked round.

"Is Mary at home?"

"I'm not sure," Mrs Sinclair said. "I'll go and see."

Five minutes later her daughter came downstairs. They embraced briefly and he felt the coolness of her kiss on his cheek.

"If you'll excuse me," Mrs Sinclair announced, "I have some letters to write."

"You're not ill, are you?" Brown said as she led him into the garden. She laughed and took his hand.

"Nothing so simple," she replied.

They sat on the patio and she asked a maid to fetch some lemonade.

"I rang you from Ballarat," Brown said, "and every evening after the Sydney game."

"Congratulations," she smiled. "I see you beat our wonderful New South Wales side."

"Yes."

"Even without your Larwood and Voce. Or even Jardine," she added. "Was that a strategic or diplomatic decision?"

He began to fidget uncomfortably.

"They were all in need of a rest," he explained.

The lemonade arrived.

"I was hoping to see you at the match," he went on, sipping the astringent, freshly squeezed cordial.

She looked at him steadily.

"After the game at Adelaide, Daddy thought it might be too dangerous," she said.

"Oh, come on, Mary." He felt himself becoming impatient. "What on earth do you mean?"

"Are you saying he exaggerated?" she asked innocently. "You came as close as dammit to a full-scale riot. He was terrified that he and Robert would get trampled."

"There were some nasty moments, yes," he answered, unable to find the correct words for what he wanted to say. "But nobody got hurt."

She stirred her drink with the straw.

"One player taken to hospital with a fractured skull, half a dozen others bruised and bleeding because of the way you bowled," she observed. "And you say no one was hurt? Freddy, were you even there?"

"I meant," he snapped, "nobody in the crowd. Of course I know about Bertie Oldfield, Woodfull and Ponny, and the others. But the wicket was springy and anyway, Oldfield has said it was his fault he got the crack on the head."

"I suppose," she said, her manner becoming colder each time she spoke, "that you approve of your methods?"

"If I said I didn't, no doubt I'd be quoted in the papers tomorrow," he grunted, then repented the second the words were out.

"You think I'd tell them?"

"Look, Mary, this is ridiculous," he protested. "Why are we talking about bloody cricket? I came here to get away from it. I'm sick of the whole tour. We're spat on in the street, get things chucked at us wherever we go. Poor old Larwood was at the theatre the other night when some ghastly child comes over and says to her mother: 'Why, mummy, he doesn't *look* like a murderer!' You can't

184

turn a page in the press without reading someone else's studied opinion about our iniquities. Is *this* why I've been unable to reach you on the telephone?"

"I can't say bodyline has been totally ignored in this household," she replied. "I mean, it's rather like talking about world affairs without mentioning the Depression."

"And what's your view?"

"Well," she smiled briefly, "put it this way. I hope no one has slipped any cyanide into your lemonade."

He gazed around the garden. The recent rains had revived the sun-weary flowers and there was a tang in the air from the newly mown lawn.

"Are we going to fall out," he asked, "because of cricket?"

"We got a letter from Robert last week," she said. "He said all the chaps at school are bowling short, just like Larwood. He said the sports master has suspended one of the First XI boys who wouldn't stop, even when he was told by the umpire. Oh, Robert thinks it's a heck of a thing. He said the boy's become a hero. When Daddy read that, his jaw sort of went rather tight, if you know what I mean."

"Very soon you're going to blame us for the Northern drought and the crime rate," Brown muttered, turning his glass round between his fingers.

"I read that a judge has decided sportsmen can be charged with assault if they play dangerously," Mary recalled.

"You read a lot, don't you?"

"I like to keep informed."

There seemed no more to be said and he stood up.

She walked with him to the car.

"It's not because of the effect you are having on schoolboys," she said. "It's not because of the newspapers screaming horrors at the tops of their voices. It's not even because we are losing. I promise you, Freddy, none of this matters to me."

"Then what *does* matter to you?" he asked miserably.

She looked him straight in the eyes.

"The fact that *you* don't think you're doing anything wrong," she replied.

It was rather late to give her his views on the matter, and anyway, he didn't think she would listen.

"I'm part of a team," he said as he climbed into the car. "I'm bound by a sort of loyalty. What I think is neither here nor there. All I can say is I support my fellow players. Give my regards to your mother and father. Tell them I had a wonderful time at Christmas and I'm only sorry I won't have the chance to reciprocate their kindness. Goodbye."

The car backfired into life and he drove away in a cloud of smoke. He looked back as he went through the gate. She was still watching, and when she saw him turn she waved. He wished he could have found the courage to wave back.

The Englishmen arrived in the torrid humidity of Brisbane for the Fourth Test as the ground staff were laying barbed wire around the stands at the Woolloongabba stadium. Instructions were given that the England dressing-rooms would be out of bounds to everyone except the players, and a squad of policemen, including a batch of dog handlers, would patrol the area until the match was finished.

They were given a security lecture at the Brisbane Hotel where they were staying, alerting them to the dangers of walking alone, particularly at night. They had already been bombarded at Sydney, and Paynter and Larwood had been chased along a street by a crowd of youths.

Of the Australian players, they saw nothing. The traditional off-field fraternity had died at Adelaide and they didn't even know if they had arrived in Brisbane yet, or where they were staying.

Tommy Mitchell, Voce, Larwood and Les Ames checked into their rooms and escaped to the hotel bar where a ceiling fan gave a slight relief from the crushing heat. A huge, broken-nosed barman, Mick MacGuire, an ex-prize-fighter, welcomed them, telling Larwood, whom he had met on the previous tour, that they served anyone here, even homicidal maniacs. Larwood grinned and they ordered beers.

Fingleton walked in.

"Is this where they keep the dangerous animals?" he said, and they gathered with relief around him.

186

"You shoon't be seen wi' the likes of us," Larwood grinned, leading him to the bar. "You'll get done."

"Ah, you know me," Fingleton said. "I'm not proud. I'll drink with anyone if they're paying."

"Sorry to hear you're not playing," Ames said.

"No, you're not," he chuckled. "You know I'd have made mincemeat of you all. I bet when you read I was dropped, you all breathed a sigh of relief."

"Then what are you doing up here?" Voce said, wiping his forehead. "I berrit's not for t'climate."

"No," he said, taking his beer and rolling the ice cold glass across his forehead before drinking half in one swallow. "As you might know, I'm trying to follow our esteemed and highly praised D. G. Bradman into the higher realms of literature. I refer, of course, to the world of newspapers."

"Didn't know you could write," Mitchell grunted.

Fingleton licked two fingers, reached down and smeared his glasses.

"Pick on someone your own size, half-pint," he grinned, then expanded on his theme. "Well, as every person who goes to the pictures knows, to get on in newspapers, you have to have what they call a scoop. Now I think there's just such a thing about to happen at the Gabba."

"What kind of scoop?" Voce asked.

Fingleton drew a line in the air like a headline: "'Brisbane Massacre,'" he announced. "'Entire England Team Lynched' by your roving reporter J. Fingleton. Yes, folks, I was there as the Australian sports-loving public finally saw to it that justice was performed at the Woolloongabba ground this afternoon, when they strung up the England side to the rafters of the pavilion. In his final words,'D. R. Jardine asked to be allowed to hang on Larwood's legside, along with six others—"

The street door was thrown open and a man came in. He was about 6 feet 4 and weighed somewhere around 15 stones. From the look of his deeply lined leathered face, bulging arms the colour of cedar, he was a bushman. He looked thirsty and, by the forward inclination of his head, spoiling for a fight. And he appeared to reckon that this bar was as good as any in which to find one. He was also drunk.

Reaching the counter, he brought the flat of his hand down and bawled: "Beer!"

Even Mick looked small alongside him. He pulled a beer out of the icebox and picked up a glass, but the customer grabbed the bottle, palmed the top off by trapping the neck against the edge of the counter and drank it off in one go.

"Another!" he yelled, slamming the bottle down with a crash.

Fingleton spread a look round the others that said: "Watch it, I think this one's mean."

They drank silently, keeping their heads into the glasses as the newcomer saw the next bottle off, threw some coins across and demanded a third.

"Warm out," Mick offered, taking the money. It was a gesture of conversation that made no impression at all.

"My shout," Voce said, resenting the stranger for killing their good humour. "Loll, gi'us your glass, and yourn Fingo—Tom, Les, sup up—"

His voice carried to the big newcomer. He stopped sucking on his third bottle and looked round.

"Same again, squire," he said to Mick.

The bushman wiped the back of his hand across his mouth and set the bottle down, gently this time.

"Well, well, well," he growled. "Look what we got here—if it ain't the Pommy cricket bastards—"

"Afternoon," Voce nodded briskly.

"Drinking here, in a public place," breathed the big man. "Large as life. How d'you like that?"

Mick, bracing himself as he smelled damage, put on a friendly face.

"Anyone can drink here, mate," he said. "Long as they're old enough and they behave."

The bushman took three paces down the bar, holding on to his bottle. He squinted at Fingleton:

"Well, I'll be—! That you, Fingo?" he said, surprised.

"No, mate, not me," Fingleton said. "Funny thing, everyone

188

mistakes me for Jack Fingleton. Dugson's my name."

"Don't come the old dog, Fingo," the man said and his voice took on an edge. "What are you doing, drinking with these pisspots?"

Mitchell was the only one who had not moved. He took off his glasses and huffed on the lenses, cleaning them with a handkerchief.

"With these lily-livered, knock-kneed, cross-eyed bastards, after what they did to your mates," he continued fluently. "After putting Bertie Oldfield in hospital. I come in here and what do I find—you and them laughing away like you was all old cobbers."

"So we are," Fingleton said. "Look, mate, it's hot and we're tired. Why don't we just sit quietly and drink our beers—?"

"To think a load of chicken-livered—" the bushman went on. He was running out of original invective, beginning to repeat himself, "bastards like this lot here, these Pommy scum, these, these—no wonder the bloody Empire's going down the bloody drain, with bleedin' scrawny little buggers like these—"

"Why don't you shut you big mouth, you fat sod," Mitchell said quietly.

For a second it seemed as if the bushman hadn't heard. The others looked on in horror as he slowly turned his head.

"What was that?"

"I said," Mitchell declared, removing his glasses and laying them on the counter, "that you've got a big mouth, you great lumbering gorilla. You've also got a brain the size of my budgerigar's willie."

Even Mick MacGuire looked startled.

"Here—!" the bushman gasped, peering down at the Derbyshire man whose head came barely up to his chest.

"I came in to have a quiet drink," Mitchell announced. "I didn't come in to listen to a drunken piss artist like you. So either shut your trap—or put up your dukes."

He raised his fists like an old-fashioned prize-fighter. The others froze in their tracks. The bushman stared in silence for a few seconds. Then, putting his hand into a back pocket, he pulled out a revolver and fired a shot through the ceiling.

Everyone except Mitchell hit the floor. MacGuire ducked

behind the counter, crawling on his knees up the bar to where he kept a truncheon beside the till.

Fingleton and Larwood cracked heads diving under the same table while Ames and Voce threw themselves to one side as the bushman waved the gun at Mitchell, who stood his ground without flinching.

"You talk like that—I'll fill you full of holes!" the huge man bellowed. "I'll shoot your ears off! I'll—"

Mitchell brought back a leg and kicked him in the shin. With a howl of pain the bushman dropped the gun, and hopped up and down. MacGuire leaned across and brought the billy stick down on his head while he was nursing his leg. It bounced off. Concentrating on his raging shin, the man didn't even notice. Mitchell remained with his fists up.

Nothing happened for a long time.

The bushman eventually straightened and hobbled across towards the Derbyshire man.

"That hurt!" he boomed.

"I don't like fools who point guns at me," Mitchell snapped.

The bushman looked blank. Then, slowly, a broad smile spread across his face.

"You know, mate," he roared, rattling the glasses on the rack above the bar, "you're all right. Here, have a drink—" And he picked the little man up in a bear hug and sat him on the counter.

"Beer!" he roared. Mick MacGuire surfaced, this time without the truncheon. "For me and my friend here!"

Cautiously the players stood and replaced their chairs upright. They watched Mitchell take the beer from his new friend and clink glasses.

"As long as you ain't Jardine or Larwood," the big man boomed, "you can drink with me any time."

Mitchell lowered his glass.

"You're speaking about friends of mine," he said severely. The others quailed. "I'll not have anything said against either of them."

The bushman scratched his head.

"Sorry, mate," he replied. "No offence. Any friend of yours is a friend of mine."

"Then cheers," Mitchell beamed. He raised his glass in front of the big man and drank.

The Fourth Test was played in scorching heat and a sapping humidity that made even the reporters in the press box feel as if they had performed for eight hours in the field.

"I know I've played in these conditions," Hobbs sighed, mopping his face with a soaked handkerchief, "but I could no more go out there today than fly to the moon."

He watched Jardine lead the men out after losing the toss and for once felt no envy. After the confrontation in the bar with the gun-happy bushman, Mitchell must have felt the gods were on his side since he took Voce's place, and for the first time in the series found himself in a Test match.

Jardine scarcely heard the wave of booing and catcalls that greeted him as he set foot on the turf. The reception was a background noise he had grown used to, rather like a mindless melody; as a matter of fact it gave him a kind of comfort. Tranquillity bored him, that much he had learned about himself on this trip. If he had to admit to a single regret, then it would be for his reaction after the Woodfull incident at Adelaide. Why had he gone over to Larwood and ostentatiously patted him on the back? Did he *really* enjoy making people dislike him? If not, why did he feel at ease, content with the world at large now it was showing its hatred of him as he strolled into the centre?

Never mind that now. This game must be won. To let Australia level the score and have everything hang on the Fifth and last Test, only a week away, would be a burden he knew might well prove too much for his tiring side. Voce was unfit and anyway had done nothing at Adelaide, while Larwood and Allen had virtually bowled themselves into the ground. They had recently played a game on the Gabba and he had doubted whether the pitch would stand up to a five- or six-day pounding. So he had brought in Mitchell, putting his faith, reluctantly as always, in spin.

Dammit, why did he have to lose the toss? Nothing ever comes easily—wasn't that one of the cardinal rules Winchester had thrust down his youthful throat?

It was less than twenty minutes into the game when he realized the wicket was lifeless. It would be Melbourne all over again, with the added torture of temperatures well over 100°. The climate soon had an effect on Larwood and when Jardine went over to have a word about the field, he received a bad-tempered shake of the head which forestalled any further discussion. The leg-trap stood like a languid spinney of autumn trees around Woodfull and Richardson who had all the time in the world to lean out of the way of anything short, and it was not until mid-afternoon that the first wicket fell when Richardson left after a whippy stumping by Les Ames, who almost alone appeared to be unaffected by the crippling heat. By the end of the day Australia had made 251 and had lost only three wickets.

Few players slept during the night. The thermometer went down only a few notches and Larwood, along with some others, decided that there was no point lying listlessly on a sweat-soaked bed when they could down a few jars. He tried to dragoon Eddie Paynter, but he was complaining of a sore throat and said if it got worse, he might even see a doctor.

"It's just t'bloody weather," Larwood consoled him. "Listen, a couple of beers'll do it good. Lubricate it."

But Paynter was not one for the beer and, as Larwood whispered to Voce as they headed for a party laid on by the reporters, the lad did look pale.

The hard core of drinkers stayed until four o'clock, lying on a balcony trying to squeeze some balm from a night air that clung to their faces like a damp cloth.

"Did you ever hear the tale," Fingleton said, "of the Brisbane bloke who died and fetched up in Hell? When his wife got in touch with him through a spiritualist, she asked if there was anything he needed. 'Aye,' he said. 'Send down a few blankets. Compared with Brisbane, this place is freezing.'"

"They used to say the test of a real cricketer," Arthur Mailey remarked, "was to spend all night up on the razzle, then go out and play a full day at the Gabba. Reckon you're a real cricketer, Loll?"

Perhaps it was the booze that spoke but he replied:

"I'll tek any bet that says I won't get Bradman out inside three overs tomorrow."

This created a long silence. Bradman was 71 not out. In the past, that usually meant an innings of 200 or more, since overnight breaks did not seem to affect him.

"I'll take that," Mailey nodded. "A quid."

"You're daft as a brush," Voce murmured to Larwood. "T'wicket's dead as mutton. Three overs? Three days, more like."

Unhappily for the human condition, the number of times a wildly improbable prediction comes true is very small. Some men go through life without ever enjoying that moment of excitement as the 100 to 1 outsider beats the favourite in a manner they had foretold. However, the next day, off the fourth ball of Larwood's third over, Bradman stepped back to cut a ball on the leg stump to avoid the leg trap, and was bowled.

"If a schoolboy had made that shot," Hobbs remarked to Mailey in the press box, "you would smack his head."

"Don't ever try and tell me bodyline doesn't work," Mailey grunted, thinking less of his forfeited pound than of the consequences of Bradman's extraordinary dismissal. He knew of the talk with Johnny Moyes, of Bradman's decision that this was the only way to counter England's tactics. Now he had been proved wrong. He had no answer, none at all. And it was reasonable to suppose that Larwood would be around for at least two more series. Was he looking at the eclipse of the Boy Wonder?

A few balls later Ponsford stepped across his wickets to avoid another Larwood thunderbolt and lost his leg stump. The crowd, which had slumbered in the heat without any direct hits on the batsmen to yell about, came back to life, but this time to pillory their own men. The "six-out-all-out" gibe was heard around the ground as Australia slid from 263 for 3 to a total of 340. Larwood took 4 for 101, bowling thirty-one overs in the torrid heat of the Tropic of Capricorn.

Jardine watched Paynter driven away to hospital with what the doctor had diagnosed as acute tonsillitis.

Inwardly he fumed. Why couldn't the bloody man have told him he was feeling unwell before the game started? 340 was not going to be any walkover, not in this climate and with a pitch he was convinced would soon start to break up.

He and Sutcliffe put on 99 for the first wicket, moving at a dreary pace that left the spectators fighting to stay awake, until bad light stopped play. The following day was Sunday and Jardine telephoned the hospital every two hours to hear about Paynter. What he learned gave him no comfort; the tonsillitis was getting worse and hospital treatment was essential. By Monday, the patient was no better, despite a series of gargles and throat-painting which had left him exhausted and feeling wretched.

The openers took the score to 114 before the first wicket fell. Then there followed a rout which had Jardine regretting he had referred to the Saturday play as the greatest day English cricket had known for twenty years. From 157 for 2, Ironmonger, McCabe and O'Reilly skittled the middle order until they were 198 for 5 with no recognized batsmen left.

Jardine found Voce lounging in the dressing-rooms.

"Get down to that hospital," he commanded, "and don't come back without Paynter."

Voce looked up in surprise. He half-grinned, convinced Jardine was making one of his rare jokes.

"Aye," he agreed, "if only Eddie were here."

He saw Jardine continue to stand over him and noticed he wasn't smiling.

"Did you hear me?"

"You—you don't mean it, skipper?" Voce faltered, but Jardine was already stalking outside.

"Get him."

When he reached the Brisbane General, he found Paynter already pacing round his bed as the wireless brought him the news of England's collapse: 216 for 6.

"You may see the patient," said a ward sister who was only a few inches shorter than Voce, "but on no account must he get overexcited. In fact, you might try and calm him down. He already seems determined to force an operation, the way he's behaving."

"Eddie," Voce whispered as the nurse left the room, "T'skipper wants you back at t'ground."

Paynter swung round and his tortured larynx croaked a few words: "Keep an eye on the door."

His clothes had been removed but he shrugged on a dressing-gown and slippers and edged out of the room.

"Nip out and get a taxi," he rasped and Voce ran on tiptoe until he was lost from sight at the end of the corridor. Paynter thought, don't act guilty. You're dressed in hospital gear. You're a patient on a stroll round the wards. Go on, that's the way—"And where d'you think you're going?"

The ward sister stood behind him, hands on hips. Her size worried him. If he had to wrestle with her, the combination of his weak state and her poundage would mean there would be no contest.

"Sorry, sister," he breathed. "but I've got to go. Nothing can stop me, I'm afraid."

"How about death?"

"Well, if you have to go, there are worse ways," he grinned and shuffled away down the corridor. He felt as if he were turning on a man with a gun. Would he be felled by a bullet in the back?

"You realize, I suppose," she boomed, "that you are forcing me to call the doctor. If you leave now, you are putting yourself in great danger."

Not half as much danger as ignoring old Sardine's call to arms, Paynter muttered to himself as he continued, finding the stairs and running outside. Voce had a taxi ticking over by the gate and ten minutes later they disgorged at the side entrance to the ground where a doorman put out a hand.

"Where do you two think you're going?" he demanded.

"This is Eddie Paynter," Voce explained. "He's playing."

The doorman looked them both up and down and laughed.

"I've heard some things said to try and get in here," he exclaimed, "but this is easily the best. I suppose you're Larwood."

"No, Bill Voce."

"And I'm Don Bradman. Go on, sling your hook, both of you—"

They heard a roar from the ground that could only be signalling another English wicket. Voce took hold of Paynter's arm and, using his size, pushed past the doorman and continued, despite a roar of protest, towards the rear entrance of the pavilion.

Jardine saw them fall into the dressing-room and yelled with delight.

"Eddie, what kept you?" he said, taking a jeroboam of champagne from a bench and filling a beer mug. Allen came in and threw down his bat.

"Quickly," Jardine snapped, "Get changed. You're in. Here— knock this back." Jardine had fed his side on a diet of vintage champagne, paid for by himself, and, as he had predicted, in such heat the best champagne always gives a lift. While Paynter struggled into his flannels, Sutcliffe buckled up his left pad, Hammond his right and Jardine held the mug steady to his lips. Minutes passed and a slow handclap started outside.

"Get going," Jardine ordered, "or they'll claim the wicket by default. Good luck. Don't come back without at least 20. We've got 100 to go to overtake their score. I know that's a long haul with only two wickets left, but let's try and get half-way there. Off you go."

A scene like this was not out of place on a village green, when players often have to be winkled out of the pub to go in, but seen on one of the most hallowed of Test match grounds, there was an incongruity to the sight of Paynter struggling to button up his trousers, players carrying his bat as he clattered down the steps, looking for gloves and coming up with two left handed ones before finding a pair that matched. That bordered on farce. When he did finally appear under a panama hat, a roar of ironic applause greeted him.

The Australians watched him approach the wicket in astonishment. The last they heard, he was lying in hospital, and they were looking forward to some shelter from the sun after one more tail-end wicket. Still, he looked awful; he couldn't possibly last.

There was an hour and a quarter left of the day and at the end Paynter was still there with 24. Back in the pavilion, Jardine force-fed him more champagne and had a taxi return him to the hospital where he cringed at the thought of meeting the ward sister.

She was standing at the door when Voce and Leyland propelled him along the corridor. At least I have safety in numbers, the Lancashire man thought as he watched her fold her arms and look down at him as if he had just been caught scrumping apples. Then her mouth softened.

"Well done," she smiled. "Now get back in that bed."

The following day his temperature had dropped enough to allow him to return to the Gabba without subterfuge, his pockets rattling with pills. He went to the crease with Hedley Verity, and when he was finally out, caught off a skier, he had made 83 and taken England 16 runs ahead. His innings captured the hitherto grudging heart of the spectators and they applauded him all the way. From Jardine he received a brief smile, a nod and a warm grip on his shoulder, the most intimate acknowledgement of gratitude he could bestow.

Paynter's performance won the Ashes for England. Australia were all out for 175, Bradman caught off Larwood for 24, once again stepping backwards to cut off the leg stump and this time lobbing the ball gently to Mitchell at deep point. England won by six wickets and Jardine had his wish granted: the Fifth Test didn't matter.

For those who played in the game, the heat was less memorable than the security imposed inside the ground. The rolls of barbed wire laid around the noisier regions of the stands and the policemen patrolling the England dressing-room area with dogs straining at the leash were the images the players took away, even more than the sight of a deathly pale Eddie Paynter writing himself into the history books. The game had come to this—?

The sullen resentment shown by the crowd may have been due to the enervating effect of the constant humidity, but many thought it represented more the gulf which now divided the two countries.

The newspapers pointed out that bodyline, irrespective of the ethical questions, had been successful. Since the First Test, McCabe had made no score higher than 32. Fingleton was dropped after scoring one run in three innings while Bradman and Woodfull, despite some respectable scores, showed they had no real answer to it. Except at Melbourne, Jardine's tactics had worked because of the unpredictability of the wickets. And if they worked this time, there was no reason why they should not work again. There was no reason why they should not always work. The Australian spectators must prepare to watch a different type of game in future.

And while Harold Larwood was still effective, there was no cause to doubt that England could win the next series down under. And the next. It was apparent to every sporting journalist in the country that unless Australia found bowlers of the same calibre, they might never win at home again for years.

The question the newspapers left open was whether Australia *should* adopt the England methods. Fingleton spoke for many players when he said he would never enjoy the game again. War had been a gentleman's pursuit until someone invented the Browning gun. Then it became professional and deadly. Opposing nations might agree not to use it, abide by rules that restricted them to cavalry charges or jousting contests, but they could not forget it existed. Similarly, a man throwing a hard ball at an opponent might invent a new technique whereby he aimed at his head and hoped to win by default. Opposing teams might agree not to use the new theory, but they would never be able to pretend it had never been discovered.

Jardine had applied the rules of war to a sport and by doing so had won. Underneath all the sermonizing and the pious sentiments, the desire, the urge, the *need* to win gnawed at the heart of every sportsman. The insistance that the game, not the result, was important, was devised by losers to cover their shame. Jardine had been the first to point out that the Emperor was not wearing any clothes. His was the voice of truth, which, like the boy in the story, exposed the cant but embarrassed the subject. Perhaps the Emperor became a better man for knowing he had been made to look a fool. Perhaps cricket was a better game for having the sentimentality removed.

The newspapers couldn't make up their minds at all.

Chapter Seventeen

"I am naturally delighted that we have won the Ashes, but I congratulate the Australian team on a well-fought and highly competitive series. I trust that we can all agree with Kipling—'to look at triumph and disaster, and treat those two impostors just the same'. In closing, I would just like to add—"

Except for the press and the players, the room was virtually empty. Row upon row of untouched champagne glasses stood forlornly on a trestle table along one wall. The Australian team stood in one corner, the England men in another. Both groups fidgeted, tried to avoid looking at each other, longed for the formalities to be over. While Jardine went on to thank people for their hospitality and kindnesses, the press edged closer and took photographs. One reporter asked Woodfull if he would shake hands with Larwood and he obliged. So did Bertie Oldfield, giving the only gesture of warmth by holding Larwood's right hand and resting his left on his shoulder, grinning broadly.

There was a smattering of applause, mainly from Warner and Palairet, as Jardine bowed curtly and stepped down from the podium. Then it was Woodfull's turn.

"I congratulate England on a convincing win and look forward to 1934 when I hope it will be our turn to prevail."

Voce gazed about at the disconsolate scene.

"Bit different from when we came, intit?" he muttered. Larwood nodded.

"Seems like ten years ago," he remarked. "Lot's happened, Tangy."

"Well, I don't give a bugger. I don't regret owt, not one tiny bit, and nor should you."

Larwood shrugged. Regrets? His left foot was hurting like blazes and he wanted to sit down. The doctors had found a broken bone, caused by the incessant pounding during the long series on the rock-hard wickets, and he had had to leave the field in the second innings of the final Test at Sydney. He hadn't wanted to play at all but Jardine had insisted.

"But we've won the Ashes," he had protested. "For once in me life I'd rather like to *watch* and not play."

Jardine had pressed his thumb on to a table.

"I don't care if we've won the series," he had said. "We've got the bastards there, and I'm going to keep them there till the very end."

And so he had played and taken four wickets in the first innings, bowling Bradman for 48. Then England had gone in and towards the end of the day Jardine had yanked him out of the showers and told him to pad up and go in as a nightwatchman. Seething, convinced he was deliberately being overworked by Jardine as a punishment for wanting to stand down, he had flailed at the ball and tried to run himself out. But the next day he reached his highest-ever score in Test cricket. Two short of a century when he was caught on the boundary, he was both amazed and gratified to hear the crowds stand and roar their approval until he was in the dressing-room and unstrapping his pads. He had expected at least a bottle or two at his head. But here he sat, the hero of Sydney, not only to his own side, but to those who had come within an ace of lynching him at Adelaide.

Regrets? Although he could no longer bowl because of the excruciating pain in his foot, because Bradman was in, he was refused permission to go off.

"Field at cover-point," Jardine had said.

Then, when Verity removed Bradman two overs later, he was allowed to leave, ironically limping alongside the Boy Wonder as he made his way back to the pavilion. England won the match by eight wickets, but not before Jardine had worked up the crowd a final time by complaining to the umpire that Alexander was running on to the wicket during his follow-through. The bowler's response was to bounce a few at the England captain until he scored a direct and painful hit in his ribs, much to the delight of the spectators. Nevertheless, Jardine defied both the bowling and the taunts from the Hill. Later Larwood saw the bruises on his side and they made him understand what he had done to men like Kippax, forced out of the game after the First Test because he was unable to withstand bodyline. Then Ponsford and Fingleton had gone the same way. And Woodfull, grievously struck under the heart, was another casualty. Regrets? Perhaps there were a few.

Someone had told him after he had left the field that Jardine had said, "I knew the little bastard would not last the series." Well, that was the skipper all over. He didn't mind. The Jekyll and Hyde some people saw in his own nature, he could detect in Jardine. When things went well, it was "Harold this" and "Loll that", but present a problem, split a boot, ask for a rest, and it was "that little bastard".

There was no denying the team had played wonderfully together, and for that they had to thank the "Iron Duke". If he thought anyone was slacking, he used the big stick or, as in the case of poor old Pataudi, made sure they never got another game. It was the discipline that had inspired them. He could be quite fearful when he wanted. Listening to him now, quoting Kipling and behaving as if nothing untoward had happened at all, he couldn't help warming a little to this complicated man. The newspapers were calling it "Larwood's Series". Well, if it was, the reason was Jardine. He it was who told him right at the start that the fate of the Ashes was in his hands.

But then, looking round again, at the undrunk glasses, the unsmiling faces, the silent, sneaking glances at watches, the fidgety embarrassment—was it worth ending like this? He recalled the farewell reception on the Percy Chapman trip. There wasn't a sober man in the room. And the songs! Such scenes were now a thing of the past. A memory to foster a little nostalgia in later years. He imagined the game twenty years hence. The batsmen wearing helmets and reinforced vests. The fielders barracking, as in baseball. Metal railings 20 feet high to keep the spectators back. He imagined a team of only fast bowlers, where guile gave way to brute force. He imagined a game he wanted no part of.

"I have no complaints," Bradman was saying. "The game of

cricket is a contest between batsman and bowler. Should the bowlers develop an effective way to contain the batsmen, then the batsmen are honour bound to find an answer. . . ."

Fine words, Don, Fingleton thought. True, he scored more runs than anyone else in the Tests, but only 11 more than McCabe. True, his average was 56.5, but that was a long way behind the 139 of 1930. True, he had never complained about bodyline, but he didn't like it because it had brought him back to the ranks of the mortal in the eyes of the nation. Worse, he hadn't found a way to deal with it. All that stepping back to cut the ball through covers! It had never worked.

"The hell with this, it's like a bloody wake in here," Fingleton said to McCabe and marched across the room.

"Good to see you again, Loll," he called loudly. Everyone turned and watched. He pumped his hand vigorously. "But you wait till '34. I'll be in my prime then and you'll be way over the hill. Then you'll see some batting."

Larwood grinned, delighted that finally someone had broken the ice. Always count on Fingo.

"We'll see, Jack," he said. "When you come up to Nottingham, me'n Tangy'll have the welcome mat out for you—"

"Goodbye, Wally, Maurice, Gubby, Bill—" Fingleton went round shaking each by the hand. Bertie Oldfield was the next to move. Soon the others followed and the separate groupings in the room disappeared.

Warner shook Fingleton's hand.

"The very best of luck to you, Mr Fingleton," he smiled gratefully. "Both in cricket and journalism."

"I reckon you had the worst job of all Mr Warner," Fingleton said, ignoring the dig. "I don't know how you managed to stay so cheerful."

The docks were deserted except for a couple of photographers when the England team embarked. Suddenly they were joined by a car that came to a lurching halt. Mary jumped out and Brown, seeing her, ran back down the gangplank.

"I just came to say have a good trip," she said. She held out her hand but he ignored it, reaching out and hugging her fiercely.

"I'll be back," he said. "Or you could find a reason to come to England. One way or another, I don't think this is goodbye."

She looked at him and smiled.

"Was I awfully pompous the last time we spoke?" she asked.

"Yes."

"Don't beat about the bush. Tell me honestly."

"You were incredibly pompous," he said. "Pompous, opinionated, boring and utterly wrong."

She stopped smiling.

"But there again," he added, "so was I."

The ship's funnel dinned their ears with a mournful wail. They kissed and he returned to the deck where he kept his eyes trained on her until the ship had sailed beyond the harbour.

* * *

Thomas was in a buoyant mood and his step showed it as he strode through St James's Park on his way from the House of Commons to his office. That little sod in Australia House had finally shut up now they had lost the series or the Ashes or whatever they called it.

"If this don't bring down the price of lamb," he had chirruped to Marsh when the news from Brisbane arrived, "nothing will."

There had been a deafening silence from the Guv Gen and his underlings. Suddenly the days seemed warmer, not only because of an early spring, but because he knew when he arrived at his desk these days, he wouldn't have a busload of demands from the ex-convict brigade, acting like God Almighty.

For a while the whole thing had been in danger of getting out of hand. Questions in the House, all those Winchester types banging on about the need to give Jardine every support. How the game brings all these pompous old buggers out of the woodwork! Talking as if it was the only passport to respectability. Acting as if a lack of concern about its finer points was the mark of someone who wasn't, basically, a gentleman. That's why he had always liked the Welsh. They didn't give a damn about any of that. They just sang.

At the office, he threw open the windows and breathed in deeply. He always liked coming back after a session in the House.

Too much noise, too many people, too many fools and time-servers, and hardly enough space to swing a cat. That was politics. Here, he could pursue his other life. He could pretend for a while that he was part of the policy-making process of Whitehall, a member of the faceless, nameless club that tells people they are to go off the gold standard or wage a war, or go to work or be idle. He knew he was fooling himself, but it bolstered his spirit.

"I think you should cast an eye over these, sir," Marsh was saying. He was standing in the doorway holding a large folder from which several pieces of paper were protruding.

"What's all that?"

"From Australia, sir."

"What from Horstralia?"

"Well—ah—complaints."

"Oh, they're whining again, are they," he muttered and left the window.

"Not so much *they*, sir," Marsh explained, laying the folder on the desk, "as we."

"We?"

"I feel you should read the letters, sir. They're self-explanatory."

The policeman on duty saluted him as he reached Number Ten and he waited in the hallway until the Prime Minister's private secretary came downstairs.

"Would you follow me, Minister?" he said, in a reverent voice that made the place feel like a church.

Thomas handed his hat, cane and overcoat to a manservant, saying, "It's all right, son, I can find my own way up," and bustled up the stairs.

Ramsay MacDonald sat in the half-light of the late afternoon, behind a desk that had borne the headaches of generations of Prime Ministers. He was tired. Not just from a hard day's work: weariness had seeped into the very marrow of his bones. The country was drifting and he had no suggestions, nor any enthusiasm to find any. He had long since realized that dreaming of being a celebrity was much, much more pleasant than being one. The aristocracy's pet poodle: that was what they called him now.

His decision to form a National Government had been forced upon him; his Labour administration had broken into pieces. But the result was abuse from all sides: from the Socialists who accused him of selling out, and from the Tories who saw him as an intruder. Only the upper classes liked him, but all he got from them were invitations to spend the weekend.

Twenty years ago he could have pulled himself together, set his jaw and waded into the In tray with vigour. Oh, to have back the old energies! To have one single, clear view and to pursue it to a logical conclusion. But the days of simplicity were gone. Everything was so complex now, complex and ultimately insuperable.

Thomas entered briskly. He always walked quickly when he was in trouble. It gave him the feeling that he was doing something positive. He also found it useful for pushing the P.M. into action, an achievement that was becoming more difficult every passing day.

"Afternoon, Mac."

"Sit ye down, Jimmy."

Thomas blinked in the gloom. Why doesn't that lad on the stairs organize some light? Or perhaps Mac preferred the crepuscule. Gave him an excuse not to read things. Reading what the country had to say about Ramshackle Mac was not an uplifting experience for any of the Cabinet, who saw their star waning alongside his. To read it about himself, however, must be terrible.

"I'd like to feel this was just a social visit," the Prime Minister said. "That ye'd come to chat about old times. But I fancy there has to be something else."

"'Fraid so," Thomas said breezily. "It's them bleeding convicts again."

"What is it this time—sheep or butter?"

"Cricket."

Ramsay MacDonald raised his heavy eyebrows.

"Cricket?" For a fleeting moment his face creased, softening.

"No laughing matter, Mac," Thomas warned. "I've had letters from the Governor-General, and Hore-Ruthven in Adelaide— they're both complaining about the same thing."

205

"And what is that?"

"They reckon this bodyline business 'as caused serious damage to Hanglo-Horstralian relations."

The Prime Minister made a scornful sound.

"It's caused *what?*" he retorted. "Jimmy, are ye seriously trying to tell me that we have a political crisis on our hands all because of a game?"

"I'm telling you just that, yes."

The mantelpiece clock ticked mournfully while Ramsay MacDonald read the letters Thomas passed across, holding them to the light from the window.

. . . furthermore, representatives of British economic interests have lost the close personal relations they have hitherto enjoyed with many influential businessmen here. Everywhere the complaint is the same. Namely that England has brought the game of cricket into disrepute, showed a flagrant and bigoted disregard for Australian opinion and were heedless of repeated warnings that such behaviour abroad could only do serious damage to long-term political and economic associations.

He removed his eyeglasses and stared at the letter as if it were about some arcane matter he had never even heard of, let alone knew anything about. "Jimmy," he asked, "do I detect a hint that Australia might go its own way? Sever ties with us? *Leave the Empire*—?"

Each rephrasing came with a little more incredulity than the last.

"When you've been dealing with the Colonies as long as I 'ave," Thomas said, "you'll realize they're capable of anything. It's their way of getting back at us, Mac. Canada, Horstralia, South Africa—we dumped all our rejects on them. Sent off our black sheep sons, our ugly daughters. They teach their children about those things. They teach 'em to rebel. They're all Irish at heart. I tell you, old friend, I wish to God you'd give this job to someone else. Just leave me something nice and uncomplicated. Say the Foreign Office."

Ramsay MacDonald was not listening. He reread the letter.

"What's to be done?" he asked.

"I'd 'ave thought a gesture of goodwill."

"Such as?"

Thomas moved uncomfortably in his chair. By now the Prime Minister was almost a silhouette in the darkness. Why the hell doesn't someone turn on the lights?

"What constitutes good will?" the Prime Minister repeated.

"I—ah—I think perhaps, well, a sacrificial goat would do it," Thomas replied, entwining his fingers together across his stomach. "Or two."

"Out with it, Jimmy," Ramsay MacDonald ordered softly. "Who's for the chop?"

This was not the first time Thomas had come in and with a shrug ended a man's career. He wished he had been capable of such ruthlessness. If he had, perhaps he wouldn't be so depressed, unable to eat, or sleep. Politics is no pursuit for the sensitive.

"It seems to me," Thomas mused, "that all this commotion was caused by Jardine." A pause, then a hint of a smile: "Another Scot."

"Get on with it, Jim."

"Well, it seems to me 'e went a bit too far. Not that I understand much about cricket—"

"Welshmen seldom do—"

"Quite so. But my chap Marsh keeps me posted and well, 'e says Jardine is hutterly 'ated Down Under. They can't stand 'im at any price, and 'e goes out of 'is way, so I'm told, to put their backs up. I think if 'e went—"

"You said two."

"What?"

"You said 'a goat—or two'," the Prime Minister emphasized.

"Ah, yes, the other bloke." Thomas began to feel grateful for the darkness now. He hadn't fidgeted like this in long time.

"Larwood."

"Why him?"

"He's the one who knocked 'em out," Thomas explained. "I don't think we can ignore 'im. 'E caused riots at Hadelaide, so I'm told."

"You know, Jimmy," Ramsay MacDonald sighed, long and sorrowfully. "It does seem hard. These fellows played and won. And you want me to punish them for it."

"Prime Minister," Thomas said, leaning forwards, "George the Third lost America. 'Ow'd you like to go down in 'istory as the one who lost Horstralia?"

"I don't like giving in to blackmail," he muttered, irritated.

Thomas smiled in the gloom.

"Now then, Mac," he remarked. "Politics is all about giving in to blackmail. You ought to know that."

"Still, it's wrong to sack men for winning."

"Of course," Thomas said, standing, "if they win *fairly*."

He moved to the door. Ramsay MacDonald managed a weary smile.

"Politics is all about winning unfairly, Jim," the Prime Minister said. "You ought to know that."

He waited a long time after Thomas had gone before picking up the telephone.

"I'd like to speak to the President of the M.C.C.," he said.

Chapter Eighteen

Miss Stevenson opened the door. "Mr Jardine is here to see you, sir," she announced.

"Oh good, show him in," he replied.

Jardine walked through and they shook hands.

"Douglas, good to see you. How fit you look," he exclaimed. "With that tan, you make the rest of us seem like ghosts. No calls, Miss Stevenson," he called.

"Very good, sir," she replied and closed the door.

He brought over the whisky decanter, two glasses and a syphon.

"Well, Douglas," he said, "it worked. I told you it would."

Jardine took the drink he offered.

"Yes, it did."

"I give you English cricket," he said, raising his glass.

Jardine nodded briefly and they drank. "Sit down and tell me all about it."

"There's nothing more to tell than you've seen in the newspapers," Jardine replied. "Larwood bowled like a dream. The fielding came up to par. So did our batting. Nothing went wrong at all."

There was a catch in his his voice and it was detected.

"What went wrong, Douglas?"

"Nothing, I've told you."

"What went wrong?"

Jardine placed his glass slowly down on the edge of the desk.

"Do you know what those bastards at Lord's have done?" he asked.

"What?"

"They've held an enquiry," he said, barely keeping his voice level. "And they've decided that although they don't condemn the methods we used, nevertheless it would only seem proper for Larwood to apologize."

"Oh, he'll say he's sorry, and that'll be that."

Jardine fixed him with the look he reserved for only the very worst situations.

"How can you take that line?" he demanded.

"Listen, I know Loll. Stroppy little bugger, but he knows which side his bread is buttered."

"He's refused."

"What?"

"He's refused to apologize," Jardine repeated. "And I'm bloody glad he has."

"You have to make him change his mind."

"Not me," Jardine shook his head. "You're supposed to have this Svengali effect on him. You try. But I know if I were him, *I* wouldn't."

"But you're not him, Douglas. You can go off and be a lawyer or make a fortune or play golf all day. If Larwood gives any trouble he's out of the game for good. It's down the pit quicker than you can say breadline."

Jardine stood up.

"I've heard it on extremely good authority," he said as he walked to the door, "that he'll never play for England again."

"That's ridiculous! There's another five good years in the man yet. We'll need him when those sods come over next year. We've *got* to have him."

"Then I wish you luck," Jardine called from the door. "Oh, and by the way, you could put in for the captain's job while you're at it. You're not too old for a come-back."

"What do you mean?"

"I mean there's a vacancy," he said. "I'm finished too. Goodbye."

"Douglas, wait—!"

He reached Miss Stevenson's office as Jardine was retrieving his hat and overcoat. He wanted to say something, but for the life of him he couldn't think what. Miss Stevenson looked

210

nervously in his direction. She had never seen him agitated like this before.

Jardine draped the coat over his arm and opened the door. He went out without turning round.